# MATT JENSEN:
# THE LAST MOUNTAIN MAN
# SNAKE RIVER SLAUGHTER

This Large Print Book carries the
Seal of Approval of N.A.V.H.

# MATT JENSEN:
## THE LAST MOUNTAIN MAN
# SNAKE RIVER
# SLAUGHTER

# WILLIAM W. JOHNSTONE
## WITH J. A. JOHNSTONE

**WHEELER PUBLISHING**
*A part of Gale, Cengage Learning*

GALE
CENGAGE Learning

Detroit • New York • San Francisco • New Haven, Conn • Waterville, Maine • London

## GALE
### CENGAGE Learning

**LIBRARY OF CONGRESS CATALOGING-IN-PUBLICATION DATA**

Johnstone, William W.
    Matt Jensen, the last mountain man. Snake River slaughter / by William W. Johnstone with J. A. Johnstone.
      p. cm. — (Wheeler Publishing large print Western)
    ISBN-13: 978-1-4104-3237-7 (softcover)
    ISBN-10: 1-4104-3237-8 (softcover)
    1. Mountain life—Fiction. 2. Large type books. I. Johnstone, J. A. II. Title.
PS3560.O415M4 2010
813'.54—dc22                2010031542

Published in 2010 by arrangement with Pinnacle Books, an imprint of Kensington Publishing Corp.

Printed in the United States of America
2 3 4 5 6       19 18 17 16 15

# MATT JENSEN:
# THE LAST MOUNTAIN MAN
# SNAKE RIVER SLAUGHTER

# CHAPTER ONE

*Sweetwater County, Wyoming*

The Baker brothers, Harry and Arnold, were outside by the barn when they saw Jules Pratt and his wife come out of the house. Scott and Lucy McDonald walked out onto the porch to tell the Pratts goodbye.

"You have been most generous," Jules said as he climbed up into the surrey. "Speaking on behalf of the laity of the church, I can tell you that every time we hear the beautiful music of the new organ, we will be thinking of, and thanking you."

"It was our pleasure," Scott said. "The church means a great deal to us, more than we can say. And we are more than happy to do anything we can to help out."

"We'll see you Sunday," Jules said, slapping the reins against the back of the team.

Lucy McDonald went back into the house but before Scott went back inside, he looked over toward the barn at the two brothers.

"How are you two boys comin' on the wagon?" Scott called toward them.

"We're workin' on it," Harry called back.

"I'm goin' to be needin' it pretty soon now, so you let me know if you run into any trouble with it," McDonald replied, just as he went back inside.

Harry and Arnold Baker were not permanent employees of the MacDonalds. They had been hired the day before for the specific purpose of making repairs to the freight wagon.

"Did you see that money box?" Harry asked.

"You mean when he give that other fella a donation for the organ? Yeah, I seen it," Arnold replied.

"There has to be two, maybe three hunnert dollars in that box," Harry said.

"How long would it take us to make that kind of money?" Arnold asked.

"Hell, it would take the better part of a year for us to make that much money, even if we was to put our earnings together," Harry said.

"Yeah, that's what I thought," Arnold said. "Harry, you want to know what I'm thinkin'?"

"If you're thinkin' the same thing I'm

thinkin', I know what it is," Harry replied.

"Let's go in there and get that money."

"He ain't goin' to give up and just give it to us," Harry said.

"He will if we threaten to kill 'im."

Harry shook his head. "Just threatenin' him ain't goin' enough," he said. "We're goin' to have to do it. Otherwise, he'll set the sheriff on us."

"What about the others? His wife and kids?"

"You want the two boys to grow up and come after us?"

"No, I guess not."

"If we are goin' to do this thing, Arnold, there's only one way to do it," Harry insisted.

"All right. Let's do it."

Pulling their guns and checking their loads, the two brothers put their pistols back in their holsters, then crossed the distance between the barn and the house. They pushed the door open and went inside without so much as a warning knock.

"Oh!" Lucy said startled by the sudden appearance of the two men in the kitchen.

"Get your husband," Arnold said, his voice little more than a growl.

Lucy left the kitchen, then returned a moment later with Scott. Scott wasn't wearing his gun, which was going to make this even easier than they had planned.

"Lucy said you two boys just walked into the house without so much as a fare thee well," Scott said, his voice reflecting his irritation. "You know better than to do that. What do you want?"

"The money," Harry said.

"The money? You mean you have finished the wagon? Well, good, good. Let me take a look at it, and if I'm satisfied, I'll give you your ten dollars," Scott said.

Harry shook his head. "No, not ten dollars," he said. "All of it."

"I beg your pardon?"

Harry drew his pistol, and when he did, Arnold drew his as well.

"The money box," Harry said. "Get it down. We want all the money."

"Scott!" Lucy said in a choked voice.

"It's all right, Lucy, we are goin' to give them what they ask for. Then they'll go away and leave us alone. Get the box down and hand it to them."

"You're a smart man, McDonald," Arnold said.

"You'll never get away with stealing our money," Lucy said as she retrieved the box from the top of the cupboard, then handed it over to Harry.

"Oh, yeah, we're goin' to get away with it," Harry said as he took the money from the box. Folding the money over, he stuck it in his pocket. Then, without another word, he pulled the trigger. Lucy got a surprised look on her face as the bullet buried into her chest, but she went down, dead before she hit the floor.

"You son of a bitch!" Scott shouted as he leaped toward Harry.

Harry was surprised by the quickness and the furiousness of the attack. He was knocked down by Scott, but he managed to hold onto his gun and even as he was under Scott on the floor, he stuck the barrel of gun into Scott's stomach and pulled the trigger.

"Get him off of me!" Harry shouted. "Get him off of me."

"Mama, Papa, what is it?" a young voice called and the two children came running into the kitchen. Arnold shot both of them, then he rolled Scott off Harry and helped his brother back on his feet.

"Are you all right?" Arnold asked.

"Yeah," Scott answered. "I've got the money. Come on, let's get out of here."

*The next day*
Matt Jensen dismounted in front of the

Gold Strike Saloon. Brushing some of the trail dust away, he tied his horse off at the hitching rail, then began looking at the other horses that were there, lifting the left hind foot of each animal in turn.

His action seemed a little peculiar and some of pedestrians stopped to look over at him. What they saw was a man who was just a bit over six feet tall with broad shoulders and a narrow waist. He was young in years, but his pale blue eyes bespoke of experiences that most would not see in three lifetimes. He was a lone wolf who had worn a deputy's badge in Abilene, ridden shotgun for a stagecoach out of Lordsburg, scouted for the army in the McDowell Mountains of Arizona, and panned for gold in Idaho. A banker's daughter in Cheyenne once thought she could make him settle down — a soiled dove in The Territories knew that she couldn't, but took what he offered.

Matt was a wanderer, always wondering what was beyond the next line of hills, just over the horizon. He traveled light, with a Bowie knife, a .44 double-action Colt, a Winchester .44-40 rifle, a rain slicker, an overcoat, two blankets, and a spare shirt, socks, trousers, and underwear.

He called Colorado his home, though he had actually started life in Kansas. Colorado was home only because it was where he had reached his maturity, and Smoke Jensen, the closest thing he had to a family, lived there. In truth though, he spent no more time in Colorado than he did in Wyoming, Utah, New Mexico, or Arizona.

At the moment, Matt was on the trail of Harry and Arnold Baker for the murder of Scott McDonald, his wife, Lucy, and their two young sons, Toby and Tyler. Before he died, Scott McDonald managed to live long enough to scrawl the letters B-A-K on the floor, using his finger as a pen, and his own blood as the ink. McDonald had hired the Baker brothers, not because he needed the help, but because he thought they were down on their luck and needed the job.

Matt had known the McDonalds well. He had been a guest in their house many times, and had even attended the baptism of one of their children. When the McDonalds were killed, Matt took it very personally and had himself temporarily deputized so he could hunt down the Baker brothers and bring them to justice.

One of the Baker brothers was riding a horse that left a distinctive hoof print and that enabled Matt to track them to Burnt Fork. That brought him to the front of the Gold Strike Saloon where he was checking the shoes of the horses there were tied off at the hitching rail. On the fourth horse that he examined, he found what he was looking for. The shoe on the horse's left rear foot had a "V"-shaped niche on the inside of the right arm of the shoe.

Loosening his pistol in the holster, Matt went into the saloon.

A loud burst of laughter greeted him as he stepped inside, and sitting at a table in the middle of the saloon were two men. Each of the men had a girl sitting on his lap and the table had a nearly empty whisky bottle, indicating they had been drinking heavily.

Matt had never seen the Baker brothers, so he could not identify them by sight, but the two men resembled each other enough to be brothers, and they did match the description he had been given of them.

"Hey, Harry, let's see which one of these girls has the best titties," one of the men said. He grabbed the top of the dress of the girl who was sitting on his lap and jerked it down, exposing her breasts.

"Stop that!" the girl called out in anger and fright. She jumped up from his lap and began pulling the top of her dress back up.

"Ha! Arnold, you done got that girl all mad at you."

They had called each other Harry and Arnold. That was all the verification Matt needed. Turning back toward the bar, he signaled the bartender.

"Yes, sir, what can I do for you?" he asked.

"I need you to get the women away from those two men," Matt said, quietly.

"Mister, as long as those men are paying, the girls can stay."

"I'm about to arrest those two men for murder," Matt said. "If they resist arrest, then I intend to kill them. I wouldn't want the women to be in the way."

"Oh!" the bartender said. "Oh, uh, yes, I see what you mean. But I don't know how to get them away without tellin' what's about to happen."

"Go down to the other end of the bar and take out a new bottle of whiskey. Tell the men it's on the house, you're giving it to them for being good customers. Then call the women over to get it."

"Yeah," the bartender said. "Yeah, that's a good idea."

Matt remained there with his back to the men while the bartender walked down to the other end of the bar. He put a bottle of whiskey up on the bar.

"Jane, Ellie Mae," he called. "Come up here for a moment."

"Hey, bartender, you leave these girls with us. They're enjoyin' our company," one of the men said. This was Arnold.

"We are enjoying your company too, sir," the bartender said. "You've spent a lot of money with us and you been such good customers and all, we're pleased to offer you a bottle of whiskey, on the house. That is, if you'll let the girls come up to get it."

"Well, hell, you two girls go on up there and get the bottle," Harry said. "And if you are good to us, why, we'll let you have a few drinks. Right, Arnold?"

"Right, Harry," Arnold answered.

From his position in the saloon, Matt watched in the mirror as the two girls left the table and started toward the bartender. Not until he was sure they were absolutely clear did he turn around.

"Hello, Harry. Hello, Arnold," he said.

"What?" Harry replied, surprised at being addressed by name. "Do you know us?"

"No, but I know who you are. I was a good friend of the McDonalds," Matt said.

"We don't know anyone named McDonald," Harry said.

"Sure you do," Matt said. "You murdered them."

The two men leaped up then, jumping up so quickly that the chairs fell over behind them. Both of them started toward their guns, but when they saw how quickly Matt had his own pistol out, they stopped, then raised their hands."

"We ain't drawin', Mister. We ain't drawin'!" Arnold said.

When Matt returned to Green River, Harry and Arnold were riding in front of him. Each man had his hands in iron shackles, and there was a rope stretching from Harry's neck to Arnold's neck, then from Arnold's neck to the saddle horn of Matt's saddle. This was to discourage either, or both, from trying to bolt away during the return journey.

# CHAPTER TWO

Within a week of their capture, the two brothers were put on trial in the Sweetwater County Courthouse. Although seats were dear to come by, Sheriff Foley had held a place for Matt so he was able to move through the crowd of people who were searching for their own place to sit. Rather than being resentful of him, however, those in the crowd applauded when Matt came in. They were aware of the role Matt had played in bringing the Baker brothers to trial.

Matt had been in his seat for little more than a minute when the bailiff came through a little door at the front of the courtroom. Clearing his voice, the bailiff addressed the gallery.

"Oyez, oyez, oyez, this court of Sweetwater County, Green River City, Wyoming, will now come to order, the Honorable Judge Daniel Norton presiding. All rise."

As Judge Norton came into the courtroom and stepped up to the bench, Matt Jensen stood with the others.

"Be seated," Judge Norton said. "Bailiff, call the first case."

"There's only one case, Your Honor. There comes now before this court Harry G. Baker and Arnold S. Baker, both men having been indicted for the crime of murder in the first degree."

"Thank you, Bailiff. Are the defendants represented by council?"

The defense attorney stood. "I am Robert Dempster, Your Honor, duly certified before the bar and appointed by the court to defend the misters Baker."

"Is prosecution present?"

The prosecutor stood. "I am Edmund Gleason, Your Honor, duly certified before the bar and appointed by the court to prosecute."

"Let the record show that the people are represented by a duly certified prosecutor and the defendants are represented by a duly certified counsel," Judge Norton said.

"Your Honor, if it please the court," Dempster said, standing quickly.

"Yes, Mr. Dempster, what is it?"

"Your Honor, I object to the fact that we are trying both defendants at the same time,

19

and I request separate trials."

"Mr. Dempster, both men are being accused of the same crime, which was committed at the same time. It seems only practical to try them both at the same time. Request denied."

Dempster sat down without further protest.

"Mr. Prosecutor, are you ready to proceed?"

"I am ready, Your Honor."

"Very good. Then, please make your case," Judge Norton said.

"Thank you, Your Honor," Gleason said as he stood to make his opening remarks.

Gleason pointed out that the letters BAK, written in the murder victim's own blood, were damning enough testimony alone to convict. But he also promised to call witnesses, which he did after the opening remarks. He called Mr. Jules Pratt.

"Mr. Pratt, were you present at the McDonald Ranch on the day of the murder?" Gleason asked.

"Yes," Jules replied. "My wife and I were both there."

"Why were you there?"

"We went to see the McDonalds to solicit a donation for the church organ."

"Did they donate?"

"Yes, they did. Very generously."

"By bank draft, or by cash?"

"By cash."

"Where did they get the cash?"

"From a cash box they kept in the house."

"Was there any money remaining in the cash box after the donation?"

"Yes, a considerable amount."

"How much would you guess?"

"Two, maybe three hundred dollars."

"Was anyone else present at the time?"

"Yes."

"Who?"

Jules pointed. "Those two men were present. They were doing some work for Scott."

"Let the record show that the witness pointed to Harry and Arnold Baker. Was it your observation, Mr. Pratt, that the two defendants saw the cash box and the amount of money remaining?"

"Yes, sir, I know they did."

"How do you know?"

"Because that one," he pointed.

"The witness has pointed to Arnold Baker," Gleason said.

"That one said to Scott, 'That's a lot of money to keep in the house.'"

"Thank you, Mr. Pratt, no further questions."

21

Gleason also called Pastor Martin who, with four of his parishioners, testified as to how they had discovered the bodies when they visited the ranch later the same day. Then, less than one-half hour after court was called to order, prosecution rested its case.

The defense had a witness as well, a man named Jerome Kelly, who claimed that he had come by the McDonald ranch just before noon, and that when he left, the Bakers left with him.

"And, when you left, what was the condition of the McDonald family?" the defense attorney asked.

"They was all still alive. Fac' is, Miz McDonald was bakin' a pie," Kelly said.

"Thank you," Dempster said. "Your witness, Counselor."

"Mrs. McDonald was baking a pie, you say?" Gleason asked in his cross-examination.

"Yeah. An apple pie."

"Had Mrs. McDonald actually started baking it?"

"Yeah, 'cause we could all smell it."

"What time was that, Mr. Kelly?"

"Oh, I'd say it was about eleven o'clock. Maybe even a little closer on toward noon."

"Thank you. I have no further questions

of this witness." The prosecutor turned toward the bench. "Your Honor, prosecution would like to recall Pastor Martin to the stand."

Pastor Martin, the resident pastor of the First Methodist Church of Green River City, Wyoming, who had, earlier, testified for the prosecution, retook the stand. He was a tall, thin man, dressed in black, with a black string tie.

"The court reminds the witness that he is still under oath," the judge said. Then to Gleason he said, "You may begin the redirect."

"Pastor Martin, you discovered the bodies, did you not?" Gleason asked.

"I did."

"What time did you arrive?

"It was just after noon. We didn't want to arrive right at noon, because Mrs. McDonald, kind-hearted soul she was, would have thought she had to feed us."

"You testified earlier that you and four other parishioners had gone to thank the McDonalds for their generous donation to the organ fund?"

"Yes."

"And that all five of you saw the bodies?"

Pastor Martin pinched the bridge of his nose and was quiet for a moment before he responded. "May their souls rest with God," he said. "Yes, all five of us saw the bodies."

"You have already testified as to the condition of the bodies when you found them, so I won't have you go through all that again. But I am going to ask you a simple question. You just heard the witness testify that Mrs. McDonald was baking a pie when they left, just before noon. Did you see any evidence of that pie?"

Pastor Martin shook his head. "There was no pie," he said. "In fact, the oven had not been used that day. It was cold, and there were no coals."

"Thank you. No further questions."

"Witness may step down," the judge said.

In his closing argument to the jury, the defense attorney suggested that the letters BAK were not, in themselves, conclusive.

"They could have referred to Mrs. McDonald's intention to bake an apple pie. After all, the letters b-a-k, are the first three letters of the word bake. Perhaps it was a warning that the oven needed to be checked, lest there be a fire," he said. "Don't forget, we have a witness who testified that the Bakers left the McDonald Ranch with him on the very day the McDonalds were killed. And, according to Mr. Kelly, the McDonalds were still alive at that time they left. The burden of proof is on the prosecution. That means that, according to the law, in order to find Harry and Arnold Baker guilty you are going to have to be convinced, beyond a shadow of a doubt, that they did it. Prosecution has offered no evidence or testimony that would take this case beyond the shadow of a doubt."

During Gleason's closing, he pointed out that Kelly was not a very reliable witness, whereas the two witnesses who had seen the Baker brothers at the ranch on the morning of the murder were known citizens of good character. He also reminded the jury that the witness said that the donation had come directly from a cash box and that Arnold Baker had commented on the money.

"Mr. Pratt said he believed there was at least three hundred dollars left in the box, and maybe a little more. An affidavit from the bartender in Burnt Fork says that the two men spent lavishly while they were in the saloon, and Matt Jensen, acting as a duly sworn deputy, found two hundred sixty-eight dollars on them when he made the arrest."

In addition, the prosecuting attorney pointed out that, according to Pastor Martin, whose testimony was also unimpeachable, that there was no evidence of any apple pie having been baked, which cast further doubt on Kelly's story.

"With his own blood, as he lay dying, Scott McDonald scrawled the letters, BAK. BAK for Baker. He hardly had time to actually leave us a note, so he did what he could to see to it that those who murdered him, and his family, would pay for their act. We owe it to this good man to make certain that his heroic action is rewarded by returning a verdict of guilty of murder in the first degree for Harry and Arnold Baker."

Less than one hour after the court had been called to order, the jury returned from their five minute deliberation.

"Gentleman of the jury, have you selected a foreman and have you reached a verdict?" Judge Norton asked.

"We have, Your Honor. I am the foreman," a tall, gray-haired man said.

"Would you publish the verdict, please?"

"We find the defendants, Harry and Arnold Baker, guilty of murder in the first degree."

There was an outbreak of applause from those in the gallery, but Judge Norton used his gavel to restore order. "I will not have any demonstrations in my court," he said sternly. The judge looked around the court room. "Bailiff, where is the witness, Jerome Kelly?"

"He's not present, Your Honor."

"Sheriff Foley?"

"Yes, Your Honor?" the sheriff said, standing.

"I'm putting out a bench warrant on Jerome Kelly for giving false testimony. Please find him, and take him into custody."

"Yes, Your Honor."

"Now, Bailiff, if you would, bring the convicted before the bench."

The two men were brought to stand before the judge.

"Harry Baker and Arnold Baker, I have presided over thousands of cases in my twenty-six years on the bench. But never in my career, have I encountered anyone with less redemptive tissue than the two of you. Your crime in murdering an entire family, a family that had taken you into their bosom, is particularly heinous.

"You have been tried and found guilty by a jury of your peers. Therefore, it is my sentence that, one week hence, the sheriff of Sweetwater County will lead the two of you to the gallows at ten of the clock in the morning. Once upon the gallows, ropes will be placed around your necks, all support will be withdrawn from under your feet, and you shall be dropped a distance sufficient to break your necks. And there, Harry Baker and Arnold Baker, you shall continue to hang until it is obvious that all life has left your miserable bodies. May God have mercy on your souls, for I have none."

# CHAPTER THREE

*One week later*
The gallows stood in the middle of Center
Street, well constructed but terrible in the
gruesomeness of its function. A profession-
ally painted sign was placed on an easel in
front of the gallows.

**On this gallows**
**At *ten o'clock* on Thursday morning**
**Will be hung**
**The murderers Harry and Arnold**
**Baker.**
**→ All are invited.**
***Attendance is Free.***

The idea of a double hanging had drawn
visitors from miles around, not only because
of the morbid curiosity such a spectacle
generated, but also because the McDonald
family had been very well liked, and the
murders the two condemned had commit-

ted, including the murder of Scott Mc-Donald's wife and children, were particularly shocking

The street was full of spectators, and the crowd was growing even larger as they all jostled for position. Matt glanced over toward the tower clock in front of the courthouse to check the time. It was five minutes after ten.

The judge had said they would be hanged at ten o'clock, which meant that the prisoners should have been brought out by now. Some in the crowd were growing impatient, and more than one person wondered aloud what was holding up the proceedings.

Matt began to have the strange feeling that something was wrong, so he slipped away from the crowd and walked around into the alley behind the jail. He was going to look in through the back window but he didn't have to. The moment he stepped into the alley he saw the Baker brothers and the man who had given false testimony on their behalf, Jerome Kelly, coming through the back door.

"Hold it!" Matt called out.

"It's Jensen!" Harry Baker shouted, firing his pistol at the same time.

The bullet hit the wall beside Matt, sending little brick chips into his face. Matt returned fire and Harry went down. By now both Arnold Baker and Kelly were shooting as well, and Matt dived to the ground, then rolled over and shot again. Arnold clutched his chest and went down.

Kelly, now seeing that both Bakers were down, dropped his gun and threw up his hands. At that moment Sheriff Foley came out of the jail, holding his pistol in one hand, while holding his other hand to a bleeding wound on his head.

"Jensen, are you all right?" the sheriff called.

"Yes, I'm not hit. How about you?"

"They killed my deputy, and I've got a knot on my head where this son of a bitch hit me," Foley said. The sheriff looked at Harry and Arnold Baker, then chuckled. "I wonder if you saved the county the cost of the execution, or if we will have to pay the hangman anyway? Or, maybe we can just go ahead and have the hanging, only it'll be Kelly instead of the Baker brothers."

From the Boise, Idaho, *Statesman:*

### *Deadly Shootout in Wyoming!*
### MURDERERS KILLED WHILE TRYING TO ESCAPE.

Last month the brothers Harry and Arnold Baker committed one of the most heinous crimes in recent memory when they murdered Scott McDonald, his wife, Lucy, and their two young sons, Toby and Tyler. The crime, which happened in Sweetwater County, Wyoming, raised the ire of all decent citizens who knew Scott McDonald as a man of enterprise, magnanimity, and Christian faith.

The murderers were tracked down and arrested by Matt Jensen, who had himself deputized just for that purpose. Jensen brought the brothers back to Green River City for a quick and fair trial, resulting in a guilty verdict for both parties. They were sentenced to be hanged, but moments before they were to be hanged, Deputy Sheriff Goodwin was killed, and Sheriff Fred Foley knocked unconscious, resulting in the prisoners being broken out of jail. All this was accomplished by Jerome Kelly, a cousin of the Baker brothers. Jerome Kelly was himself wanted for having provided false testimony at the trial of Harold and Arnold Baker.

Had Matt Jensen not discovered the escape in progress, the two brothers would have made good their getaway. In the ensuing shootout Matt Jensen dispatched both murderers with his deadly accurate shooting. The accomplice, seeing that further resistance was futile, threw down his gun and surrendered. A quick trial found him guilty and he is to be hanged for murdering Deputy Goodwin.

Some readers may recognize the name Matt Jensen, as he has become a genuine hero of the West, a man about whom books and ballads have been written. Those who know him personally have naught but good things to say of him. Despite his many accomplishments, he is modest, a friend of all who are right, and a foe to those who would visit their evil deeds upon innocent people.

*The Boise Statesman,* being published in the territorial capitol, was the largest newspaper in Idaho. And though only five thousand copies were printed, it was circulated by railroad and stage coach throughout the territory so that a significant number of the thirty-two thousand people who lived in Idaho were aware of, and often read, the newspaper.

*Sawtooth Mountains, Idaho Territory*

Colonel Clay Sherman was a tall man with broad shoulders and narrow hips. He had steel gray eyes, and he wore a neatly trimmed moustache which now, like his hair, was dusted with gray. He was the commanding officer of the Idaho Auxiliary Peace Officers' Posse. The posse consisted of two officers and thirty-two men, all duly sworn as functioning, though unpaid, deputies to the Idaho Territorial Task Force. Clay Sherman had received his commission from the assistant deputy attorney general of the territory of Idaho, and, as such, was duly authorized to deputize those who joined the posse. Sherman and his Auxiliary Peace Officers wore deputies' badges, but because they were not paid by the territorial government, the posse supported itself, and supported itself very well, by acting as a private police force. Most of the posse's income was generated when it was hired by the disgruntled to get justice where they felt justice had been denied.

So far the posse had managed to avoid any trouble with territorial or federal law agencies because they managed to find loopholes to allow them to operate. But their operations always walked a very narrow line between legality and illegality, and had either the territorial or federal government taken the trouble to conduct a thorough investigation, it would have discovered that in fact, the posse often did cross over that line.

There were many citizens, and quite a few lawmakers, who felt that the posse was little more than a band of outlaws, hired assassins who hid behind the dubious authority of deputies' badges. It was also pointed out by these detractors that very few of the wanted men they went after were ever brought back alive, including even some who were being pursued for the simple purpose of being served a subpoena to appear in civil court. *The Boise Statesman* and other newspapers had written editorials critical of the Idaho Auxiliary Peace Officers' Posse, pointing out that, despite its name, it had nothing to do with "peace." Some of those newspapers had paid for their critical observations by having their offices vandalized by "irate citizens who supported the posse," or so it was claimed.

At this moment, Sherman and few members of the posse were engaged in one of the many private police force operations by which it managed to earn its keep. They were operating in the Sawtooth Mountains, and Colonel Sherman stepped up on a rock and looked down toward a little cabin that was nestled against the base of the sheer side of Snowy Peak. The posse had trailed Louis Blackburn to this cabin, and now their quarry was trapped. The beauty of it was that Blackburn had no idea he was trapped. He thought he was quite secure in the cabin.

Part of the reason for Louis Blackburn's complacency was due to the fact that he didn't even know he was being trailed. Two weeks earlier, Louis Blackburn had been tried for the murder of James Dixon. At least three witnesses testified that Dixon not only started the fight, but he had also drawn first. The jury believed the witnesses, and found Blackburn not guilty, and not guilty by reason of self-defense. The judge released him from custody and Blackburn went on his way, a free man.

The problem with the court finding was that not everyone agreed with the verdict, and principal among those who disagreed was Augustus Dixon, James Dixon's father. And because the senior Dixon had made a fortune in gold and was now one of wealthiest and most powerful men in Idaho, he was able to use both his money and influence to find an alternate path to justice, or at least the justice he sought.

Dixon managed to convince a cooperative judge to hold a civil trial. It was Augustus Dixon's intention to sue Louis Blackburn for depriving him of his son. No official law agency of the territory of Idaho would serve a subpoena for the civil trial, but then, Dixon didn't want any official law officer involved in the process. Dixon hired Clay Sherman and his Idaho Auxiliary Peace Officers' Posse to run Blackburn down and bring him back for civil trial.

Sherman had eight men with him and as he looked back at them he saw that everyone had found a place with a good view and a clear line of fire toward the cabin.

"Lieutenant," Sherman said to Poke Terrell, his second in command.

"Yes, Colonel?"

"It is my belief, based upon our conversation with Mr. Dixon, that he doesn't particularly want us to bring Blackburn back alive."

"Yes, sir, that is my belief as well," Poke replied.

"You know what that means then, don't you?"

"Yes, sir," Poke said. "We have to get him to take a shot at us."

"You know what to do," Sherman said.

Poke nodded, then cupped his hand around his mouth. "Blackburn!" he called. "Louis Blackburn! Come out!"

"What?" Blackburn called back, his voice thin and muffled from inside the cabin. "Who's calling me?"

"This is Lieutenant Poke Terrell of the Idaho Auxiliary Peace Officers' Posse. I am ordering you to come out of that cabin with your hands up!"

"What do you mean, come out with my hands up? Why should I do that? What do you want?"

"I have a summons to take you back for the murder of James Dixon!" Terrell shouted, loudly.

"You're crazy! I've already been tried, and found innocent."

"You're being tried again."

"My lawyer said I can't be tried again."

"Your lawyer lied. And if you don't come out of your cabin now, I'm going to open fire," Poke called.

"Go away! You ain't got no right to take me back."

"You are going back, whether it's dead or alive," Poke said.

As Sherman and Poke expected, a pistol shot rang out from inside the cabin. The pistol shot wasn't aimed, and was fired more as a warning than any act of hostile intent.

"All right, boys, he shot at us!" Sherman called.

"Beg your pardon, Colonel, but I don't think he was actual aimin' at us. I think he was just tryin' to scare us off," one of the men said.

"That's where you are wrong, Scraggs," Sherman said. "He clearly shot at us, I could feel the breeze of the bullet as it passed my ear." Smiling, Sherman turned to the rest of his men. "That's all we needed, boys. He shot at us, so now if we kill him, it is self-defense. Open fire," he ordered.

For the next several minutes, the sound of gunfire echoed back from the sheer wall of Snowy Peak as Sherman, Poke, and the other men with them fired shot after shot into the cabin. All the windows were shot out, and splinters began flying from the walls of the little clapboard structure. Finally Sherman ordered a cease-fire.

"Lieutenant Terrell, you and Scraggs go down there to have a look," Sherman ordered.

With a nod of acceptance, Poke and Scraggs left the relative safety of the rocks then climbed down the hill to approach the cabin. Not one shot was fired from the cabin. Finally the two men disappeared around behind the cabin and, a moment later, the front door of the cabin opened and Poke stepped outside, then waved his hand.

"He's dead!" Poke called up.

"Dead — dead — dead!" the words echoed back from the cliff wall.

"Gentlemen, we've done a good day's work here, today," Sherman said with a satisfied smile on his face.

## Boise City

For a time during the gold rush, Boise had prospered and boomed. After the gold rush, Boise began declining in population, and had shrunk to less than one thousand people in 1870. But now, with both the territorial prison and the territorial capital in Boise (some wags suggested that there was very little difference in character between the prisoners and politicians), there had been a rather substantial rebirth and, once again, Boise was a booming community.

Clay Sherman had an office in Boise, boldly placing it right next door to the Territorial Capitol building. He had no reservations about advertising his location, and a sign, hanging from the front of the office read:

## IDAHO AUXILIARY PEACE OFFICERS' POSSE
*Colonel Clay Sherman, Commanding*
### PRIVATE POLICE SERVICE

At the moment, Sherman was meeting with Poke Terrell, his second in command. Poke had brought him a proposal for a job down on the Snake River in Owyhee County.

"What do you think, Colonel? Should we take the job?" his first lieutenant asked.

"I don't know," Sherman answered. "It's not the kind of thing we normally do."

"No, but he's offerin' fifteen hunnert dollars, and the job don't seem all that hard to do. I just don't think we should walk away from it."

"Who is it that's wantin' to hire us?"

"His name is Marcus Kincaid. He's a rancher down in Owyhee County."

Sherman, who had once been an Arizona Ranger, stroked his jaw for a moment as he contemplated the suggestion his second in command had made.

"If you ask me, I think we should do it," Poke said. "I mean, we don't need ever'one. I could prob'ly take care of it myself."

"All right, I'll tell you what," Sherman said. "How about you go down there and

41

meet with this fella? If it looks like something you can handle, go ahead and do it."

"By myself?"

"Why not? You just said you could probably handle it by yourself."

"Well, yeah, I think I can. But maybe I should take a few of the men with me?"

"No. Because of the type operation it is, I want to keep as much separation as I can between that job and the posse," Sherman said. "In fact, I think you should quit the organization."

"What? No, now wait, I didn't have nothin' like that in mind," Poke said. "I was just suggestin' that it might be a good way to make some money."

Sherman held up his hand to halt the protest. "Don't worry, you won't really be quitting," he said. "We'll just make everyone think you have quit. In fact, we can let it out that I fired you."

"Oh. All right, whatever you say. As long as you ain't kickin' me out, I mean."

"Now why would I want to kick you out, Poke?" Sherman asked. "You are one of the best I've ever ridden with. I told you, you leavin' us would be just for show, just to keep anyone from tracing your operation back to us."

"What if I need help?"

"If after you get down there, you decide that you need help, hire some locals. If the job is really worthwhile, you should be able to afford it."

"Oh, the job will be worthwhile, all right," Poke said. "I don't see how it can miss."

*King Hill, Idaho Territory*
Joel Matthews, president of the Cattleman's Bank and Loan of King Hill, was sitting behind his desk, reading a newspaper. To some, Matthews's office might have been considered messy, but because it was the office of a bank president, it was just considered busy. The bank president's desk was filled with stacks of paper, though he did manage to keep enough room left on his desk for an ink blotter and an inkwell and pen. The walls of his office were festooned with pictures, including one of a 4-4-2 engine with steam gushing from its piston rods as it thundered beneath a plume of smoke, pulling a string of passenger cars across a high trestle that afforded a grandiose mountain vista. There was also a portrait of the bank president, Joel Matthews, as well as a calendar with a picture of a brightly colored array of pumpkins, corn, apples, peppers, and pears. A grandfather's clock stood against the wall, its pendulum mark-

ing each passing second with a loud tick tock.

"Mr. Matthews?"

Matthews looked up from the paper to see someone standing at his desk. The man was medium height, slender and well groomed. His hair was very light, almost blond, and his eyes were such a pale blue that one could almost say they had no color at all. Matthews recognized him at once.

"Ah, Marcus Kincaid," he said. "It's so good to see you."

"I came to talk about that proposal we discussed."

"Good, good, I'll be happy to answer any questions you may have about it." Matthews put the paper down.

"Anything interesting in the paper?" Kincaid asked.

"An interesting story about Kitty Wellington's ranch," Matthews said. "But I'm certain, given the circumstances, that you read the story."

"I read it," Kincaid said without showing a lot of enthusiasm.

"But did you also read the article about the shootout over in Green River City, Wyoming?" Matthews asked his visitor.

"Yes, I read that as well," Kincaid answered. "The story makes this Matt Jensen

44

fellow into quite the hero, doesn't it?"

"Yes. From time to time editorial writers wax on about the spirit of the West. Most of it, I'm sure, is just hyperbole. But I have read about Matt Jensen before, and occasionally, someone like Jensen comes along and you think maybe there is something to it. Clearly, Matt Jensen is a living manifestation of the spirit of the West."

"Come on, Mr. Matthews, don't you think it is possible that the person who wrote this story may be engaging in a bit of this same hyperbole?" Kincaid asked.

Matthews chuckled. "I suppose that could be true," he said. "Still, it is reassuring to believe that there are such men out there, men who are dedicated to fighting evil, and doing what is right and true."

"I suppose so."

The bank president leaned back in his chair and hooked his thumbs into the shoulder openings of his vest. "Well, Mr. Kincaid, you are here, so, am I to take it that you have decided?"

"Yes, I have decided."

"That's good to hear. Tell me, what have you decided? Do you want to buy the loan?"

"Yes."

"You are sure, now, that you want to do this?" Matthews asked. "I don't want to be in the position of having you pushed into something that, upon further reflection, you regret."

"I am positive I want to do it," Kincaid answered. "And don't worry, there will be no regrets."

"I don't have to tell you that we are talking about a lot of money here. The original loan was for twenty-five thousand dollars. With interest, the amount due now is considerably more."

"I just want you to tell me again what happens if the borrower cannot make payment," Kincaid said.

"You don't have to worry about it. Mrs. Wellington has pledged Coventry on the Snake as collateral. That means there are more than significant assets against the note to cover the loan. If payment cannot be made, those assets will be forfeited to the mortgage holder."

"Which will be me, if I purchase the loan right now. Is that right?"

"Yes, that would be you."

"So if I make this investment, I will be protected?"

"Oh, indeed you will."

"Do you think it is a good investment?" the bank customer asked.

"I think it is an excellent investment,"

Matthews said, gushingly. "Why, back East, banks sell off loans all the time. It is perfectly safe — as I told you, if the loan goes into default, the assets will come to you. And of course, if the loan is paid on time, which I have every reason to believe that it will be, you will recoup every cent of your money, plus the interest that will have accrued between the time of your acquisition and the time of the settlement of the loan."

"If you are sure the loan is going to be repaid, why are you willing to sell it?"

"We are a bank, Mr. Kincaid, and in order to function as a bank is supposed to function, it is necessary that we maintain a significant balance of funds. From time to time we get — well, to be honest — a little over extended. When that happens, we can't make any new loans. Selling this note will give us more flexibility in handling customers who require new loans."

"All right, I want to buy the loan. How long will this transaction take?"

"Not very long at all," Matthews said. "In fact, we can do it this very day. As soon as you make the payment, we can draw up the papers transferring the mortgage to you."

"Exactly how much money will it take at this moment, to purchase the loan?"

"The initial loan was for twenty-five

thousand dollars, but currently, with accrued interest, the amount due is twenty-eight thousand, five hundred seventeen dollars, and thirty-six cents," Matthews said with the efficiency of one who was well at home with numbers, especially as it related to money.

"And you say that she has pledged the entire ranch against the loan?"

"Yes. Mrs. Wellington being a woman and all, our board of directors insisted upon more collateral than they would had the borrower been a man. As I am sure you are aware, the assets are easily worth twenty times the face value of the note."

"Thank you," Kincaid said. "I will draw a draft for immediate payment. Oh, and Mr. Matthews, if you would, please say nothing of this to anyone else."

"You needn't worry about that. Confidentiality is the policy of the Cattlemen's Bank and Loan."

"I appreciate that," Kincaid said as he began filling out the draft.

"As a matter of fact, if you wish," Matthews added as he watched the draft being written, "for a nominal fee, we will continue to process the loan for you. That way, as far as Mrs. Wellington is concerned, the bank is still the mortgage holder. For your purposes, that might be better."

"How would it be better?"

"Well, say for example Mrs. Wellington finds out you hold the note instead of the bank. And suppose the borrower is unable to make the payment on time. It is much easier for the bank to turn down any request for extensions on the loan than it would be for you."

"Yes, I can see what you are talking about. Good, good, let's do it that way then."

Finishing the draft, Kincaid held up the document and blew on it to dry the ink. He then passed it across the desk to Matthews. "I guess that makes me a member of the banking business," he said with a broad smile.

Matthews accepted the check. "I guess it does at that," he said with a satisfied smile. "I only wish that other businessmen were as astute as you are. If we could sell more of our loans, we would have more money available to service our customers when new loans are needed."

# CHAPTER FOUR

When Poke Terrell rode into King Hill a train was sitting at the depot. The engine, painted green and trimmed in red, was glistening in the golden light of the setting sun. The engineer was leaning through the window of the cab and holding a long-stemmed pipe clinched tightly between his teeth. He watched from his lordly position as arriving passengers left the train and departing passengers boarded.

The restaurant Poke was looking for was next door to the depot, an adobe building that had recently been given a fresh coat of whitewash. There was a sign hanging in front of the restaurant that identified it as Delmonico's and a hitching rail that ran all the way across the front of the building. Poke dismounted, tied his horse to the rail, then climbed the two wooden steps to the porch.

Poke was a relatively short man, but he

was powerfully built, with a barrel chest, and muscular arms. His head was bald and round, and because one could almost imagine that Poke had no neck, it looked rather like a cannon ball resting on his shoulders.

He was greeted by an employee of the restaurant as soon as he stepped inside.

"May I help you sir?"

"I'm supposed to meet someone here, only I ain't never met him so I'm not . . ."

"Would you be Mr. Terrell?" the restaurant employee asked.

"Yeah."

"Your party is back here."

When the waiter took Poke back to the table in the corner of the restaurant, Marcus Kincaid stood to greet him. There could not have been a more dramatic contrast in the appearance of the two men. Terrell was wearing denim trousers and a white stained shirt. Kincaid was wearing a brown tweed suit. Poke was the rough-hewn log on the fireplace hearth; Kincaid was the cut flower in a vase.

"Thank you for agreeing to meet me," Kincaid said, as the two men sat down.

"Do you have the money?" Poke asked.

"Yes, I have the money. Half now, as we agreed," Kincaid said, taking an envelope from his inside jacket pocket and handing it to Poke.

Poke took the money from the envelope and began counting.

"Don't count it here!" Kincaid snapped.

Poke looked up with a frown on his face, as he continued to count the money.

"All right, it's all here, seven hundred fifty dollars," Poke said as he finished counting. He put the money back into the envelope, then put the envelope into his pocket. "What do you want me to do?"

"Have you heard of a ranch called Coventry on the Snake?" Kincaid asked. "It's near Medbury."

"Yeah, I've heard of it. Owned by a foreigner," Poke said.

"It was owned by an Englishman named Thomas Wellington. Now it's owned by an American woman. When Wellington died, it became the property of his widow. She has invested heavily into the operation and is badly in debt. She needs, desperately, to sell some horses, and she has to do it soon, or she will lose the ranch."

"And you want me to help her sell the horses? I don't know what you thought I could do for her. I'm not a salesman."

Kincaid shook his head vehemently. "No, no, it's just the opposite. I don't want you to help her save the ranch. I want you to make sure she loses the ranch."

Poke laughed. "I'm glad to hear that. I think that might be easier to do. Do you have an idea as to how I need to do it?"

Kincaid shook his head. "No, use your own initiative. I don't care how you do it, as long as you do it."

"You don't care how I do it?"

"Well, I don't want you to burn any of the buildings, or anything like that," Kincaid said. "I don't want the ranch destroyed. All I want is for it to fail."

Poke chuckled. "That's all you want, huh?"

"That's all I want. Do you think you can handle that without too much difficulty?"

"Yeah," Poke said. "As long as you stay out of my way and let me handle things."

Kincaid held up both his hands. "Trust me on this, Mr. Terrell, you shall have free reign. In fact, I would be very pleased if we never even saw each other again."

"Except for the final payment," Poke said.

"Yes, except for the final payment," Kincaid agreed.

When Poke Terrell stepped inside the Sand Spur Saloon in Medbury for the first time, 'he looked around the room until he saw the table that he wanted. It was slightly more

53

than halfway back in the room and sitting close, but not uncomfortably close, to the stove. It was also situated so as to give him a good view, both of the front door and the side door, and this was important to him. A person in Poke's business, and with his reputation, made enough enemies that it was always a good idea to know who was coming and going.

There was a cowboy sitting at the table, and he was joking with one of the bar girls. Poke walked up to the table, then stood there, staring at the cowboy. The cowboy glanced up at him briefly, then turned his attention back to the young woman.

Poke didn't move, and his presence was obviously making the young woman nervous. She had been laughing and teasing with the cowboy, but now she couldn't take her attention away from this brooding man who stood inches away from the two of them.

"Can I help you, Mister?" the cowboy finally asked.

"You have my table," Poke said.

"What are you talking about, your table? I ain't never even seen you before."

"I've just arrived," Poke said. "I want this table."

"What if I don't want to move?"

54

"Prew, come on, let's go to another table," the young woman said.

"I'm not goin' to let some son of a bitch just come in and order me away from this table," Prew said.

"Prew, please," the young woman said. "If you want me to talk to you, you'll change tables."

Prew stared at Poke for a moment longer, then he got up. He pointed at Poke. "All right, I'm movin'," he said. "But it ain't none of your doin'. I'm movin' 'cause of Jenny."

Poke didn't answer, but as soon as Prew left, Poke sat down, then took out a deck of cards and dealt himself a game of solitaire.

"Mister, you want anything to drink?" one of the other girls asked.

"Beer," Poke said, as he began playing.

Poke stayed at the saloon until it closed that night, drinking beer and playing solitaire. Except for his initial confrontation with the cowboy, and occasionally ordering a beer, Poke spoke to no one, and no one spoke to him. When he left, everyone breathed a sigh of relief and offered up a quick prayer that the strange, brooding, and frightening man not return.

To the chagrin of everyone, Poke returned the next day. This time the man who was sitting at his table got up and moved without being asked. By the third day, Poke had clearly established a proprietary right to the table, and nobody sat at it, even when Poke wasn't present.

On the third day Marshal Sparks came to see him.

"I've done some checking up on you, Terrell," Marshal Sparks said. "That's who you are, isn't it? Poke Terrell?"

"That's me," Poke replied. He continued to play solitaire all the time the marshal was talking to him.

"What I want to know is, what is a member of the Idaho Auxiliary Peace Officers' Posse doing in Medbury?"

"I ain't a member no more," Poke replied.

Marshal Sparks nodded. "Yes, that's what I found out. At least you are honest about it."

"Marshal, I have not violated any of your laws since I arrived, and I'm not wanted. So what do you want?"

"Nothing, I'm just curious as to why you are here, that's all."

"I think you have a nice little town here," Poke said. "I just thought I'd visit here for a while. Like I said, I have not broke none of your laws, and I am not wanted."

"I hope things stay like that," Marshal

Sparks said.

For the first few days, Poke Terrell was the talk of the town.

"He used to be a member of the Peace Officers' Posse. Did you know that? Leastwise, that's what the marshal says."

"Yeah, but the marshal also says he ain't a member no more."

"You know why he ain't a member no more? Because he was too violent, that's why. I mean, can you imagine someone who is too violent for the Peace Officers' Posse? The Posse makes Quantrill's Bushwhackers seem like Sunday School boys."

By the end of two weeks, though, Poke was no longer the center of conversation or even attention. Because he sat at "his" table playing solitaire he be came as ubiquitous as the heating stove. He wasn't always alone, though. Gradually Poke began to make a few friends, or at least acquaintances. Sam Logan was the first to come sit at the table with him. Al Madison and Ken Jernigan came as well, and sometimes all three would come.

The telegraph office was located in one end of the railroad depot, so located because Union Pacific Railroad provided the Western Union office in Medbury with at least ninety percent of its business.

When Poke stepped up to the telegraph window, he could hear the instrument clacking, and he saw the telegrapher writing on a tablet. A sign on the telegrapher's desk identified him as William S. Tate and, though Poke had no way of knowing, Tate was recording all the latest changes in train departures and arrivals. This was absolutely necessary in order to schedule the use of the track to avoid wrecks.

Poke waited until the clacking stopped, then saw Tate send a message. Finally Tate turned to him.

"I need to send a message."

Tate gave the man a tablet and pencil, and Poke wrote the message, then handed it back.

Found three men to work for me. Will pay from profits.

"Where does this message go?" Tate asked.

"To Colonel Clay Sherman, Idaho Auxiliary Peace Officers' Posse in Boise," Poke said.

"That will be one dollar and twenty cents," Tate said.

"Damn, that's kind of high, ain't it? Only cost three cents to send it by mail."

"A letter will get to Boise sometime tomorrow. This will get there in thirty seconds," Tate said.

Grumbling, Poke paid for the telegram, then went back to his table at the Sand Spur.

That night when Poke's three new friends were at the table with him, speaking animatedly but too quietly for anyone to hear what they were saying, Prew was standing at the end of the bar, nursing a beer and looking toward the table. Jenny, one of the young women who worked the bar, was with him.

"Logan, Madison, and Jernigan," Prew said contemptuously. "Those are three of the biggest polecats in the entire county. There can't any of them hold a job anywhere. It stands to reason they would become friends with someone like Poke Terrell."

"You're just mad because Terrell ran you away from the table the first night he was here," Jenny said.

"He didn't run me away," Prew insisted. "You did. I would have fought him for it."

"I know you would have," Jenny said. She smiled at him. "But I didn't want to see you get your face bruised." She put her hand up to his face and rubbed her fingers, lightly,

59

across his cheek. "It's such a handsome face."

Prew, who's real name was Jason Prewitt, was a ranch hand at Coventry on the Snake, a huge, 20,000-acre horse ranch that belonged to Kitty Wellington. The ranch was approximately five miles south of Medbury, and it was nearly midnight by the time Prew arrived back at the ranch. Most of the others ranch hands were already asleep when he sat down on his bunk to pull off his boots, and the cacophony of their snores filled the room.

When he first came to work at the ranch, the snoring sometimes kept him awake. Now it was just a part of the background, a part of his life on the range.

"Prew?" Tyrone called, quietly from his private room at the end of the bunk house. Tyrone Canfield was the ranch foreman.

"Yeah?"

"I just wanted to make sure it was you. Better get to sleep as early as you can. The field where the Arabians are being kept is getting grazed out and first thing tomorrow we are going to move them to fresh grass."

"How'm I goin' to get to sleep with you yapping at me?" Prew teased.

■ ■ ■ ■

By any means of measurement, Kitty Wellington was a beautiful woman. Tall and statuesque, she had blond hair and blue eyes, naturally long lashes, high cheekbones and full lips. She was a widow, still young, because when she married, she had been thirty years younger than her husband.

After her husband died, Kitty inherited the ranch, a parcel of land that was bordered on the north by the Snake River and Castle Creek, on the east by the Bruneau, and on the west and south by a network of interconnecting creeks; the Blue, the Bottle, and the Mill. It was this ready availability of water as well as a plentiful supply of good grass that made Coventry on the Snake so valuable.

It was not by mere coincidence that the name of the ranch, Coventry on the Snake, had an Old World flavor. Kitty's husband, Sir Thomas Denbigh Wellington, the Seventh Earl of Buckinghamshire, had named it after his ancestral home, Coventry on the Wye, in Buckinghamshire, England.

But Kitty was not just a beautiful woman who happened to inherit a lot of land. She had turned Coventry on the Snake into one of the finest horse ranches in the country, and she had done it all since the death of her husband.

This morning Kitty was sitting in her study working on the books when someone knocked lightly on the door frame. The door to her study being open, when Kitty turned in her chair, she saw Tyrone Canfield standing there, holding his hat in his hand.

"Yes, Tyrone," Kitty said, greeting her foreman with a smile. "Did you want to see me?"

Tyrone rolled his hat in his hand and cleared his throat, obviously not wanting to say what he had to say. The expression of concern on Tyrone's face caused Kitty to give up her smile.

"What is it, Tyrone?" she asked. "What is wrong?"

"I hate to tell you this, Mrs. Wellington, but we're missin' seventy-five head of Arabians," he said.

"What? Are you sure?"

"Yes, ma'am, I'm positive. We've been keepin' a real good count of the Arabians, especially since they are the ones you are sellin' to the army. Last count we had eight hundred and eighty-five. This mornin' we only had eight hundred and ten. And we counted them twice, just to make sure."

"This is a big ranch, with a lot of range land," Kitty said. "Maybe they just got out of the field where we were holding them."

"No, ma'am, we've looked all over the range," Tyrone said. "The horses are gone."

"Stolen?"

"Yes, ma'am. There's no doubt in my mind, but that they were stolen."

"Seventy five horses?" Kitty sighed, and leaned back in her chair. "Oh, Tyrone, that's seven thousand five hundred dollars," she said.

"Yes, ma'am, I know it is. Mrs. Wellington, if you don't mind, I think I'm going to put out night riders to keep watch from now on."

"No, I don't mind at all. I think that's a very good idea," Kitty replied.

# CHAPTER FIVE

A colt whinnied anxiously and a horse responded with a whicker. An owl hooted, while the night insects filled the air with their songs. There was no moon, but the night was alive with stars — from the brightest orbs in the heavens, all the way down to those stars which weren't visible as individual bodies at all, but whose distant presence added to the ambient glow in the velvet vault of sky.

Three young men rode around the milling shapes and shadows that made up the herd. It had been a week now since the seventy-five horses were stolen, and since that time, Tyrone had put out riders every night to keep watch over the horses. Though it would have been more efficient for them to separate, the boring aspects of the task caused the three nighthawks to ride together so they could visit. Prew was one of the riders, and he and another rider were teasing the youngest one.

"What do you mean? Are you trying to tell me you've never been with a woman?" Prew asked the youngest one.

The youngest cowboy, whose name was Hank, cleared his throat in embarrassment. "I ain't never thought I was old enough. And comin' from the orphanage like I done, I ain't never really had the opportunity to be with no woman."

"Hell, you don't need no opportunity. All you got to do is go into town and visit Flat Nose Sue," Prew said.

"Yeah," the other added. He laughed. "And bein' as you ain't never been with a woman before, that makes you lucky."

"How does it make me lucky?"

"Tell him, Prew. How does it make him lucky?"

Prew laughed. "You the one that brought it up, Timmy. You tell him."

"All right," Timmy said. "Here's why it makes you lucky. If you go into Flat Nose Sue's place and tell her you're a virgin, why, she's such a big hearted woman that on your first time, she will let you do it for free."

"I ain't no virgin," Hank insisted.

"What do you mean you ain't no virgin?" Timmy asked. "You just said you ain't never been with a woman before."

65

"I ain't never been with no woman before, but that don't make me a virgin."

"Sure it does. If you ain't never been with a woman before, then you are a virgin."

"Virgins is women, ain't they?" Hank asked.

Prew and Timmy laughed. "It ain't only women that's virgins. A woman that ain't never had a man is a virgin, yeah, but a man that ain't never had a woman, why, he is a virgin too."

"Are you sure about that? I ain't never heard of no man virgin."

"And you know all about such things do you?" Timmy asked. "I mean, bein' as you are so experienced and all."

"No, I don't really. I just thought — that is — I didn't know that men could be virgins too. All right, if that is the case then I guess I am a virgin."

"So, like I said, all you got to do is, you go into Flat Nose Sue's place and tell her you're a virgin."

"Then what?" Hank asked.

"Then, you don't have to do nothing. Flat Nose Sue will take care of that little situation for you," Timmy said. "Right, Prew?"

"Right."

"For sure?" Hank asked.

"For sure," Timmy answered. He laughed.

66

"Flat Nose Sue, she's the oldest one there and she runs the place. So she'll break you in her ownself."

"Break me in her ownself? Wait, what do you mean? Are you saying I'd have to uh — do it — with Flat Nose Sue?" Hank asked in a voice that reflected the unattractiveness of the offer. "Didn't you say she's the oldest one there?"

"That she is. How old you reckon she is, Prew? Fifty. Sixty, maybe?"

"Yeah, maybe sixty," Prew answered. "I don't think she's any older than than sixty, maybe sixty-five. And if she is any older than that, then it ain't by all that much."

"But I'm only sixteen. I don't want to do it with someone who is sixty, or maybe sixty-five years old. Couldn't I do it with one of the younger ones?" Hank pleaded.

"You don't want a young one for your first time," Prew said. "You want someone who knows what to do so they can break you in proper. Besides, why are you askin' that? You wouldn't turn her down, would you? That would hurt her feelings. You sure don't want to hurt Flat Nose Sue's feelin's because if you do that, why, you'll piss off all the women that's in the whore house, and they won't none of 'em have anything to do with any of us anymore. Is that what you want to do?"

"No, I guess not," Hank replied plaintively. "If she says I've got to do it with her, why, I reckon I will. Why do they call her Flat Nose Sue?"

Timmy and Prew both laughed.

"That's right, you ain't never seen her, have you?" Prew asked.

"No. I told you, I ain't never been to no whore house nowhere before."

"Well, sir, they call her Flat Nose Sue 'cause she's done got her nose broke so many times by drunk cowboys and the like, that when you look at her sideways, it purt' nigh looks like she don't have no nose at all," Prew explained.

"Oh," Hank said, even more dispirited than before.

"But she don't look all that bad when you are lookin' at her from the front," Timmy said. " 'Ceptin' for how old she is," he added.

"Tell you what," Prew said. "Why don't we all go into town first thing in the mornin' after we get off work? Seein' as we're goin' to be ridin' herd all night, it'll be early in the mornin' and there won't hardly be nobody else there. We can have our pick."

"Except for Hank," Timmy said. "He don't get his pick, 'cause he'll have to lay with Big Nose Sue."

"Yeah, but it'll be free," Prew said.

"You lucky dog," Timmy said, reaching over and striking Hank playfully on the shoulder. "You're goin' to get it for free."

"Yeah, I'm just real lucky," Hank said without enthusiasm.

The colt whinnied again.

"Sounds like one of the colts might have got somewhere it shouldn't be," Hank said. "I'll go take a look."

Prew waited until Hank rode out into the darkness, then he laughed.

"We got that boy so up tight that right now you couldn't drive a straw up his ass with a ten pound sledge hammer," Prew said.

Timmy laughed, then asked, "You sure Flat Nose Sue will go along with it?"

"She said she would," Prew answered. "This is going to be funnier than all hell."

"Yeah, I reckon so. But it's sort of a dirty trick when you think about it. Lord I hate to think of breakin' him in with Flat Nose Sue. I mean, she could turn a fella off women for life," Timmy said.

"She ain't really all that bad," Prew said.

"How do you know?" Timmy asked. Then he laughed out loud. "I'll be damn. You've had her, ain't you?" He laughed and slapped his hand against his leg. "I can't believe you've actually had her. Does Jenny know that?"

"What's Jenny got to do with it?"

"I thought you was kind of sweet on her. You always hangin' out with her at the Sand Spur."

"She's s'posed to hang out with me. That's her job."

"It's the job of all the girls in the Sand Spur, but she's near 'bout the onliest one I ever see you with."

"Maybe you got it backward," Prew teased. "Maybe she's sweet on me."

"Ha! I can see that," Timmy said.

Suddenly, their banter was interrupted by the sound of a gunshot coming from the darkness.

"What the hell is Hank shootin' at?" Prew asked.

"I don't know," Timmy answered.

"Hank? Hank, what is it you are shootin' at? A cougar?" Prew called out.

"Hank? Where you at?" Timmy called. "What the hell? Where's Hank? How come he ain't answerin' us?" Timmy asked.

"Maybe we'd better go see what's goin' on," Prew replied.

Timmy and Prew were both wearing guns, and though sometimes in town they liked to wear them low and kicked out in the way of a gunfighter, neither of them had ever done anything but take a few pot shots at a rabbit now and then. Nevertheless, both men drew their pistols, then rode out into the darkness to check on Hank.

Before they had gone too far, gunshots erupted in the night, the herd of horses illuminated by the muzzle flashes.

"Rustlers!" Timmy shouted.

"Let's get out of here!" Prew said.

Firing their own pistols, even though they had no target, the two young men tried to run, but within less than a minute, both had been shot from their saddles, and once again, the night was still.

Sitting quietly in his saddle after having dispatched a few other riders to take care of business, Poke Terrell saw one of those riders, Sam Logan, appear from the darkness.

"What was the shooting?" Poke asked.

"It was just like you said. She's got night riders out watchin' over her herd."

"How many of 'em was there?" Poke asked.

"They was three, but we took care of all of 'em."

"Good. Now, round up seventy-five horses, and let's get out of here."

"Say Poke, I heard that these here horses is worth a hunnert dollars apiece," Logan said. "How come we only been getting' twenty-five dollars apiece for 'em?"

"Because to us, twenty-five dollars apiece is all they are worth."

"Why is that?"

"This here is the only horse ranch in the county. You want to take 'em in Medbury to sell, do you? Or maybe to Glen's Ferry or King Hill?"

"No. More'n likely the horses would be recognized there."

"Then don't you think it would be better to sell them to someone who will give us twenty-five dollars a horse and not ask questions? Poke asked.

"Yeah, I guess you're right," Logan said.

"Maybe you aren't as dumb as I thought."

Out in the dark, Jason Prewitt crawled on his stomach until he reached Timmy.

"Timmy! Timmy!" he said, whispering as he shook the body. He was afraid to speak any louder because he was afraid he would be heard.

Helplessly, Prew lay in the dark and watched the rustlers round up the horses, then take them away.

"Son of a bitch," he said to himself.

"That's Poke Terrell." Prew reached for his pistol, but his holster was empty. He had lost his gun somewhere in the dark.

Not until they were gone did he get up. Favoring the wound in his shoulder, he found his horse, and rode back to the big house to report the robbery.

Mrs. Wellington wasn't going to like this. She wasn't going to like it at all. The only reason there were nighthawks out at all was to prevent just such a thing from happening. At least, that's what they were supposed to do. But they failed.

*The next day*

"I arranged for Timmy's body to be sent back to Missouri where his family is. He'll be goin' out on tomorrow's train," Tyrone Canfield told Kitty. Tyrone Canfield had been foreman of Coventry on the Snake for eighteen years, long before Kitty had married Sir Thomas Wellington. Thomas died three years earlier, but, at Kitty's request, Tyrone had stayed on as her ranch foreman.

"What about Hank?" Kitty asked.

"Hank, being raised in an orphanage and all, I done like you said," Tyrone replied. "I made arrangements to bury him in the cemetery in town."

"Not in Potter's Corner?"

"No, ma'am, he'll have him a spot right in the middle of the cemetery."

"Good."

"You're a fine woman, Mrs. Wellington. You've always had a soft spot in your heart for orphans."

"Yes, I have," Kitty said, without further explanation.

"How is Prew?" Tyrone asked. "The doctor was just comin' out when I left to go into town."

"The wound was in his shoulder and the doctor got the bullet out. He said Prew will be all right if the wound doesn't fester," Kitty said.

"We lost another seventy-five horses," Tyrone said with an expression of frustration in his voice. "Prew saw them this time, and he said he was sure that the leader of the bunch was Poke Terrell. I told that to the sheriff but he won't do anything about it."

"Who is Poke Terrell? I don't believe I've ever heard of him," Kitty said.

"No, he is not the kind of person you would likely meet," Tyrone said. "He is a scoundrel who hangs out in the Sand Spur Saloon. They say he used to belong to the Idaho Auxiliary Peace Officers' Posse. If so, that doesn't speak very well for him or the posse."

"Does Marshal Sparks know that Terrell is the one who has been stealing my horses?"

"I told him that Prew said he saw him."

"Is the marshal going to arrest Terrell?"

Tyrone shook his head. "No ma'am. For one thing, he says that an identification, made in the dark, wouldn't hold up. To tell the truth, Mrs. Wellington, I think the marshal would like to do something about it, but it is just too overwhelming for him."

"If you ask me, the whole thing is just too overwhelming, not just for Marshal Sparks, but for all concerned," another man said, coming into the room then. "I have told Kitty that the best thing she can do is sell all the horses off, now. In fact, I think she should sell the land too."

"Hello, Mr. Kincaid," Tyrone said.

"Tyrone," Marcus Kincaid replied with a nod.

"Sell the land to who, Marcus?" Kitty asked. "To you?"

"If you would like to sell it to me, I would be happy to buy it," Kincaid replied. "After all, it was my land long before it was ever yours."

"It was never your land," Kitty said with the long suffering sigh of someone who had been through this argument many times before. "It was Tommy's land, to do with as he saw fit, and he saw fit to leave it to me."

"He left the land to you after only one year of marriage," Kincaid replied. "He was your husband for one year, he was my stepfather for twelve years."

"He was never your stepfather."

"He was my stepfather in all but name."

"I will admit that after he married your mother, he treated you as his own son, but he never adopted you. Anyway, why are you complaining? It isn't as if he abandoned you. Even before he died, he divided all of his holdings in two, and gave you half."

"Yes, including all his money in England which he gave half to me, and half to you," Kincaid said. "That would have been over half a million dollars for each of us. But the family back in England has prevented either one of us from collecting our rightful inheritance."

"Then your anger should be with those in England, not with me."

Kincaid held up his hand. "Kitty, Kitty, I don't want to fight. We're on the same side here. I just heard that you had another episode of rustling, and I came out to see how you are doing. And to be honest, I am also suggesting that you may have taken a bigger bite than you can swallow."

"So you are willing to come to my rescue,

right, Marcus?"

"In a matter of speaking. Just think about it, Kitty. If you sold everything to me, just the land mind you, I'm not interested in the house, you can keep the house, why, you would have enough money to live comfortably for the rest of your life." Kincaid chuckled. "That would show the Wellingtons back in England that neither one of us need them."

"And you would do what? Get rid of the horses and raise cattle?"

"You have to admit, that raising cattle is a lot more practical," Kincaid said.

"I appreciate the offer, Marcus, I really do," Kitty said. "But raising horses was a dream that Tommy and I had together. If I don't follow through with it, I would feel as if I had let him down."

"I've only got one more thing to say," Kincaid said. "I happen to know that you have a considerable loan against this place. I am sure that you know that if you can't pay off the loan, you are going to be faced with losing everything. And I'll tell you the truth, Kitty, I don't see any way on earth you are going to be able to pay that loan."

"I have no intention of defaulting on the loan. I will pay it."

"How?"

"I'll pay it," Kitty said.

"By July fourth? That is when your loan is due, isn't it? July fourth?"

"Yes."

"That's just over a month from now."

"What if I am a few days late with my payment? It isn't going to make that much difference," Kitty said.

"What makes you think that?"

"Think about it, Marcus. The bank wants the money I owe them. They don't want the ranch. Anyway there's no problem. I have a contract to sell some horses in Chicago. Once I deliver those horses I will have more than enough money to pay off the loan, and I'll have the property, and the horses, free and clear."

"You have a contract to sell horses in Chicago?"

"Yes."

"But even so, how many horses can you sell in Chicago?"

"My contract calls for five hundred."

"Five hundred? That's a lot of horses. Who would buy five hundred horses?"

"The U.S. Army," Kitty replied with a satisfied smile. "So you see, Marcus, there is no problem. I will get the bank paid off."

"In time?"

"Yes, in time. That is, assuming I have no

problems in getting the horses to Chicago."

"Ahh, well, therein is the rub. Kitty, I don't want to be the naysayer here, but just what makes you think you are going to be able to get your horses to Chicago? You haven't even been able to protect them when they are on your own property."

Kitty walked over to a table and picked up a copy of *The Boise Statesman.* "Did you read this article?" she asked, showing the paper to Kincaid, and pointing to the article in question.

"About the shootout over in Wyoming? Yes, I read it. What about it?"

"Read the last sentence," Kitty said. "The one that says Matt Jensen is a friend of what is right, and a foe of those who would visit their evil deeds upon innocent people."

Kincaid read the sentence, then he laughed out loud.

"What is so funny?" Kitty asked.

"Do you really think Matt Jensen, this — hero — will come to your rescue, wearing shining armor and riding on a white horse?" Kincaid asked.

"Well, not the shining armor, and maybe not even the white horse. But yes, I really think he will come to help me."

"What makes you think that he save the day?"

"Because he is Matt Jensen," Kitty replied. Marcus Kincaid left the house then, laughing out loud at Kitty's innocent naïveté about someone she had only read about in the newspaper.

# CHAPTER SIX

*Coventry Manor*

George Gilmore was a small man, five feet
three inches tall, and weighing but 120
pounds. What he lacked in size, though, he
made up for in intelligence, having gradu-
ated from Washington University in St.
Louis with full academic honors. After
graduation he read for the law, and was now
a practicing attorney in Medbury, Idaho.

At the moment he was standing in the
entry hall at Coventry Manor, having been
summoned by Kitty Wellington. As he
waited there, he studied the colorful ban-
ners that hung over the hall, including the
Union Jack of Great Britain, the Stars and
Stripes of the United States, and the Wellington family crest.

Gilmore was a little nervous about the
visit because he had recently represented
the plaintiff in a lawsuit against Mrs. Wellington. Mrs. Wellington won the lawsuit, so

he hoped she hadn't sent for him to give vent to her anger. Mrs. Wellington was a very important woman in Owyhee County, and someone in his position could not afford to make such a powerful enemy.

"Mr. Gilmore," Mrs. Wellington said, smiling sweetly when she came to greet him. "Thank you so much for coming."

Gilmore was a little taken aback by the smile. It seemed genuine. He relaxed a little.

"Yes, well, you said you had need of my services. I must confess to being a little surprised."

"Why surprised?"

"I thought you might be angry with me."

"Because you represented the other party in a lawsuit against me? Don't be silly. I know that's what lawyers do. I also know that you are an honest and trustworthy man. You could have bent the facts in the case, but you did not."

"That wouldn't have been ethical," Gilmore said.

"Exactly," Kitty said. "And right now I need someone who is both ethical and discrete. Can you be both?"

"As long as the two requirements aren't contradictory," Gilmore replied.

Kitty laughed. "Good, good, that is exactly the answer an honest man would give. Now

I know I have the right man."

"What is the task, Mrs. Wellington?"

Kitty picked up a folded copy of *The Boise Statesman* from the hall table. "Have you read this paper?"

Gilmore glanced at it, then he looked up. "Yes, it has a very nice article about you."

"It also has an article about Matt Jensen," Kitty said. "The task I am assigning you, Mr. Gilmore, is to find Matt Jensen. Once you learn where he is, I want you to contact him and tell him that an old friend needs help, and ask him to meet you in American Falls. Once you meet him, bring him to me."

"You tell me to bring him to you, but I can only bring him if he is willing to come," Gilmore said. "I have heard of Matt Jensen. I get the feeling that he is not a man who can be coerced into doing something he doesn't want to do."

"I will give you a personal letter to carry from me to him. Once you show him the letter, he will come," Kitty said, confidently.

"All right, I'll contact him, and I'll carry your letter to him," Gilmore replied. "But I'm curious. Why do you want me to meet him in American Falls? Why not meet him in Medbury?"

"I want to keep the meeting secret," Kitty replied. "I think we can better do that in

American Falls. Besides if, after you meet him, he doesn't want to get involved, he won't have come so far. That is, assuming he is still in Green River."

"I'll do what I can."

"Mr. Gilmore, I especially do not want Poke Terrell to find out about this. If Prew is right, if Mr. Terrell is the one behind the rustling of my horses, he might try and stop Matt from coming."

"Matt? You are on a first name basis with Matt Jensen?"

"I was once," Kitty said.

"Well, in that case, maybe he will come," Gilmore said. "And don't worry, I will be extremely guarded in my mission."

*Cattleman's Bank and Loan, two days later*
"You sent for me, Joel?" Marcus Kincaid asked.

"Yes," Matthews said. He slid a letter across the desk, and Marcus picked it up.

"What is this?"

"This is a letter from Kitty Wellington. I thought it might give you comfort to know that the loan will be repaid and you will recoup your investment, as well as the interest due. It's addressed to me but, under the circumstances, you being the one who now owns the loan, it is really your letter."

Dear Mr. Matthews:

As you know, within the last two weeks, Coventry on the Snake has been the victim of the foulest rustling, resulting in the loss of more than one hundred and fifty head of fine horses, worth a total of fifteen thousand dollars.

I fear that you may be worrying about whether I will be able to retire the loan your bank so generously advanced, so I undertake the writing of this letter to ease any worries you may have on that score. I have recently signed a contract to deliver enough horses to the U.S. Army to allow me to easily discharge the debt I owe the bank. In order to help me accomplish this, I am calling upon Matt Jensen, an old friend, to help me, and I am sending my agent to American Falls to meet with him.

I'm sure you can understand that, for the time being, I would prefer that the details of my contact with Mr. Jensen be kept in the strictest confidence.

Sincerely,
Mrs. Katherine Wellington
Coventry on the Snake

"Yes, I heard she had signed a contract to sell enough horses to pay off the loan," Marcus said. "That's good. That's very good."

"I thought you might appreciate that, knowing that the money will be repaid, in full, and with interest."

"Yes, that's very — comforting." He set the word comforting apart from the rest of the sentence.

"As the bullfighters say, it is the moment of truth for all bankers, when the loans are repaid in full," Matthews said. "Perhaps after the successful conclusion of this project, you would be interested in purchasing more loans."

"Perhaps."

*Mountain Home, Idaho*
When Sam Logan, Al Madison, and Ken Jernigan first stepped into the Cow Palace Saloon, they didn't see the person they were looking for.

"You sure this is the place?" Madison asked.

"Yeah, I'm sure," Logan answered.

"What makes you so sure?"

"How many saloons are there in Mountain Home named Cow Palace?" Logan asked.

"There's only one saloon in Mountain Home," Jernigan said.

"And it is named Cow Palace," Logan said.

"So, if this is the right place, how come

86

Poke ain't here?"

"There he is," Logan said.

"Where?"

"Back there in the corner, sitting with his back to us."

"Why is sittin' like that? We damn near didn't see him," Jernigan said.

"Maybe that's why he's sittin' like that," Logan answered. "Maybe he don't want to be seen."

Logan led them to the back of the saloon to the table where the man they were to meet was sitting.

"Did you see anyone else from Medbury outside?" Poke asked.

"No," Logan answered. "Poke, why we meetin' here, 'stead of in the Sand Spur?"

"It's better to meet here," Poke said without further explanation.

Matt Jensen was in Southeastern Idaho, riding north and sloping down a long slant from the Sublett Mountain range. The green covered mountains loomed up behind him, a long impressive range that ran south, all the way down to the Utah border. The Subletts were interspersed here and there with canyons and draws which made the mountain range look much larger than it actually was.

Matt was following a little dry wash that was, appropriately called Rock Creek, because only during the spring run offs did it have water. Now, as in most of the year, Rock Creek had only rocks. He had not been worried though, because he knew that soon he would come upon the Snake River, and now that confidence was rewarded. Ahead of him he spotted a narrow, snaking band of green, cutting across the amber desert floor. This, he knew, was the Snake River.

"You thirsty, Spirit?" he asked. He reached down to pat the second horse to bear the name. "Well, I am too, but to tell you the truth, I'm thirstier for something that tastes a little better than water."

Spirit whickered.

"I know, I know, after the ride we've put in today, water will taste awfully good."

As Matt rode on across the stretch of desert, Spirit's hoof falls raised clouds of dust to hang in the air behind him. Those little puffs of dust marked his trail to the patch of green. There, in the middle of the patch of green, the river, some one hundred feet wide at this point, moved in a surprisingly swift flow, the surface showing white water here and there as it passed over the rocky bottom.

Matt dismounted, then got down on his stomach and stuck his mouth into the water. It was cool, almost too cold, and as he sucked in great draughts of water he felt a stab of pain behind his eyes from drinking something too cold, too fast.

Raising his head from the water he saw Spirit drinking as well, but Spirit seemed to be approaching it more cautiously.

Matt laughed. "Looks like you knew better than to drink too fast," he said. "I guess that's where they come by the term horse sense."

Matt filled his canteen, then looked across the river. About a mile on the other side he espied a cluster of buildings, gleaming crimson now in the sun that was slowly sinking in the west. To the east, the sky was already growing darker, whereas a band of clouds, belly lit and glowing brightly in vivid golds and reds, still illuminated the sky to the west.

"Spirit, if you've had your fill, what you say we go on into town, and see what this letter is about?" Matt asked, swinging back into the saddle.

Because the bottom of the creek was clearly visible, Matt had no difficulty finding a place to ford. The water was about twelve inches deep, and Spirit pranced through quickly and easily, his hooves making but little splash in a stream that was already running rapidly.

As Matt approached the town from the south, he saw a train coming from the east, a long, rumbling, string of cars following behind the powerful locomotive, the puffs of which could be heard even from this far away.

*American Falls, Idaho Territory*
Because George Gilmore was a lawyer, he felt that he owed a certain degree of decorum to the profession he had chosen. Therefore, even when he wasn't arguing a case in the courtroom, or dealing directly with one of his clients, he believed that he should still dress the part. For that reason, as he stood here in the Red Horse Saloon, dressed in a three piece suit, but surrounded by denim and homespun, he stood out like a flower among cabbages.

Gilmore was in American Falls to meet Matt Jensen, though Jensen didn't know he was coming here to meet Gilmore. Gilmore had written a letter to Jensen, offering to hire him to "provide security for an old friend." Responding to Kitty Wellington's request, he did not tell Jensen who the old friend was, nor did he tell him how much the job would pay. He was depending entirely upon Matt Jensen's curiosity and known appreciation of adventure to provide the catalyst needed to get him here.

Gilmore ordered a mug of beer, then found a table back in the far corner under the balcony. He had just taken his first swallow when he saw Al Madison, Ken Jernigan, and Sam Logan come in. He knew all three of them because he was an officer of the court over in Owyhee Count, and the three of them were often in trouble. Also, of late, he heard that the trio had allied themselves with Poke Terrell. Jason Prewitt was certain that Poke Terrell was the one behind the rustling of Coventry's horse, and Gilmore believed him. However, Gilmore did not blame Marshal Sparks for not doing anything about it because, as a lawyer, he knew that there wasn't enough evidence to support Prew's accusation and thus, make the case in court.

Gilmore had never actually met Poke Terrell, but he had seen him, and he could recognize him on sight. He was aware of Terrell's background and of his former connection with the Idaho Auxiliary Peace Officers' Posse. He knew, also, that because of that connection, and because Terrell seemed to be a brooding and unpleasant man, the

91

majority of the residents of Medbury tended to keep their distance from him. The exceptions were Logan, Madison, and Jernigan, who were now here in American Falls. Gilmore wondered what they were doing here.

At this precise moment, they appeared to be in the midst of an argument, though Gilmore was too far away to be able to ascertain the cause of their argument. Finally, Logan shook his head as if in disgust and left the saloon. Madison and Jernigan stepped up to the bar and ordered a drink.

As Matt approached the town, he saw a crudely painted sign on a narrow board that was just wide enough to display the name of the town:

## AMERICAN FALLS

Passing the sign, Matt encountered a cluster of white painted clapboard houses, some with well-tended lawns and colorful flowers, others with dirt yards. It was getting close to supper time, and he could smell the aromas of meals being cooked.

"Johnny, wash your hands and come to supper," a woman called through the door.

"Yes, Mama," a young boy's voice replied.

For a moment — just a moment, Matt could remember a time when his own mother would call him in to supper. That was before she, his father, and his sister were murdered as they were going out West to seek a new life after the war. Matt was just a boy when that happened, and one of the reasons he was a wanderer today was that wondering what lay just beyond the horizon in front of him tended to blur memories of what was behind him. That helped to prevent periods of painful and nostalgic recollection, such as the one he just had.

Matt continued on into town, and as he rode down Idaho Street, the hollow clopping sound of his horse's hooves echoed back from the buildings that crowded down to the boardwalks that lined each side of the road.

Most of the business establishments were closed now, the only exceptions being a couple of restaurants, a hotel, and the saloon. The restaurants and saloon were all brightly lit and, through the windows, he could see people inside.

He pulled up in front of the saloon, a false fronted building that bore a painting of a prancing red horse. The name of the saloon, in gilt edged, bright red letters, was the Red Horse Saloon.

Matt swung down from his saddle, then looped the reins around the hitching rail. He patted Spirit on the neck.

"You be a good horse, now," he said.

A woman's high-pitched squeal of laughter spilled through the bat wing doors, followed by a man's loud guffaw. There had been no piano playing when he dismounted, but as he started up the two wooden steps that led to the boardwalk in front of the saloon, the music began again, a loud, bright tune that was more to provide ambience than to entertain. Matt wasn't a musician, but even he could tell that the piano was badly out of tune.

The saloon was well lit with two dozen or more lanterns, in addition to a wagon wheel chandelier that had a dozen or more candles set around the rim. The smell was a familiar one — burning kerosene, stale beer and whiskey, cigar and pipe smoke, and the odor of dozens of bodies, too long between baths.

A few looked toward him, but most paid him no attention. The bar was to his left, long, polished, with a brass foot rail and silver hooks every five feet or so, from each of which hung a towel, all of them soiled. Just in front of the bar, at approximately the same intervals as the towels, were spittoons. A spattering of tobacco quids on and around the spittoons indicated that the customers weren't particularly careful with their expectorations.

A young woman, heavily made up and wearing a low-cut dress, was standing by the piano. She might have pretty before the too many years on the line took its toll on her. She started toward Matt with an inviting smile and, while Matt responded with a polite nod of his head, he made it obvious by his action that he wasn't particularly interested in her company tonight, so she turned and walked back to the piano.

A mirror, almost half as long as the bar itself, was on the wall behind the bar. There was a flaw in the mirror so that the reflections were somewhat distorted. A man was wiping the bar as Matt approached. He wore a low crown black hat, with so many red and yellow feathers sticking up from the hat band that they almost formed a crown.

"Yes, sir," he said. "What can I do you for?"

"I'll have a beer," Matt said, putting a nickel on the bar.

The bartender pulled a clean glass from under the bar, then held it under the spigot of a beer barrel. He cut it off when the head reached the top of the glass.

"Interesting hat," Matt said, pointing to the feather festooned chapeau. "Couldn't make up your mind what color feather you wanted?"

The bartender chuckled, then removed his hat and held it out for Matt's closer appraisal.

"I'll have you know, sir, that these feathers come from the little known, golden beak twitter, a bird that is adorned with beautiful red and yellow feathers. It is said that, many years ago, the golden beak twitters were as thick as flies, but the Zapmonog Indians treasured their feathers so much that the noble creature was made extinct."

"Or maybe they are just dyed chicken feathers," Matt suggested.

The bartender laughed. "I can't get one over on you, can I, friend?" He put the hat back on his head. "Stranger in town, are you? I haven't seen you in here before."

"I just got here." Matt blew some of the foam away, then turned the mug up and took several deep swallows."

"You must've been ridin' some," the bartender said. "You've worked yourself up a real beer thirst there."

Matt finished the beer, set the mug down,

then wiped his mouth with the back of his hand.

"You're right," he said. "That one was for thirst. Now I'll have one for taste." He put another nickel on the bar.

The bartender chuckled. "Yes, sir, I hear you," he said, taking the mug, then turning around to refill it.

Gilmore had never met Matt Jensen before, so he didn't know if this was Jensen or not. But it could be. There was a rather heroic aura about his appearance, and he did say he had been riding.

Gilmore got up from his chair and started to approach the stranger, but he saw Madison say something to Jernigan. Jernigan nodded, then went upstairs to the balcony. Going back to his chair, Gilmore looked up toward the balcony and, from his position, was able to see Jernigan step around a corner in the hall, then pull his gun. While he was wondering what that was about, he heard Madison address the man who had just come in.

"Mister, would your name be Matt Jensen?"

Matt looked around and saw that the question had come from a man who was standing at the opposite end of the bar.

The man who asked the question had a pock-marked face, beady eyes, and a drooping moustache. And from the tone of the man's voice, Matt perceived the question to be more confrontational than a mere request for information. Is this the man who sent him the letter? He decided to give the man the next move, so, saying nothing, he turned his attention back to his beer.

"I asked you a question, Mister!" the man at the other end of the bar said. "Is your name Matt Jensen?"

"Have we met?" Matt asked, without looking back toward the man.

"No, we ain't never met."

"Do you have business with me?" This time, Matt did look at him.

"Yeah," the man answered with what might have been a smile. "Yeah, I got business with you."

"What business would that be?"

"I aim to kill you," the man said. "That's what my business is."

Those who were close enough to hear the challenge in the man's voice had already grown quiet in order to better hear where this conversation was going. Now, with the man's declaration of his intent to kill Matt Jensen, they moved quickly to get out of the line of fire, should shooting begin.

Matt turned to face his challenger. Maybe this was the man who had sent him the letter. Maybe the letter was just a ruse to get him up here, just for this purpose.

"Mister, this ain't the place for somethin' like that," the bartender said. "Why don't you have another beer, on the house?"

"And why don't you mind your own business?"

The bartender started to say something else, but as he looked at Matt Jensen, he saw that, despite the tension of the moment, Matt was exhibiting no nervousness.

"You don't really want to do this," Matt said.

"Oh yeah, I do want to do it. I very much want to do it."

"I don't want to sound like a braggart, mister, but there have been a lot of men who tried to kill me, and a lot of men who died trying."

"I ain't a lot of men. I'm just me."

"What is your name?"

"My name is Al Madison. I reckon you've heard of me."

Matt shook his head. "No, I can't say that I have."

"Well, after this little fracas, I expect ever' one will know the name Al Madison. They will all know that Al Madison is the man who kilt Matt Jensen."

"Or they will know that you were the man who was killed by Matt Jensen," Matt replied, easily. "We don't have to take this any further, Madison. You don't need to die tonight. You can stop now, and live to see the sun rise tomorrow."

"Oh, I ain't the one that's goin' to die, Mister," Madison said confidently. "You are."

In the corner of the saloon, Matt saw another man sitting all alone at a table back under the balcony. He was a rather smallish man, and he was wearing, not the denims and shirts most of the other patrons were wearing, but a suit with a vest and a tie. Matt had noticed this man when he first stepped into the saloon, not only because he was dressed differently from the others, but also because he had been one of the few who had paid particular attention to him.

But as Matt glanced toward him now, the well-dressed man pointed up toward the balcony, doing so with a movement of his hand that was almost imperceptible. Matt wasn't sure he would have even caught the signal at all had the man not also glanced up.

Responding to what he perceived as a warning of some sort, Matt took a quick peek toward the upstairs balcony where he saw someone kneeling behind the railing. He also saw that the man behind the railing upstairs had drawn his pistol.

"Is there any way I might be able to talk you out of this?" Matt asked, continuing the effort to diffuse the situation.

Madison stretched his mouth into what might have been a smile, though it was a smile without mirth or pleasantness. "No, I don't think so," Madison said. "I've come to the ball — I reckon it's time we danced." Without further discussion, Madison's hand dipped toward his holster.

At the same time Madison made a ragged grab for his pistol, Matt saw the man on the balcony stand up with his pistol raised and pointed directly at him. Considering the man aloft to be the greater danger, Matt drew and fired. The man on the balcony pulled the trigger, but it was too late. Matt's bullet had already plowed into his heart and the would-be assailant's pistol shot shattered Matt's beer mug but missed him. The man fell through the railing, doing a half somersault on his way down and landing on his back on the piano below. The impact caused a discordant ring of the piano strings. The piano player, as well as the soiled dove who had been standing beside the piano, were in no danger because, like the others, they had moved to get out of the way as soon as Madison made his declaration known.

Realizing that his backup had not only been discovered, but killed, the expression on Madison's face changed quickly from one of easy confidence to shock and fear over the fact that he no longer had an edge. Frightened now, he pulled the trigger on his pistol, even before he could bring it all the way up to bear. The bullet from Madison's gun hit a spittoon that was sitting on the floor halfway between him and Matt, causing a fountain of noxious brown liquid to erupt from the container.

Matt's second shot hit Madison in the forehead, and he fell back.

Matt continued to hold his pistol at the ready as the smoke from the four gun discharges drifted toward the ceiling, then spread out to collect in a bluish gray, nostril-burning cloud that hovered just above the wagon wheel chandelier. He looked around quickly to make certain there were no other challengers.

Seeing none, he holstered his pistol, then looked over at the bartender who had ducked down behind the bar when the shooting started.

"You can stand up now," Matt said, easily.

"Is it all over?" the bartender asked in a nervous voice.

"It's all over, and it looks like I'll be needing another beer," Matt said.

Like everyone else, Gilmore had been shocked by the sudden drama that had erupted in here. Unlike everyone else, Gilmore knew Madison and Jernigan, and he knew they were unpleasant characters, but he did not realize they would actually commit, or at least attempt to commit, murder.

Logan, the third man of the group, had watched the whole thing from just on the other side of the bat-wing doors. He came back into the saloon now, to have a closer look at his two dead friends. Gilmore held his breath while he waited to see what Logan was going to do. To his surprised relief, Logan did nothing but look around for a moment, then, turning, he left the saloon.

# CHAPTER SEVEN

After he served Matt another beer, the bartender leaned over the bar to look at the two bodies. Madison was lying on his back at the end of the bar, his arms thrown out to either side of him, his pistol a few feet away from his right hand.

The second shooter was also on his back, but he was draped across the piano with his head hanging down. His hat and pistol were on the floor just in front of the piano bench. Gradually, cautiously, the others in the bar began approaching the two bodies.

"Are they both dead?" the bartender asked.

"This here'n is deader'n shit," someone said as he poked at Madison's body with his foot.

"This one is as well," the piano player said, returning to his instrument. He lifted the shooter's hand, then let it go. It fell against the keyboard, striking several keys inharmoniously.

"Damn, Floyd, that feller plays the piano better dead than you do alive," someone said, and a few of the others laughed, nervously, not from the humor of the comment, but from the fact that it tended to relieve the tension.

Only the women of the bar did not gather around the two bodies. Instead, the one who had smiled at Matt when he first came into the saloon, and the other two who had been working the bar with her, now stood in a frightened cluster back in the far corner of the barroom, near the large, upright clock.

"Did you all you see what I just seen?" someone asked. "That feller at the bar took 'em both out."

"Damndest thing I ever saw."

"I seen Hickock in action oncet. He war'nt nowhere near as fast as this here fella was."

"I've hear'd tell of a feller named Matt Jensen, but this here is the first time I ever actual saw him."

For a long moment nobody approached Matt, and he was glad. He had come in here for a beer, and that was all. He had no idea he would get involved in a gun fight, and he still had no idea why he was challenged. It couldn't have been, as Madison said, to

105

make a name for himself. For if that had been the case, there would not have been a second shooter on the balcony. And if there was a second shooter that meant this was planned. But how could they have planned it? Nobody knew Matt was coming to American Falls.

Nobody except the person who had offered him the job. Was Madison the one who wrote the letter? Had he written it just to get Matt to come American Falls? That would explain how they were able to set up an ambush for him, but it did not explain why.

The life Matt Jensen lived was full of desperate and deadly encounters, and those encounters invariably left enemies. But as far as he knew, he had never encountered Madison before. On the other hand, he also realized that there was no way he could ever know just who every enemy might be.

Matt looked over in the corner toward the smallish man who had given him the warning of the second shooter. Seeing a nearly empty beer mug sitting on the table in front of him, Matt turned to the bartender.

"Give me another beer," he said, again putting a nickel down.

The bartender drew a third beer, and Matt took the full mug over to the little man at the table.

"I'd like to buy you a beer," Matt said.

"Thank you."

"Why did you do it?" Matt asked.

"Why did I do what?"

"You know what. You gave me a signal about the second shooter."

"I suppose I did."

"Why?"

"Because, Mr. Jensen, if you had been killed, I would not have been able to fulfill my obligation to my client."

Before the little man could explain his comment, a deputy sheriff came into the saloon. He stopped just inside and looked around at the saloon patrons who were now gathered in a knot around the two bodies.

"What the hell happened here? Did these two fellers shoot each other?" the deputy sheriff asked.

"Not hardly," the bartender answered.

"Well then, what did happen?"

Everyone wanted to tell him, and they all started talking at once, each one shouting over the other in order to be heard.

"Hold it! Hold it!" the deputy called, loudly. He put his hands over his ears. "I can't hear you if you are all goin' to shout at the same time. You, Ben," he said to the bartender. "Did you see it?"

"Yeah, I seen it." Ben offered nothing else.

"Well?" the deputy asked.

"Well what?"

"Tell me what happened."

"That feller sittin' at the table over there," Ben said, pointing to Matt. "The big one, not the little one. Anyhow, he just come into the saloon a couple minutes ago and ordered hisself a beer. I drawed him one — from that barrel there, the other'n bein' just about empty and it gets some bitter when you get to the bottom. And you know me, Pete, I figure the first beer anyone orders should be the best 'cause otherwise, how are you goin' to keep 'em as a customer?"

"For God's sake, Ben, will you get on with it?" the deputy said. "I don't give a damn which barrel you served him from."

"Yes, sir, but you asked what happened, and I'm just tellin' you in my own way. Now if you want to hear what happened, just hear me out an' let me speak my piece. Now, like I was sayin', I drawed him a beer, and that feller was just drinkin' it, all peaceful like, when that feller down there" — he pointed to Madison's body — "he says, 'Would you be Matt Jensen?' And the big feller, he says, 'Yes I am.' And then that feller lyin' on the floor, he says 'I'm goin' to kill you.' And the next thing you know, the shootin' commenced."

"What about the other one over there?" the deputy asked, pointing to Jernigan's body. The deputy looked up at the balcony and saw the busted rail. "Did he just get so excited watchin' that he fell through the railing?"

"No, sir. To tell you the truth, Pete, now that's the mystifyin' thing of it. That feller was up on the balcony, and he shot at Mr. Jensen too," Ben said.

"Did he also challenge Jensen to a gunfight?"

"No, sir. What he done is, he just commenced a' shootin' without no word of warnin' at all."

"Ben's tellin' it right, Deputy," a patron said. "It all happened just like he's a' tellin' you it happened."

"So what you are sayin' is, there was two men shootin' at him, one from up on the balcony, but the big man sittin' back there took 'em both on and kilt 'em both?

"Yeah," another said. "I ain't never seen nothin' like it. This here Jensen fella is as fast as greased lightnin'. I mean, when you think about it, it was all over in not much more than the blink of an eye."

"Jensen?"

"Matt Jensen is who it is. I reckon you've

heard of Matt Jensen."

"Yeah," the deputy said. "I've heard of him."

During the entire conversation between the deputy, the bartender, and the other patrons of the bar, Matt had remained seated at the table with the small man who had warned him about the second shooter.

"You want to come over here, Mister Jensen?" the deputy called to Matt.

"Excuse me," Matt said to the little man at the table. He pushed his chair back, then walked over to join the deputy.

"Is that pretty much the way you'd tell the story?" the deputy asked Matt.

"Yes."

"Folks are sayin' you are Matt Jensen. Is that right? Are you really Matt Jensen?"

"Yes."

"I've heard of you, Mr. Jensen. Fac' is, I seem to recall seein' a book that was writ about you. Would you be that Matt Jensen?"

"I wouldn't put much store in any of those dime novels," Matt replied.

"But you are the one them books is about, ain't you?"

"I suppose."

"Didn't I just also read somethin' about you bein' involved in a shootout over in Green River City, Wyoming last month?"

"You may have."

"You bein' the real Matt Jensen and all, it makes me wonder what you are doin' in American Falls," the deputy said. "Is there a reason for you bein' here?"

"There's no reason for me not to be here," Matt answered in a matter of fact tone.

"I reckon not," the deputy agreed. "But the thing is, Mr. Jensen, we don't get that many famous folks in our little town. And we most especial don't get folks that's famous 'cause they are so all fired good with a gun. Accordin' to them dime novels, you are always on the right side of the law. Is that true?"

"I try to be a law abiding citizen," Matt replied.

"Yes. Only, you come here to American Falls and the first thing you do after you get here is, you get yourself involved in a gunfight. Ain't that about the size of it?"

"I didn't start the gunfight."

The deputy waved his hand in dismissal. "I know, I know, ever' one says you didn't start it. But that still don't tell me what you're a' doin' here."

"Deputy, since I am not breaking any law, nor am I wanted by the law, the truth is, I can be just about anywhere I want to be," Matt replied.

"I'm just curious, that's all," the deputy said. "I reckon you are right, I reckon you do have the right to be anywhere you want. And, from what all the folks are saying, I don't see any need for an inquiry. It was self-defense, pure and simple."

"You're doin' the right thing, Pete," the bartender said.

"Anybody know these two men?" the deputy asked, looking toward the bodies.

"This one here said his name was Madison. Al Madison," the bartender said. "I seen him and the other fella together earlier. And if I recall, there was a third one with them too."

"Is that a fact? Is he still here?"

The bartender looked around the saloon, then he shook his head. "I don't see him."

"I seen him a while ago," one of the other saloon patrons said.

"Where did you see him?"

"He was standin' just outside the door there," the man said. "He was watchin' what was goin' on. And like Ben said, he come in with them two fellers. For a moment, I was afraid he might start in a' shootin' seein' as how he was with them before. But all he done was watch. He come in for a few seconds, just long enough to look at his two dead pards, then he left."

"You ever heard of a fella named Al Madison, Deputy?" the bartender asked.

"Yeah, to tell the truth, I think I have heard of him," the deputy replied. "I think I might have seen some paper on him once. Only I believe he's from over in Owyhee county. What do you reckon he's doin' here?"

"Well sir, from the way he was talkin', I'd say he come here especially to kill Mr. Jensen," the bartender answered.

"Did you know him?" the deputy asked Matt.

Matt shook his head. "No."

"I ain't never heard that you ran bad, Mr. Jensen, but I have heard that you've come out on the standin' up side of an awful lot of gunfights, just like you done with this one. Could this maybe be some feud you brought in from somewhere else?"

"Like I said, I've never laid eyes on either one of them before today."

"Uh huh," the deputy said. He stroked his chin as he studied Matt. "Well, I reckon when you come right down to it, somethin' like this is bound to happen, pretty much anywhere you go, ain't it? I mean people like you just seem to breed trouble."

"What do you mean 'people like me'?"

"You know what I mean. I mean people

113

who have a reputation like you have. There's always someone all full of himself, someone who thinks that killin' you will make him famous."

Matt had encountered many such people before, so he couldn't argue with the deputy's logic.

"You've got me there, Deputy," he said. "It's not something I want — it's just something that happens."

"Ahh," the deputy said with a dismissive shake of his head. "It ain't your fault. It's just that — well, for small towns like American Falls, we simply ain't prepared to deal with it. Adam," the deputy called to one of the others, "go get Mr. Prufrock. Tell him he's got some undertakin' business to do. We got us two bodies to take care of."

"Yes, sir, Deputy."

The young man charged off on his errand. The deputy hung around for a moment or two longer, then he started for the door, but before he reached the door, he turned back.

"I'd appreciate it, if those of you who can write, would stop by the office tomorrow and write out a statement about what you seen here tonight. There ain't goin' to be no inquiry, but the sheriff and the judge are goin' to need to know the facts."

"We'll do it, Deputy," someone called back.

# CHAPTER EIGHT

Matt waited until the deputy left, then he returned to the table where the little man sat, quietly waiting. Matt had some questions for him, and began, by asking him his name.

"My name is George Gilmore."

"Just before the deputy came in, you said something about fulfilling an obligation to your client. What were you talking about?"

"I am a lawyer, Mr. Jensen. The client I was talking about is Mrs. Kitty Wellington of Coventry on the Snake."

"You are the one who sent me the letter," Matt said. It was a statement, not a question.

"I am."

"What is Coventry on the Snake?"

"It's a ranch over in Owyhee County."

"Owyhee County is in West Idaho," Matt said. "If your client wanted me to come over there, why did you ask me to meet you here, in American Falls?"

"We didn't want anyone to know we were hiring you," Gilmore said. "That's why Mrs. Wellington suggested that we meet here, in American Falls. Evidently our ruse didn't work, because as you can see, Madison, Jernigan, and Logan found out, not only that we were attempting to hire you, but also where we would be meeting."

"You knew these men?"

"Not personally, but I know who they were. The moment I saw them here, I knew there was likely to be trouble."

"How did you know they would mean trouble?"

"Mrs. Wellington has recently had some trouble with rustlers. One of her hands said that Poke Terrell was behind the rustling, and these three men are associates of Poke Terrell."

"Is Terrell in jail?"

"No."

"Why not?"

"It was one ranch hand's word against Terrell's. And Terrell had witnesses who provided them with an alibi."

"But you believe the ranch hand?"

"I do. And what happened here, tonight, proves it, as far as I'm concerned. I believe they were trying to keep you from going to help Mrs. Wellington."

"How did they know?"

"I beg your pardon?"

"I know how you knew I would be here, since you are the one who sent me the letter. But how did these two men know that I would be here?"

"That is a good question, Mr. Jensen" Gilmore admitted. "I don't have any idea how they knew I was going to meet you here."

"I have another question for you. Why did Mrs. Wellington pick me?"

"At one time Mrs. Wellington knew you, and she remembers you fondly."

Matt shook his head. "I don't recall ever meeting anyone named Kitty Wellington."

"That is her married name," Gilmore said.

"If she is married, why is she trying to hire me? Shouldn't her husband be the one doing the hiring?"

"Her husband is deceased," Gilmore said. He chuckled. "But the truth is, Mrs. Wellington is such a remarkable woman, that even if her husband was still alive, she might very well be the one involved in these negotiations."

"She sounds like an interesting woman."

"Oh, indeed she is, sir. Have you had your dinner yet, Mr. Jensen?"

"No, Matt replied.

"Let me buy you dinner. And over dinner I shall show you a newspaper article about her. Then, I will show you the letter that Mrs. Wellington wrote to you. I think that will explain everything."

Matt smiled. "I've never turned down a free meal," he said.

The undertaker arrived just as Matt and Gilmore were leaving the saloon. He had two workers with him, and he began directing them through the grim business of recovering the bodies.

As they left the saloon they saw the undertaker's wagon parked out front, not the elegant and polished glass sided hearse, but the more pedestrian wagon he used to pick up bodies for preparation.

The two men walked up the street, past the leather goods store, the apothecary, a dry goods store, and a hardware store until they reached a restaurant called Morning Star Café. They were greeted by an attractive brunette, who showed them to a table in the back of the room.

"Now then," Gilmore said, after they ordered, "we'll start with the newspaper article. This particular article happens to be from *The Boise Statesman.* When you read it, perhaps you will have an idea as to who

Mrs. Kitty Wellington is."

Gilmore took an envelope from his pocket, then removed the newspaper article. Gingerly unfolding the article, he handed it across the table to Matt. "Read this."

Matt unfolded the article, spread it out on the table in front of him, and began to read.

### Coventry on Snake Will Be Ready
TO SHIP HORSES SOON.

Mrs. Kitty Wellington of Coventry on the Snake now has upward of one thousand horses on the Range. These are the finest animals one can imagine.

Mrs. Wellington is a strikingly handsome woman, tall and graceful. Her face shows great strength of character and a wealth of blond hair makes a striking frame for it.

Few persons are more entertaining conversationalists. In speaking about her ranch interests, Miss Wellington stated that the ranch was the vision of her late husband, Sir Thomas Wellington, who was the Seventh Earl of Buckinghamshire. However, he died before his ambition could be realized. While some may think that starting a horse ranch may be unseemly for a woman, Mrs. Wellington says that she considered it her obligation to bring his dream to fruition.

Readers may know of Coventry Manor, Wellington's palatial estate located on the Snake River at the conflux of the Bruneau. The ranch itself, Coventry on the Snake, comprises some 20,000 acres of the best grazing range in Idaho. Among the horses are several fine Arabian saddle horses, as well as imported stallions, including Normans and French coach horses.

Her prize horse is a Hanoverian, which she brought out to the ranch from the East last year. Prince William, a champion jumper, stands sixteen hands high, weighs 1,200 pounds, and has a bright brown coat. Mrs. Wellington is breeding draft, coach, and saddle animals that are as magnificent as any that appear upon the parade grounds of the U.S. Cavalry, or the boulevards of the great cities of the world. Though she has spent the last three years developing her stock, this will be the first year she will actually ship her animals to market.

It may be added that Miss Wellington has quickly established the reputation of being a perfect judge of horses There is no man in Idaho who is her equal and few anywhere who are as good as she. Moreover she is an ideal horsewoman; there is probably no woman in the world who can excel her in the saddle.

"She sounds like quite a lady," Matt said, handing the article back to Gilmore. "But it still doesn't ring any bells as to why I should know her."

"Read this letter, then we'll talk," Gilmore said.

Dear Matt:

Please forgive me for addressing you by your Christian name, but it is the way I remember you. You will remember me, if you remember me at all, as Katherine. I slept in the bunk next to Tamara when she and I, and you, were residents of the Soda Creek Home for Wayward Boys and Girls.

Of course, you may not remember me at all. I was younger than you, and not nearly as courageous. But then, nobody at the home was as courageous as you were. You had no way of knowing, but I was so in love with you then. Well, I was as in love as a nine-year-old girl can be.

It took me a while to find you, and if you are reading this letter, then the first part of my quest has been accomplished. The second, and most difficult part of my quest, will be in getting you to agree to come work for me. Don't get me wrong, I don't mean work for me in a permanent position. I would love that, but from what I have learned about you, you are a man who moves about in a restless drift that neither proposes a particular destination nor has a sense of purpose.

Perhaps, for a short time, I can provide you with both a destination and a sense of purpose.

I believe Mr. Gilmore, who is the bearer of this letter, also showed you a newspaper article that will provide you with some information about me. If so, then you know that I am undertaking to fulfill a dream that I shared with my late husband.

Although my husband owned the land, he did not have any livestock, and when he died, I was denied access to his funds by the English courts. As a result, I have had to borrow money against the land and the house in order to build the ranch. I am about to make a shipment of horses which will make enough money to pay off the loan, but recent events have caused me to worry as to whether or not I will be able to do this. Rustlers have twice struck the ranch, and I have been losing stock at an alarming rate. I have asked the city marshal, who is also the deputy sheriff of the county, for help, but there is only so much he can do.

Marcus Kincaid has suggested strongly that I sell the ranch to him. Kincaid was the son of my husband's first wife and inherited half of Thomas's holdings. I believe he was hurt that he did not inherit Coventry, so I think his offer to buy the ranch is made as much out of his desire to own the ranch, as it is out of genuine concern over my welfare.

Despite his offer, I intend to keep the ranch. That is, I shall keep it if I am successful in fighting the rustlers. And that is why I am contacting you, now. From what I have learned about you, Matt, the courage and resourcefulness you showed as a youth in the orphanage has now manifested itself in your adulthood. I have read about you. You are a fearless defender of what is right and a brave foe of all that is evil.

I am calling upon you for help, believing that the aforementioned virtues, as well as any residual feeling you might have for one who shared with you those terrible days in the orphanage, will lead you to respond favorably.

Should you decide in the affirmative, Mr. Gilmore will provide you with rail passage to Medbury, the nearest railhead to Coventry. From there, it is but a short ride to my home.

Sincerely,
Your Friend, Katherine

Matt smiled as he finished the letter. "I do remember her," he said.

"Oh, thank Heavens," Gilmore said. "If you had not remembered her, I fear it would have been impossible to talk you into coming to her aid. Though I am prepared to tell you what a wonderful woman she is, and how . . ."

"I'll do it," Matt said, interrupting Gilmore in mid-sentence.

"Oh, my, this is a little unusual," Gilmore said. "Is there to be no negotiation? Don't you want to know how much Mrs. Wellington is willing to pay for your services?"

"Not particularly."

Gilmore smiled. "Mrs. Wellington said this would be your reaction. I didn't believe her — I thought you, well, that is, I thought any man would want to know what was in this for them before they made a commitment."

"When do we leave?" Matt asked.

"We will leave on the morning train,"

125

Gilmore replied.

"My horse?"

"I have rooms for us at the hotel. The hotel also provides a stable. You can put your horse there for tonight, and I will secure passage for him on the train tomorrow."

"Mr. Gilmore, you are a very efficient lawyer," Matt said.

"Thank you, sir. I try to be," Gilmore replied.

That night, Matt dreamed. It had been a long time since he had actually thought of the orphanage, and even longer since he had dreamed about it. But the contact with Katherine had brought back the memories that caused the dream. And in the dream the years rolled away so that it was a real as if he were reliving the first day he became a resident of the Soda Creek Home for Wayward Boys and Girls.

"I thought this was the orphanage," Matt said. "Maybe I'm in the wrong place. I'm sorry." He turned and started to leave.

"Did you come with Landers?" the man asked.

"Yes, sir."

"Then I already paid for you. You are in the

right place."

"You paid for me?"

"Twelve and a half good dollars," the man said. "You'll be workin' that off."

"But he took my rifle."

"Who took your rifle?"

"Brother Landers. He said he paid you so I could stay here, and he took my rifle to pay him back."

The man chuckled. "Let that be a lesson to you," he said. "Don't trust somebody, just because they tell you they are a preacher."

"Isn't he a preacher?"

"He is sometimes, I reckon. What's your name?"

"Matthew Cava . . ."

The man held up his hand. "Your ma and pa alive?"

"No, sir."

"Then you don't have a last name."

"But my last name is . . ."

"You don't have a last name," the man said again. "Do you understand that?"

"Yes, sir."

"Yes, Captain Mumford."

"What?"

"When you talk to me, you will always address me as Captain Mumford."

"Yes, Captain Mumford," Matt said.

"You're awfully small for twelve years old."

"I'm not twelve," Matt said.

Mumford slapped Matt in the face, not hard enough to knock him down, or even bring blood, but hard enough that it stung.

"What did you say?"

"I said I'm not twelve," Matt repeated.

Mumford slapped him again. "You don't learn very well," he said. "Now, I'm going to ask you again. What did you say?"

"I said I'm not twelve — Captain Mumford," Matt said, getting the last part out just before Mumford slapped him again.

Mumford smiled. "Well, maybe you aren't so dumb after all. Not twelve, huh? How old are you?"

"I'm ten, Captain Mumford."

"Ten, huh? Well, you are a big enough boy for ten. I'm sure I can find something for you to do. Connor!" he called loudly.

An older boy came into the office from the back of the house.

"Yes, Captain Mumford?"

"Here is a new boy," Mumford said. "His name is Matthew. Take him into the back and," Mumford paused, "break him in."

Matt awakened in the middle of the night and for just a second or two, he could almost imagine that he was back in the Wayward Home for Boys and Girls.

128

Despite what Captain Mumford had told him, he did have a last name. At that time, his last name was Cavanaugh. He was ten years old, and he had already killed the first man — killing one of the outlaws who had killed his parents and his sister.

He escaped from the Home a few years later, and was found in the mountains, half frozen to death. The man who found him was Smoke Jensen, and the legendary mountain man not only saved Matt's life, he raised him, and taught him how to ride, shoot, and track. But mostly, he taught Matt how to be a man and a grateful Matt took Smoke Jensen's last name to honor his friend and mentor.

Then he used every skill Smoke taught him to track down, and bring to justice, the men who had killed his entire family.

Now, several years later, he lay in bed, in the hotel room in American Falls, Idaho, separated from the reality of his dream by both time and distance, until finally sleep overtook him.

The rest of the night was deep and dreamless.

# CHAPTER NINE

*Medbury, Idaho*

Poke Terrell woke up with a ravenous hunger and a raging need to urinate. The whore still asleep beside him had the bed-cover askew, exposing one of her breasts. One leg dangled over the edge of the bed and she was snoring loudly as a bit of spittle drooled from her vibrating lips. She didn't wake up when Poke crawled over her to get out of bed and get dressed.

The whore was not one of the women who worked at the Sand Spur, nor even at Flat Nose Sue's. She did business out of a very small, one-room house called a crib. Poke walked through the alley to the Sand Spur, which was about two blocks from the whore's crib.

He used the toilet behind the Sand Spur, holding his breath against the terrible odor. As he started into the saloon, he saw someone lying in the alley behind the building.

At first he thought he might be dead, then he saw him move, and knew that it was just a saloon patron sleeping off last night's drunk.

Once inside, Poke took a seat at his table. The main room of the Sand Spur saloon was big, with exposed rafters below the high, peaked ceiling. Although there were several tables in the saloon, most of them were empty as it was still fairly early in the morning and there were only a few patrons at this hour. A couple of all-night customers for the whores came down the stairs, looking a little sheepish at being seen by the few who were in the saloon. A few minutes later the two girls came downstairs, laughing uninhibitedly. There were several large jars of pickled eggs and pig's feet on the bar, and the two women walked over to the bar, then stuck their hands down inside the jars to pull out a couple of pickled eggs each for their breakfast.

The Sand Spur was one of two saloons in town. The other saloon was called the Mud Hole, and it catered to a lower class clientele, serving cheaper whiskey and beer in an establishment that no amenities of any kind. It was behind the livery, whereas the Sand Spur had the more choice location, at the end of Meridian Street, right next to the

Union Pacific track.

Poke had ordered breakfast and it was just being brought to his table as the morning train rolled in. With its whistle blowing and its bell clanging, the heavy engine caused the saloon to shake. As a result of the shaking, the bottles of whiskey that were lined up behind the bar began to rattle when they banged together. It sounded, and felt, as if the train was about to come right through the building, but the arrival and departure of the daily trains, both freight and passenger, was such a routine event that no one in the saloon paid any attention to them.

After a few minutes of sitting in the station, the train blew its whistle then moved on. Shortly after the train left the station, Sam Logan stepped into the saloon. Seeing Poke, he walked back to his table. Yesterday, Poke had sent Logan, Madison, and Jernigan to American Falls to deal with the Matt Jensen issue.

Poke didn't interrupt his breakfast and he took a bite of biscuit as Logan approached his table.

"Well, you are back I see. Any trouble?"

"Yeah, we had trouble. We had a lot of trouble," Logan said.

"What kind of trouble?" Poke looked toward the door, expecting to see someone else. "Where are the others? Where are Madison and Jernigan?"

"That's the trouble. Madison and Jernigan? They're dead, Poke."

"Dead? Are you sure?"

"Damn right, I'm sure. I seen both of 'em lyin' out on the floor of the Red Horse Saloon back in American Falls. And they was both of 'em deader 'n a door nail."

"How did that happen? There were three of you. Matt Jensen is only one man. How hard could it be for three of you to take care of one man?"

"Yeah, well, Madison had his own way of doing things, only it didn't work out quite like he planned."

"What happened?"

"Matt Jensen is what happened. You ever run into him, Poke? Or heard tale of him?"

"I've heard of him, I've never run into him," Poke replied. "Why do you ask?"

"Well let me tell you somethin' about him that maybe you don't know. Matt Jensen is faster'n greased lightnin' I believe he's got to be about the fastest man with a gun there is — I mean the way he shot 'em both."

"So, you did see it?" Kincaid asked. "By that, I mean you were a witness to it?"

"Yeah, I seen it. I had left the saloon a minute earlier but I come back and was standin' just outside the door, watchin' it when it happened, so yeah, I seen it all right."

"What do you mean you were standing just outside the door watchin'? I sent all three of you over to take care of him. If you were there with them, and they are both dead, how is it that you are not?"

"I ain't dead, 'cause I ain't a fool, that's why. You can't blame me. Like I told you, it's all Madison's fault," Logan said. "Madison, what he wanted to do, was brace Jensen head on. He figured, what with Jernigan up in the balcony and all, that he'd have an edge."

"Why did Madison want to do such a fool thing as that?"

"Why? Because he wanted to become a big shot, that's why," Logan answered.

"Even so, that sounds like a pretty good plan, what with Jernigan bein' up in the balcony and all. So, what happened?"

"Somehow or the other, and I don't know how, Jensen figured out what was goin' on. And once he figured it out Madison didn't have the edge no more. Jensen shot Jernigan first, then after that, he still had time to shoot Madison before he could even get his gun out. The next thing you know, Jensen was standin' there holdin' a smokin' gun, and Madison and Jernigan was both of 'em layin' dead on the floor. It was all over before you could even blink your eyes."

"Where were you during all this time?"

"Like I told you, I was standin' just outside the door, watchin'."

"Why didn't you help?"

"I tell you true, Poke, if I had stuck my nose into it, I'd be dead too. Jensen is that fast. Besides, I didn't figure you sent us over there for no duel."

"I sent you over there to take care of Jensen, and I didn't care how you did it."

"Your complaint is with Madison, it ain't with me."

"Really," Poke said sarcastically. "How am I going to complain to Madison if he is dead?"

"You can't, I guess," Logan admitted.

"That leaves only you."

"But think about this. Iffen I had got myself kilt as well, then how else would you know that Jensen and Gilmore will be takin' the train to Medbury this mornin'?"

"How do you know they will be taking this morning's train?"

"What I actual know is just what I found out from the station agent. And that is, that Gilmore bought hisself two tickets for this mornin's train. I'm just figurin' that the other ticket is for Jensen."

"I think you are right. Good job, Logan."

"Thanks."

"I just imagine that if you were on the train most of the night, then you probably haven't eaten, have you?"

"No, I ain't. I ain't et nothin' since lunch time yesterday."

"Would you like breakfast?"

"Yeah, I believe I would."

Poke spread some butter on his biscuit but as Logan reached for it, Poke took a bite of it himself. "Go over to the bar and grab yourself a pickled egg and pig's foot," he said. "Then after you eat, come back and see me. I've got another job I want you to do."

"If it has to do with Matt Jensen, there ain't no way I'm goin' to do it by myself," Logan said.

"You won't have to be by yourself."

Although the tracks of the Union Pacific generally follow the Snake River west across Idaho, when they reach a point twenty miles west of American Falls, the railroad is at the farthest distance from the river and the Snake can no longer be seen. On the north side of the tracks is a lava desert that is black and craggy, leading northward toward a barren and ugly escarpment that thrust upward as if in some way the land had formed waves, like the sea.

Matt sat next to the window, looking out at the barren land. He had read, somewhere, that this desert was what the surface of the moon might look like if one could take a balloon high enough to ever reach that heavenly body. But as he continued to study the denuded and uninviting terrain, he wondered how anyone could ever suggest that this was similar to the moon. The moon was bright and shiny, sometimes silver and sometimes gold. This was dark as coal.

"When you see land like this, it makes you wonder what would ever have attracted someone to settle out here, doesn't it?" Gilmore asked, noticing the intensity with which Matt was studying the terrain outside the train.

"Oh, I don't know," Matt replied. "In a way the area holds some appeal just in its awesome starkness, and, if not appeal exactly, then it certainly creates interest."

Gilmore chuckled. "I've never heard it put that way before, but you may have a point."

"Tell me about this man, Poke Terrell," Matt said.

"He used to be on the right side of the law," Gilmore said. "Sort of," he added.

137

"What do you mean, sort of?"

"Poke Terrell used to ride with Clay Sherman and the Idaho Auxiliary Peace Officers' Posse."

"The Idaho Auxiliary Peace Officers' Posse? What is that? I've never heard of it."

"Supposedly, they are sort of a permanent posse, and from time to time they have made their services available to one sheriff or another. But there are some who say they are nothing but a bunch of mercenaries, willing to sell their guns to the highest bidder."

"What do you think about them?"

"If Poke Terrell is any example of the caliber and quality of the men who belong to the Idaho Auxiliary Peace Officers' Posse, then I would say that mercenary is not a strong enough word for them. I would say they are a band of hired assassins."

"What about Marcus Kincaid?"

"Marcus Kincaid? He isn't a problem. Why do you ask about him?"

"Katherine mentioned in her letter that he wanted her ranch."

"Yes, but he isn't her problem. Poke Terrill is. Poke is the dregs of the earth, and one wonders how he has avoided prison all these years. But Marcus Kincaid is totally different. If you met him in a social setting, in someone's home, say, or at a club, or in the lobby of an elegant hotel, you would no doubt think him to be a fine fellow. He is affable, charming, wealthy, well-read, everything one needs to be a first class citizen," Gilmore replied.

"That's the kind of description you would give to someone who is running for governor," Matt said.

"Yes, I suppose it is, isn't it? But Idaho is sure to be a state some day and when it is, I would not be the least bit surprised to see Marcus Kincaid running for governor."

"And he is Katherine's stepson?"

"Katherine? Oh, you mean Kitty Wellington. No, he was never her stepson." Gilmore chuckled. "That would have been awkward at any rate, since Marcus Kincaid is two years older than Mrs. Wellington.

"The way this relationship came about, is that Kitty was married to Sir Thomas Wellington, and prior to his marriage to Kitty, Sir Thomas Wellington was married to a woman named Mary Kincaid. Mary Kincaid came into the marriage a widow, and with a young son, Marcus. Sir Thomas never officially adopted Marcus Kincaid, but he treated him as his own.

"Mary died four years ago, and shortly thereafter, Sir Thomas married Kitty, but by that time, Marcus Kincaid was on his own, having received a ranch and a rather large sum of money, in the form of an outright gift, from Sir Thomas.

"Sir Thomas and Kitty were married for only one year before he died. His will left Coventry on the Snake to Kitty, and that is what started the trouble. Marcus Kincaid was convinced that the ranch should have gone to him."

"Katherine's husband was called Sir Thomas?"

"Yes, he was British, and since he never became an American citizen, he was able to keep his title. I must say though, that he wasn't vain about it. He never insisted upon being addressed by his title, though his friends and business acquaintances did so out of respect for him. He was a fine man."

"What, exactly, did he leave to Katherine?"

"He left her Coventry on the Snake and Coventry Manor. Unfortunately, as you read in the letter, he left her land rich and liquid asset poor. He had less than five thousand dollars in his American account — he was used to transferring funds here from England, as he needed them. But once his brother learned that Sir Thomas had died, he went to court and got an order preventing any more funds from being transferred."

"What is Coventry Manor?"

"It's the house where Mrs. Wellington lives. That is, if you can call it a house. It's bigger than any house, or hotel for that matter, that I've ever seen."

"If I understood her letter, Katherine didn't start raising horses until after her husband died."

"That is true, and she had to take out a loan in order to do it," Gilmore said.

"Is she having trouble meeting the loan?"

"She is not in default yet. But don't get me wrong, Mr. Jensen, taking out the loan was not an imprudent thing to do. Mrs. Wellington is a very good businesswoman. In fact, she is a much better business person than Sir Thomas ever was. And, of course, that makes Marcus Kincaid's claim that it should all belong to him, even more untenable. He actually took his claim to court, you know, suing Mrs. Wellington for ownership of the ranch. The court decided in Mrs. Wellington's favor."

"Good job," Matt said. "I take it you represented her."

Gilmore cleared his throat before answering. "Uh, no, I didn't," he said. "I — uh —

141

represented Marcus Kincaid in that petition."

"And now you represent Katherine?"

"Yes."

"That's interesting."

"It may be even more interesting, once Kincaid learns that I am working for Mrs. Wellington."

Matt laughed.

"What is it?"

"Even if I didn't know Katherine from before, I would be tempted to take this job, just for the sheer fascination of it."

*Coventry Manor*

The ornate and baronial home looked more like a castle than a house, and that was by design. Though smaller than the Coventry Palace, Coventry Manor had the same design as the Palace on the Wey River, back in England. It was complete in every detail, including the towers, lacking only the moat that surrounded the original building.

As spectacular as the house was though, it was the grounds that attracted the most attention. The lawn spread out over at least five acres, with an artfully designed maze of shrubbery, neatly trimmed, weed-free grass, and flowers, which grew in colorful profusion in several well-tended islands. At the moment almost a dozen groundskeepers were working on the lawn, a few pushing lawn mowers, others sculpturing shrubbery, while still others were digging out a new flower garden.

Kitty Wellington was in one of the flower gardens, cutting flowers in order to make a bouquet. She was being assisted by the head of her household staff, Frederica Bustamante.

"Señor Yensen must be a very important man," Frederica said.

"Why do you say that?"

"You have Maria cook a big meal, you have Manuel find the best wine in the cellar, and now you take the most beautiful flowers for a bouquet. I think you would not do this if he would not be a very important man."

"He is an important man," Kitty said.

"Have you met him before?"

"Yes," Kitty said.

"Has he been here before? I do not remember him."

"No, he has never been here before. I met him, many years ago. I met him when I was a young girl."

Frederica chuckled. "You were in love with him then, I think."

"Don't be silly, Frederica. I was only nine

years old."

"But you were in love with him, I think," Frederica insisted.

Kitty laughed, easily. "Well, maybe I was," she said. "I thought he was the most handsome boy I had ever known. He was brave too."

"Brave?"

"Yes. I told you once that I lived in an orphanage, remember?"

"Si, Señora, I remember."

"We were always hungry then. Pease porridge, that's all they ever fed us. Pease porridge, except for one time. One day, Matt told us to follow his lead and eat none of our supper.

"No one asked why we should do such a thing, everyone knew and trusted Matt. So when we went through the line for supper, we accepted our bowls of pease porridge, then went back to our tables. Looking toward Matt, he let it be known by sign and signal that we were not to eat our porridge.

"There were two other orphans who were different from all the others. Their names were Connor and Simon and, because they worked for Captain Mumford, who was the head of the orphanage, they never had to go through the line. Instead, they were served at their seats.

"On that night, one of the kitchen workers brought two bowls of pease porridge out to them and set them on the table in front of Simon and Connor."

As Kitty told the story, she relived the moment so that it was as real to her, as it had been on the day it actually happened.

"Here, hold on!" Simon called out as the woman started back toward the kitchen. "Is this a joke? What is this?"

"It's your supper," the woman answered.

"The hell it is. We're having ham tonight."

The kitchen worker shook her head. "No ham," she said. "We didn't cook a ham tonight."

"You didn't have to cook it, it was already cooked. What's going on here? What happened to our ham?"

"I haven't seen any ham," the woman answered.

Though none of the other residents laughed out loud, they all repressed giggles and smiles while they watched the frustration of the two oldest of their number as they tried to eat the pease porridge.

"What is this?" Connor shouted in anger. "Nobody can eat this shit!"

Again, there were repressed giggles from the other residents. Then, at a nod from Matt, everyone got up from the table and took their untouched bowl of porridge to the garbage can. There, they dumped the porridge, turned the bowls in, then filed out of the dining room.

"Connor, did you see that?" Simon asked.

"Did I see what?"

"None of them ate."

"Yeah, well, who can blame them?" he replied, looking at his meal with disgust.

"No, you don't understand," Simon said. "None of them ate so much as one bite. They always eat."

"Yeah," Connor said. "Yeah, you're right. I wonder why not. Why don't you follow them, Simon, and see if you can figure out what's going on?"

"Yeah," Simon said. "I will."

Simon slipped out of the dining room, then hanging back a little, watched as the others went into the chapel. Curious, he moved up to the door of the chapel, then looked inside. Everyone was sitting quietly in the pews, with their heads bowed and their eyes closed.

"Simon," Matt called, seeing Simon standing at the door. "It's so good to see you here. Come on in."

"What?" Simon asked.

"Why don't you go get Connor and bring him with you? We would love to have you two join us."

"Join you for what? What are you doing? What's going on, here?"

"You may have noticed that we ate none of our food tonight."

"Yeah, I did notice. Why didn't you eat?"

"Because we are having a night of fasting and prayer," Matt said.

"What do you mean fasting and prayer? How can you have a prayer service if there ain't no preacher here."

"You don't need a preacher to have a prayer service," Matt said. "Remember, the Lord said 'When two or three are gathered in my name, there I shall be.' I noticed that you fasted as well tonight. Won't you please join us?"

Matt reached out as if to grab Simon and pull him into the chapel.

Simon held out his hands as if warding off Matt. He shook his head no.

"No," he said. "I ain't doin' no prayin'."

"What about Connor? Won't you ask him to join us?"

"You're crazy," Simon said. "There ain't neither one of us goin' to be comin' in here and sayin' a bunch of prayers."

"Then we will pray for you," Matt said.

"You're crazy, I tell you. Every last one of you."

Matt waited for a moment, then he looked over at Eddie. "Make sure he's gone."

Eddie went to the door, looked through it, then turned back. "He's gone," he said.

"Let's eat," Matt said, and with that, everyone crowded up to the altar where, from beneath the pulpit, Matt pulled out a large ham.

"Oh, this looks so delicious," Tamara said. "Where did you get it?"

"The ladies of the Methodist Church cooked it especially for us," Matt said. "I just happened to be outside Mumford's office when they brought it in to him. Mumford thanked them for it, then told Connor that he and Simon could both have a little of it before he took it home."

"Took it home? He was going to keep a ham that was supposed to be for us?" Katherine asked.

Matt nodded. "Yeah. You think pease porridge is all we ever get? Churches and the like have been bringing us food ever since I got here, only we don't ever see any."

"That ain't right," one of the boys said. He had only been here about six months.

"I agree, Billy, it isn't right, so that's why I decided to do something about it," Matt said. "I waited until Mumford stepped out of the office, then I took the ham and brought it here."

"I wouldn't have had the nerve to do that," one of the others said.

"Sure you would have," Matt said. "All you would have had to do was smell it when you were hungry."

"When is anyone not hungry in here?" Katherine asked, and they all laughed.

"Oh, that ham was so delicious," Kitty said. "I have had many fine meals since that time, but never have I had a meal better than that one."

"Señor Matt sounds like a very good man," Frederica said.

"He is a good man, Frederica," Kitty said. "That's why I sent for him. I think he is just the kind of man I need now, to help me through this difficulty."

# Chapter Ten

The Mud Hole was a poor second place saloon to the Sand Spur. Whereas the Sand Spur had a real bar, a brass foot rail, a mirror, and lantern sconces, the Mud Hole bar was boards, spread across barrels. There was no mirror, the light was dim, and provided by no more than three or four lanterns that were strategically set around the room.

No bar girls worked the Mud Hole, because the clientele didn't believe in buying drinks for anyone but themselves. So different was the clientele that frequented the two saloons that even in a town as small as Mudbury, there were men who were regulars at the Mud Hole, who would not even be recognized if they stepped into the Sand Spur.

Such was the case with John "Mole" Mueller, and Harold "Cooter" Cotter, habitués of the Mud Hole, who earned their money in the most menial tasks imaginable.

Logan had met Mole and Cooter when he spent some time with them in prison.

Logan, who tended to move back and forth between the saloons, needed a couple of men to help him "take care of" Matt Jensen, so he recruited them in the Mud Hole, calling upon Mole and Cooter.

"Ten dollars?" Cooter said. "Ten dollars to do what?"

"To do what I tell you to do, without asking any questions," Logan said.

"Hell, what kind of job is that?" Mole asked.

"It's a job that will earn you ten dollars," Logan said. He waited for a moment, then added, "each."

"Wait. We each get ten dollars?" Cooter asked.

"Yes."

"That's different. I thought you was just talkin' about ten dollars for the two of us to have to share. When do we get it?"

"When the job is done," Logan answered.

Cooter shook his head. "No, we need it before we do the job."

"Why do you need it before you do the job?"

"I don't know what the job is, but since you won't tell us beforehand, it ain't likely to be all that easy," Cooter said. "Besides,

151

we may want to buy us a bottle of whiskey."

"I ain't goin' to have you gettin' drunk on me," Logan said.

"We ain't goin' to get drunk. We just want a couple of drinks."

"You got horses and guns?" Logan asked.

"Yeah, I got me a gun and a horse," Cooter said proudly.

"I ain't got either one. I used to have a gun, only I sold it in order to get enough money to buy some whiskey," Mole said.

"All right, I've got a gun I'll lend you, Mole. And we can rent you a horse from the livery."

"What about the ten dollars?" Cooter asked.

Logan stared at them for a long moment, then sighed and pulled out two ten dollar bills. "Here it is," he said. "But if you two try and run out on me before we do the job, I'll hunt you both down."

"We ain't goin' to run out on you," Cooter said, smiling as he took the money. "Come on, Mole, let's split the cost of buyin' a bottle of whiskey."

An hour later Logan, Cooter, and Mole were on the top of the Bruneau Canyon Wall. A moment earlier, Logan had ridden out onto the lip of the canyon rim and looked north toward the Snake River. That was when he saw Jensen and Gilmore coming south in a buckboard. There was a horse tied on to the back of the buckboard.

Smiling, Logan turned his horse and rode back far enough from the edge of the canyon to avoid being silhouetted against the bright, blue, sky. He dismounted and tied his horse off where Cooter and Mole had ground staked their own mounts.

The two men were sitting cross-legged, passing back and forth the bottle of whiskey they had bought with the money Logan had given them.

"Cooter, he's comin'. You two boys get ready."

"Put the whiskey away, Mole," Cooter said.

"What about it, Logan? Before I put it away, you want a drink?" Mole asked holding up the bottle. He dropped the bottle, and though it didn't break, it did turn over and some of the whiskey began gurgling out.

"Sum' bitch, Mole, you're pourin' out all our whiskey," Cooter said, angrily.

"Don't worry about it. There ain't practically none of it spilt," Mole said.

"Hah. If it had'a been spillin', like as not you would be down on your hands and knees tryin' to lick it up," Cooter teased.

"What the hell?" Logan asked. "Are you men drunk?"

"We ain't all that drunk," Cooter answered with a belching laugh.

Poke Terrell had given Logan one hundred and fifty dollars, telling him to find four men he could trust, who would work for thirty dollars apiece. Generously, he told Logan that he could keep thirty dollars for himself.

What Poke didn't know was that Logan was able to find two men who would work for ten dollars apiece. That left Logan with a total bonus of one hundred thirty dollars. But now, as he looked at the two men he had hired, he was beginning to wonder whether he made a mistake. If they weren't drunk yet, they were well on the way.

"This ain't the kind of job you can do while you are drunk," Logan said.

"Well now, you just hold on there, Mr. Sam Logan," Cooter said. "You're askin' us to kill a couple of fellas, right? For no reason in particular, just kill 'em. If that ain't reason enough to take a couple of drinks before you commence shootin', then I don't know what is."

"They're coming," Logan said disgustedly. "Get up to the edge of the rim. As soon as they come into the canyon, open fire."

The two men stood up then walked up to the edge of the canyon.

"Where are they?" Cooter asked.

"Damn it! Get down!" Logan said. "You may as well be holdin' up a sign."

"Oh, yeah," Cooter said. "You're prob'ly right."

All three men lay on their stomachs, then crawled up to the rim of the canyon so they could see.

"I don't see nothin'," Mole said.

"There's two of 'em, comin' in a buckboard with a horse tied on to the back. The buckboard is just around the bend. Be ready, you'll see it in a minute," Logan replied.

What neither Logan, Cooter, or Mole knew was that five minutes earlier, Matt had seen Logan up on the rim. He wouldn't have thought anything about it, but for two reasons. First was that the run in with the two men in the saloon back in American Falls last night told him that someone was trying to see to it that he didn't do anything to help Katherine. And second, the man on the rim was obviously trying to avoid being seen.

As the buckboard made a curve around a bend it was, for the moment, obscured from view by anyone who might be up on top of the canyon wall. Matt halted the team, then set the brake.

"Stay here until I get back," Matt said, crawling over the seat into the back of the buckboard, then stepping into the saddle.

"What is it? Where are you going?"

"There is someone up on the lip of the canyon who seems more than a little interested in us," Matt replied. "I plan to go up and see what he wants."

"Oh, my," Gilmore said. "You know, I never realized that we might actually be in danger, just by riding out to Coventry. I — I don't even have a gun."

"You won't be in any danger as long as you stay behind this promontory," Matt said, as he rode away.

Matt didn't have to ride too far back before he found a small creek coming down from the top of the canyon wall. The creek bed was much larger than the creek itself, apparently the result of spring runoffs. Any question he may have had as to whether the creek bed would lead all the way up to the top was answered when he saw the track of three horses. Fresh droppings on the trail told him that the pass had been used within the last hour or so.

Matt urged Spirit into a trot and, rather

quickly, he reached the top. Dismounting, he tied Spirit off to a low growing juniper, then, pulling his pistol and walking quietly, he started out across the relatively flat top.

"Are you sure you seen 'em? I don't think there's anybody down there at all."

"I told you, they are around there behind that point. Soon as the buckboard comes into view, start shootin'."

"I need another drink."

"You don't need nothin' of the sort. Just do what I tell you."

"Who is this fella we're supposed to be shootin' at, anyway?"

"His name is Matt Jensen."

"Matt Jensen? Are you loco? I don't know much, but I've heard of Matt Jensen, and I know he's someone you don't want to mess with."

"You took the money, now just do what I told you to do. Keep lookin'."

"Are you boys looking for me?" Matt asked, stepping up behind them.

"What the hell?" Cooter shouted. "Where did you come from?"

"Stand up," Matt ordered.

The three men did as they were directed.

"Now, this is what I want you to do. I want you to toss your guns over the edge."

"Mister, I ain't tossin' my gun over the edge of this here canyon for nobody," Logan said.

Matt fired at him and a little mist of red flew up from his earlobe. Crying out in pain, he slapped his hand up to his ear, then pulled away a palm full of blood.

"You son of a bitch! You shot my ear off!" he shouted in fear and anger.

"I didn't shoot it off, I just shredded your ear lobe some," Matt said. "If you want me to shoot your ear off, I'll do it. Now, toss your gun over like I said."

The man with the bleeding ear tossed his gun over and the other two followed suit.

"Now your boots," Matt said.

"Whoa, hold it now. Have you seen the kind of rock that is around here?" Logan asked. "Some of it is as sharp as a razor. You go walkin' barefoot on that, you're goin' to cut your feet to pieces."

"Then you'll have to walk real slow and careful, won't you?" Matt said. "That'll give my friend and me time to get through the canyon without worryin' about someone trying to kill us. Throw your boots over, like I said."

Grumbling, the three men sat down and pulled off their boots, then dropped them over the edge. They stood up again.

"I'll tie your horses off down at the bottom of the canyon," Matt said.

"The hell you will!"

Logan produced another pistol from somewhere, and he fired at Matt, the bullet coming so close that Matt not only heard the pop as it passed his ear, he felt the concussion of air.

Matt returned fire, hitting Logan in the chest. Logan dropped his pistol and put his hands over the wound as blood poured through his fingers. His eyes rolled up, and he fell back.

The other two would-be assailants looked down at him.

"Either one of you two have another pistol?" Matt asked.

"I ain't got one."

"Me neither."

"Hell, can't neither one of us afford a second pistol."

"Who was this man?" Matt asked, pointing to the one on the ground.

"His name was Logan. Sam Logan," one of the men answered.

"Logan?" Matt remembered Gilmore telling him that Logan had been with Madison and Jernigan.

"That's what he told us his name was."

"Do you men work for Poke Terrell?"

"Poke Terrell? No, there don't none of us work for Poke Terrell. Don't none of us work for nobody except odd jobs from time to time," the more talkative of the two men said. "That's how we wound up with Logan."

"What's your name?" Matt asked.

"Folks call me Cooter."

"Well, Cooter, if you aren't working for Poke Terrell, what were you doing up here, waiting to ambush me?"

Cooter pointed to the body. "Like I said, we take odd jobs from time to time. Logan, he give us ten dollars apiece to come up here with him," he said.

"Did he work for Poke?"

"He didn't say," Cooter said. "He never give us no reason for comin' up here to shoot you. All he done was give us ten dollars."

"And you agreed to kill someone for ten dollars? You consider killing somebody an odd job, do you?" Matt asked.

"He made it seem like it wasn't goin' to be all that hard to do."

Matt raised his pistol and aimed it at Cooter. "It's not much of a man who would agree to kill someone for ten dollars," he said. "The world would be better off if I just killed you now."

"No!" Cooter said, putting his hands out in front as if he could ward off the bullets. "No, don't shoot!"

"Oh, damn, I just peed in my pants," Mole said.

With a sigh, Matt lowered his pistol. "Like I told you, I'll leave your horses at the bottom," he said. "Being barefoot, it will take you a while to get there, but if you are careful, you can make it without cutting your feet up too bad. But hear this." He raised his pistol again and waved it back and forth pointing at all of them. "If I ever seen any one of you again, I will kill you."

"You ain't never goin' to see me no more, Mister. I can promise you that," Cooter said.

Ten minutes later, Matt returned to the buckboard, leading the three horses.

The buckboard was empty.

"Mr. Gilmore?" Matt called out in some concern. "Mr. Gilmore, are you here?"

"I'm here," a muffled voice answered and Matt saw the lawyer crawling out from a fissure in the side of the promontory.

Matt laughed. "It looks like you found a good hiding place there, Mr. Gilmore," he said. "I didn't even see you."

"I heard shooting," Gilmore said. "I didn't know — that is, I wasn't sure what was happening."

"It was probably a good idea for you to hide," Matt said. He found a scrub bush growing out of the side of the promontory, and he tied the three horses off, then he tied Spirit to the back of the buckboard.

"How much farther is it?" he asked climbing back into the buckboard and picking up the reins."

"Not far," Gilmore said. "We should be there in time for dinner."

About half an hour later, Matt and Gilmore approached an arched gate. The pillars were made of stone and the overhead arch that connected the pillars was made of steel. The words COVENTRY MANOR in ironwork, were worked into the arch. On the left stone pillar was a coat of arms. The escutcheon was in quarters, and in the first and fourth quarters was a golden lion rampant on a red background. In the second and third quarters was the cross of St. George.

As they passed through the gate, they drove up a long, crushed white gravel drive which led to a three-story edifice of stone, brick, and mortar. The house spread out for at least one hundred fifty feet. The house had a castellated top, with towers at each of the four corners, plus an additional tower over the main entrance to the house. Pennants flew from the top of each of the corner towers; an American flag flew from the top of the central tower.

It had been many years since Matt last saw Katherine — he never knew her last name as nobody was permitted to use last names in the orphanage — but he recognized her immediately.

It was her eyes, big, blue, and flecked with gold, that he recognized first. They hadn't changed. Appraising her as they drove up, Matt decided that she had grown up well. She was a very pretty woman.

Kitty Wellington was standing in the curved driveway, an entrance that seemed much more suited for an elegant and liveried carriage than an ordinary buckboard, pulled by a team of rented horses.

"Welcome to Coventry," Kitty said as Matt pulled back on the reins to stop the team.

"Mrs. Wellington," he said.

"Oh, please, Matt," Kitty said. "Can't we refer to each other as we remember?"

"All right," Matt said with a big smile. "Only I remember you as Katherine, not Kitty."

"Then, by all means, call me Katherine. I started calling myself Kitty as a way of totally separating myself from the orphanage. When I left I never wanted to think of it again. Although as I think back on it, I remember some people with great fondness — Eddie, Tamara, and of course, you. Eddie and Tamara are both dead now," she said with a wilting tone. Then she smiled, and brightened. "But you and I are still alive. We have done well, Matt. And when you get right down to it, I think doing well is the best way possible to put that period of our lives in its proper perspective."

"I agree," Matt said. He looked around at the house and grounds. "I must say though, Katherine, that when it comes to doing well, you seem to have excelled far above my meager accomplishments."

Kitty laughed. "Please, come in. I've had the cook prepare something special, just in your honor."

Matt and Gilmore followed Kitty up the huge, curved stone steps, across the wide flagstone porch, through the massive carved and leaded glass double front doors, and into the house. The front doors opened onto a long, wide hallway. There were suits of armor standing on both sides of the hallway, while flags and tapestries hung from above.

On one wall, lit by flanking lanterns, was a huge painting of a young man in the

164

uniform of a British colonel.

"Tommy was really proud of this painting," Kitty said.

"Tommy?"

Kitty chuckled. "He asked that I call him that. He considered it an endearment. And he was a dear man, so I did so, willingly."

"How long were you married?"

"Just over a year," Kitty said. "He was considerably older than I, but it didn't seem to matter."

From the hallway they passed through the library. There was an open door at the rear of the library and, looking through that door, Matt saw what appeared to be an office. Even as he glanced toward it, Kitty confirmed what it was.

"My office," she said.

Next door was a formal parlor with bright blue covering, from which French doors opened onto another patio that overlooked the lawn. From the formal parlor, Kitty led Matt and Gilmore into the dining room. The dining room had polished oak wainscoting, while the top half of the wall was covered in gold linen. The table was very long, and illuminated by three crystal chandeliers that hung above it in equidistant spacing. Although it looked as if it could easily seat forty diners, there were, at the moment, only three place settings of exquisite china, rimmed with a band of dark blue and edged with gold. In the middle of each plate was a crest, exactly like the crest that was on the stone pillar of the entrance gate. The dining plates had been placed on gold chargers. Sparkling crystal and shining silver completed the setting.

Matt started to sit at one of the side chairs, but Kitty demurred. "No," she said, pointing to the chair on the end. "You sit here, at the head of the table."

"I wouldn't feel good about that. This is your house," Matt said.

"A woman should never occupy the head of the table, and I never do, even when I eat alone," she said. "Please, do me the honor."

"Very well," Matt agreed, holding the side chair out for Kitty, before taking his seat at the head of the table.

Kitty picked up a small bell and rang it.

"Yes, ma'am?" a young woman said, stepping through a door.

"You may serve," Kitty said.

The first thing that was brought out of the kitchen was a glistening ham. It was set it in front of Matt.

"I thought you might enjoy carving," Kitty said. "As you did that day, so long ago."

Matt picked up the carving knife and fork,

166

then smiled as he sliced into the ham.

"You are talking about the ham the ladies of the Methodist Church gave us," he said.

"Yes. I'm glad you remember."

"There are some things you never forget," Matt said, as he lay a generous piece of ham on Kitty's plate.

*Bruneau Canyon*
When Cooter and Mole reached the bottom of the canyon, they went right to the river where they sat on the bank and stuck their feet into the water.

"Damn, this hurts more'n it did when we was walkin'," Mole said.

"Quit your bitchin', Mole," Cooter said. "The water is what's makin' it hurt now, but after a minute you'll feel better."

"Logan said this was goin' to be easy," Mole said. "Now he's lyin' up there dead, and we near 'bout walked our feet off."

"What are you complainin' about?" Cooter asked. "At least you're still alive. And we still got the ten dollars Logan give us."

"Cooter, when you looked Logan's pockets, did he have anything else on him?" Mole asked.

"I told you, all he had was ten dollars, same as us."

"The way I figure it, that ten dollars he had should belong to both of us," Mole said.

"It does. Only I can't give it to you now."

"Why not?"

"What do you want me to do? Tear the bill into two pieces?"

"Oh, no, I reckon not."

"Soon as we get into town I'll get change and we can divide the money up."

"Yeah," Mole said, smiling broadly. "Hey, you know what I'm goin' to do? I'm goin' to get myself a real café supper, a bottle of whiskey I don't have to share, and a woman with that five dollars. That'll still leave me the ten dollars I got in the first place."

"Nine dollars and fifty cents," Cooter said. "Don't forget, we put our money together to buy a bottle of whiskey."

"Yeah, well, that's still enough to do ever' thing I said and have some money left over," Mole said.

Cooter pulled his feet out of the water and rubbed them for a moment. "I don't know about you, but I intend to find my boots and pistol, then go back into town. I don't plan to be out here after dark."

"Hey, I reckon this pistol Logan loaned to me is mine, now," Mole said.

"You might as well keep his horse too, seein' as you got to turn the one you're ridin' back into the livery."

"You don't mind if I take the horse?" Mole asked.

"No, I got one, you don't."

"That's real good of you, Cooter."

# CHAPTER ELEVEN

"And what did you say your name was?" Poke asked the man who was standing nervously before him, rolling his hat in his hands.

"My real name is Cotter," the man said. "But folks has always called me Cooter."

"Cooter?"

"Yeah."

"Tell me, Cooter, how do you know that Sam Logan is dead."

" 'Cause I seen him get hisself that way," Cooter said. "This feller Jensen, he had us all dead to rights. Made us throw our guns and our shoes over the edge of the canyon. Only Logan, he didn't throw all his guns down. Turned out he had him another'n, and what he done is, he drawed that gun against Matt Jensen. That was about as big a mistake as you could make, 'cause Jensen shot him down, dead."

"Where is Logan's body?"

"As far as I know, it's still a' lyin' up on top of Bruneau Canyon," Cooter said. "What with no horses, and no boots neither, me and Mole wasn't able to bring him back home."

"What were you doing up on top of Bruneau Canyon?" Terrell asked.

Cooter's eyes widened. "Why, don't you know? I figured we was up there, workin' for you. I mean Logan never told us that, but that's what I figured. That's what Jensen figured too, only I didn't tell Jensen nothin' except that Logan give us ten dollars apiece to — uh — take care of Jensen and the other feller that was with him."

"What do you think he meant by 'take care of'?"

"Take care of. You know. Kill him."

"And you were willing to kill Jensen for ten dollars?"

"That's all the money Logan give us," Cooter answered. "Only thing is," he started, then he let the sentence hang.

"The only thing is what?"

"Well, sir, he said he'd give us ten dollars apiece once we got the job done, only he got hisself kilt, so we never got no ten dollars."

Cooter did get the ten dollars. In fact, he not only got the ten dollars, he was the one

171

who rifled through Logan's body and he got the rest of the money as well, keeping it all for himself. The fact that he didn't share the money with Mole was what enabled him to be so generous with Logan's horse.

Instinctively, Poke realized that Cooter had taken the money, if not for himself, at least for the two of them. He stared accusingly at Cooter until Cooter, guiltily, cut his eyes down.

"Why should I give you ten dollars?" Poke asked. "If you didn't have sense enough to collect the money before you started, that's your problem. Besides, if I understand the deal you had with Logan, it was that you was bein' paid ten dollars to kill Matt Jensen. Is Matt Jensen dead?"

"No, sir, he ain't dead."

"Then what makes you think you should get any money?"

"I thought maybe you would give me some money for bringin' you the news that Logan is dead."

"If Logan never showed up again, I'd have a pretty good idea that he was dead, don't you think?"

"I reckon so," Cooter said, dejectedly. He brightened as he got an idea. "Maybe you got somethin' me and my friends could do to make a little money."

"Why should I hire you?" Poke asked. "You had one simple job to do, and you couldn't do it."

"You ever seen Matt Jensen?" Cooter asked.

"Can't say that I have."

"Well, killin' him ain't a simple job, I can tell you that right now."

"Be on your way," Poke said with a dismissive wave of his hand. "And don't speak to anyone else about this until I figure out what to do."

"Don't worry, there ain't neither one of us goin' to say nothin' about it," Cooter promised.

"Stay where I can get hold of you," Poke said. "If I can find some way to use you, I'll let you know."

"Yes, sir, Mr. Terrell. We'll be ready whenever you need us," Cooter said.

Poke said nothing, but he repeated the dismissive wave of his hand.

A bottle of whiskey sat on his table, and he pulled the cork from the bottle, then poured himself a glass.

"Damn you, Jensen, you've got more lives than a cat," he said as he raised the glass to his lips.

Coventry Manor was a huge house with two

parlors, a formal dining room, a big kitchen, with servants' quarters just off the kitchen, two parlors, a library, an office, and, as Matt had just learned, ten bedrooms.

"Tyrone has his own room attached to the bunkhouse. The wranglers all sleep in the bunkhouse, there are servants' quarters downstairs, and these ten bedrooms up here," Kitty said. "I sleep up here and I must confess that it sometimes gets lonely, when I'm up here, all by myself," she said, pointedly.

"So, that brings us to where you are going to sleep," Kitty said. "Of course, now that you are here, maybe it won't be quite as lonely as it has been."

"I can see how it might be a bit over-whelming sleeping in a place this big," Matt said, not quite sure how to respond to Kitty's inference.

"Go ahead, choose your bedroom. You can have — any — bedroom you want," she said, setting apart and emphasizing the word "any."

Although Kitty didn't come right out and say so, Matt knew that the offer of any bedroom he wanted inferred her bedroom and her bed. Matt did not respond to it, acting as if he did not understand the implied invitation.

Kitty was a beautiful woman, and Matt was a healthy man. If it had been any other woman, any other situation, he would have taken her up on it in a heartbeat. With any other woman, they could enjoy each other, taking and giving no more than necessary. But Kitty wasn't any other woman, and if he accepted her invitation to his bed, she would expect more than a pleasurable interlude. And she would have a right to expect more. After all, she was someone who had shared a part of his childhood, a connection that was important to him. But Matt knew that he could not give her what she really wanted.

"I'll take this bedroom," Matt said, selecting one that he knew was not hers.

There was a momentary expression of disappointment on Kitty's face, though she recovered so quickly that Matt wasn't entirely certain he had even seen it. She smiled at him.

"You've made an excellent choice," she said. "When the Duke of Warwick visited us, this was the room he selected."

"Will sleeping in this room make me a duke?" he teased.

"Matt, as far as I am concerned, you were a duke when I first met you back in the orphanage," Kitty replied.

Matt went in to look over the room that would be his while he was here. It was quite large, and though Matt had stayed in some rather impressive hotel rooms from time to time, he had never spent the night anywhere in a room that was more elegant than this. The room had a huge, four-poster bed, a dresser, a chifferobe, and a desk. Matt chuckled softly. He didn't have enough clothes with him to fill one small drawer, let alone all the space that was available to him.

After breakfast the next morning, Kitty invited Matt to take a ride with her.

The barn where Spirit had been boarded for the night was unlike any barn Matt had ever seen. It was very big, with extremely generous size stalls. There was fresh water and feed at each stall, and the barn was kept so clean and fresh smelling that it was more like a hotel than a barn.

"Ha!" Matt said as he began to saddle Spirit. "I'll bet you've never seen anyplace like this, before."

Spirit whickered.

"Oh no you don't," Matt said with a little chuckle. "Don't go getting used to living like this. Trust me, Spirit, you won't be seeing another barn like this one."

With Spirit saddled, Matt led him outside.

He had been there only a few minutes when Kitty rode out.

"What do you think of my horse?" Kitty asked, taking in her horse with a wave of her hand.

"I would say you are particularly well mounted," Matt replied.

Kitty laughed. "You would say that, no matter what, just because you are nice."

"No," Matt replied. "I mean it. He is just what you look for in a good-bodied horse. He has long, sloping shoulders, short, strong back, long underline, and a long, rather level croup."

Kitty clapped her hands. "My," she said. "You do know horses. Where did you learn?"

"I learned from a man named Smoke Jensen."

"Jensen. Your last name is Jensen," Kitty said. "Of course, we never knew each other's last name in the orphanage. Is Smoke Jensen family?"

"You might say that," Matt said. "You will remember that I ran away from the orphanage?"

"Oh, yes, of course I remember. Captain Mumford said you had died in the mountains, but none of us believed that."

Matt chuckled. "I nearly did die," he said. "But someone found me, then took me in as if I were his own. And the funny thing is, he wasn't really that much older than I was at the time. He was a father, big brother, friend, whatever you want to call him. And he taught me everything I know."

"So you took his name?"

"Yes."

"Why, I think that is wonderful. Did he teach you how to ride?"

"Yes."

"Good, let's see how well he taught you to ride," Kitty said. "Now, catch me, if you can."

Suddenly Kitty's horse exploded forward as if it had been shot from a cannon. Matt did not expect it, so by the time he realized he was being challenged, she was some distance ahead of him. Instead of heading for the road, Kitty galloped across the lawn, the hooves of her animal throwing up divots of grass. Matt had no choice but to dash after her.

Kitty was heading directly for the stone wall that surrounded the estate. The wall was high, not insurmountable, but high. Had it been an ordinary fence, or a row of shrubbery, it would not have presented much of a challenge.

But this wall was made of stone, and it was at least three feet wide. If the horse missed the jump, it could be fatal for the horse, and possibly for the rider as well. Kitty and her horse took the jump as if the animal had wings.

"Come on Spirit, don't embarrass me," Matt said, squeezing his knees against Spirit. "Damn, I didn't mean that, boy. Embarrassment is the least of my worries. Just don't kill yourself."

Spirit made the jump as well, and Matt saw that Kitty had stopped just on the other side to look back toward the wall. She laughed when she saw Matt make the jump, then she urged her horse on, and it was all Matt could do to keep up with her.

Kitty maintained the gallop for about mile or so before she finally pulled up to a trot, followed by a cooling walk, then ending the ride at a grass-covered point that overlooked the Bruneau River. From this overlook, the river was about one hundred feet below.

It was obvious that Kitty had visited this spot many times, because there was a bench that overlooked not only the river, but also the Owyhee Mountains. Sitting on it, she invited Matt to join her.

Kitty was quite an attractive woman. Bareheaded, her blond hair glistened in the sun. Her eyes were shining, and her full-breasted figure was displayed to advantage in her riding habit.

"I'm impressed that you made the jump," Kitty said. "You are the first visitor I've had who has been able to make the jump. Most of them go around when they see the rock wall."

"I confess that I thought about going around myself," Matt replied with a laugh.

"I shouldn't do that — challenge my visitors to make that jump, I mean. I would hate to think that my vanity might cost a horse its life."

"It wouldn't be your vanity, it would be the vanity of the rider who took the jump unless they knew they could make it."

"I suppose that's right," Kitty said. She looked at Spirit. "That's a fine horse you are riding as well. You call him Spirit?"

"Actually, he is Spirit the second," Matt said. "My first horse was also named Spirit, but he was killed. He was such a special horse to me that I like to think that he — or his spirit, at least, is living on. Somehow, I think this horse understands that he is carrying on the name. I know that sounds silly."

"No, it doesn't sound silly at all," Kitty said. "Since I've become involved with horses, I've learned a lot about them. Horses understand us, not only our words, but our very thoughts. If you named this horse to honor your first, then this one knows exactly what you have done, and believe me, he carries the name proudly.

"I think that is a very nice thing to do," she added.

"Oh, I believe you all right. It's like the jump he just made. I don't think, once he saw the challenge, there is any way I could have held him back," Matt said.

"Then the two of you seem well matched," Kitty said. "You are obviously one who is up to a challenge. Otherwise, you would not have responded to my letter."

"Well, once I read the letter and knew who you were, there was no way I wouldn't come."

"I wasn't sure you would even remember me," Kitty said.

"How could I forget you, Katherine? You were the prettiest girl there."

Kitty laughed, her laughter as melodic as wind chimes stirred by the breeze.

"I think you may be doing a bit of flattery there. Especially since everyone knew how taken you were with Tamara," Kitty teased.

"Ahh, well now Tamara was an older woman, and you know how boys are often intrigued by older women," Matt replied with a laugh of his own. "As I look back on it now, it's hard to think of a fourteen-year-old as an older woman. But at the time, that's exactly what she was."

"Tamara was the oldest of all the girls then," Kitty said. "She was sort of the mother hen to the rest of us. Or at least, she was our big sister. I really missed her when she left the home."

"What happened to you, after you left the home?"

The smile left Kitty's lips. "Don't you know?"

"No."

"Matt, I went the same path as Tamara, and every other girl who left the home. Like all the others, I was sold into prostitution," Kitty said.

"What do you mean you were sold into prostitution? How can you sell somebody? Isn't that like slavery?"

"It is exactly like slavery," Kitty agreed. "But Mumford, and the people he sold us to, had a clever way of getting around it. Mumford charged all the girls for room and board, then he arranged for Madam Crockett to loan us enough money to pay off the fee we owed to Mumford."

"Madam Crockett?"

"Emily Crockett. She owned what she called a 'boardinghouse for women' there in Soda Creek. The boardinghouse was a whore house, and we were bound to Madam Crockett until the loan was paid off. And of course since we also had to make a living out of what were getting, it took quite a while to pay off the debt. Some of the girls never got it paid off."

"You did."

"Yes, I did eventually get her paid off, but it took four years. By that time I knew no other profession, so I went into business for myself. That's what I was doing when Tommy came along," Kitty admitted. "After his first wife died, Tommy became one of my regular customers. I don't know how, or why, but, for some reason, Tommy fell in love with me."

"It's not that difficult to understand why," Matt said. "You are a beautiful woman, Katherine. And I don't mean just your physical beauty."

"You are just being nice to me, for old times' sake."

"No, really, you are a very beautiful woman."

"I wouldn't have been, if Tommy hadn't come along when he did. By now I would be worn and haggard looking — or I would be dead." She sighed. "So many of the girls who were residents of Mumford's Home are dead now."

"Oh, I'm sorry," Matt said. "I didn't mean to bring up unpleasant memories."

"I don't know if I would call it unpleasant memory, as much as I would call it a simple fact of life," Kitty said. "And, for me at least, it didn't turn out all that unpleasant. I wasn't in love with Tommy, not in the way a young girl dreams of falling in love. He was very good to me, and I did love him in my own way." Kitty sighed. "But then, I'm not sure that someone like me — someone who has been on the line, can ever actually be 'in love' with someone."

"Don't sell yourself short, Katherine. You have a lot to offer. You're husband was a very lucky man."

"Marcus certainly didn't think so."

"Yes, Mr. Gilmore told me a little about Marcus Kincaid," Matt said. "I gather he was not all that pleased with the fact that you married the man who had been married to his mother."

"I think that is what you would call an understatement," Kitty replied. "I'm sure he believes that, somehow, I tricked Tommy into marriage, in order to get out of the life, and have all this," Kitty said. "And I must confess that he is half right. I was anxious to get out of the life, and Tommy seemed like a good way of doing it. I knew Tommy,

I knew that he was a very nice man, and I thought it would do no harm. But I swear to you, Matt, I didn't really know who he was, and I knew nothing about all this until after we were married," she said, taking in the land with a sweep of her arm. She laughed. "He told me that he didn't want me to know about it beforehand, because he wanted to be sure that I was marrying him for him, and not for his fortune. Bless his heart, he didn't know that I would have married him if he had been a stable hand just to get out of that situation."

They were quiet for a long moment, then Kitty chuckled. "Now I find myself in another situation, fighting off rustlers to hang on to this ranch."

"In your letter, you said the rustlers were taking their toll of your stock."

"Yes. But what is worse is that they have killed two of my riders. "I would gladly give up every horse I own if I could change that."

Kitty's eyes welled with tears and when she began wiping them with the back of her hand, Matt gave her his handkerchief. "Thank you," she said, dabbing at her eyes. "One of the riders was a boy named Hank. Hank was just sixteen years old. Matt, he was raised in an orphanage, just as you and I were. It kills me to think of that, and then to realize how young he was when he was killed."

"Think of it this way, Katherine," Matt said. "At least he was out on his own when he was killed. That means he died free and proud. And you and I, more than most, can understand that."

Kitty nodded. "Yes," she said. "I can understand that."

"I understand that one of your men was a witness to the rustling."

"Yes, Prew was out there that night, and he saw it."

"Prew?"

"His real name is Jason Prewitt, but everyone calls him Prew."

"I'd like to talk to him."

"All right. He's back in the bunkhouse now, mending from the gunshot wound in the shoulder that he got that night. He says that he is absolutely certain that the man he saw was Poke Terrell, but Marshal Sparks says that seeing him from a distance, in the dark, won't hold up in court. Especially since Terrell has witnesses who will say he was somewhere else that night. Maybe you can find some way of proving that he is the one who has been stealing my horses."

"I'll do what I can," Matt promised. "As

long as you remember that I'm not a detective."

"I'm already grateful to you, just for coming," Kitty said. "And at the risk of your own life. Mr. Gilmore said two men tried to kill you back in American Falls."

"Yes."

"And again on your drive here, from Medbury?"

"Yes."

"I would say that they tried to kill you in order to prevent you from coming here to help me," Kitty said. "But I don't know how that is possible."

"What do you mean?"

"I mean, nobody but Mr. Gilmore knew I had sent for you. And even then, he did it by ruse."

"Maybe it had nothing to do with my coming to work for you," Matt said. "I have made a lot of enemies in my life. The fact that some people tried to kill me after I received the letter from you could just be a coincidence."

"But you don't believe that, do you?" Kitty asked. "I mean, Mr. Gilmore knew the two men, and he said they were associates of Poke Terrell."

Matt was silent for a moment. "Yes, well, I didn't want you to feel responsible for it,"

187

he finally answered. "But the truth is, I think you are right. I believe they were trying to keep me from getting to you to help."

"You say you don't want me to feel responsible, but I do," Kitty said. "I don't know what I was thinking when I sent for you. I guess I was just being very selfish. I never even gave a second thought to the fact that it would put you at such risk."

"I've taken risks before, Katherine."

"A moment ago you said you weren't a detective. You don't have to worry about being a detective," Kitty replied. "I have something else in mind for you, if you will do it."

"I'll do it."

Kitty laughed. "You don't even know what I'm going to be asking you to do."

"It doesn't matter. If you want me to do it, and I am physically capable of doing it, I'll do it," Matt replied. "What do you have in mind?"

"In a few weeks I will be transporting, by train, five hundred horses to the U.S. Army procurement office in Chicago. I want you to accompany me on that train to see that the horses get through. If you will do that, I will pay you ten dollars per horse."

"Ten dollars per horse? Katherine, that's five thousand dollars," Matt said.

Kitty chuckled. "I know it's five thousand dollars. I may be a woman, Matt, but I can do figures."

"No, I didn't mean —"

Kitty laughed, and held up her hand. "I know you didn't mean anything. I was just teasing you. But, seriously, Matt, it is well worth ten dollars per horse to me to see them safely to their destination. I took out a twenty-five thousand dollar loan from the bank in order to start the horse farm. I have a contract with the army that will pay me a hundred dollars a head which is enough to get me out of debt, but that money is payable only on delivery in Chicago. So you can see why I must get this shipment through."

"All right," Matt agreed. "I'll shepherd your horses for you."

"Thank you," Kitty said. "I knew I could count on you." She stood up. "Well, shall we be getting back, then?"

"I don't know. You aren't going to jump that stone wall again, are you?"

"No, we'll go back another way. I'm sure you would like to see some of the ranch."

"As a matter of fact, I would."

# CHAPTER TWELVE

Coventry on the Snake was mostly rolling upland grassy country. As they rode back, in the distance Matt could see mountains, dark blue at their base, and rising to majestic heights where little spindrift-like tendrils of snow trailed away from the brightly gleaming snow-covered peaks, white, against the bright blue sky. The prairie below the mountains was ablaze with a colorful profusion of wildflowers: yellow Yarrow, red Indian Paintbrush, light blue Mountain Phlox, and purple Trillum.

Just ahead of them, a jack rabbit ran along with them for a short distance until it grew tired, then it stopped and watched as the two riders passed by.

The range was divided by fences, into several different pastures, each pasture area containing a specific breed of horse.

"If I didn't keep them separated, it would be no time at all until I had such a mixture of breeds that the horses would be practically worthless," Kitty explained. "As you can see, I have nothing but purebreds, specific as to their purpose: draft horses, carriage horses, horses that are best for pulling stagecoaches, and saddle horses," Kitty said.

"I see you also have a few head of cattle," Matt said, pointing to a distant field where a rather substantial herd of cattle grazed.

"Only about five hundred head," Kitty replied. "They are what is left from Tommy's original cattle operation. They are also a hedge. If my note comes due and I can't pay it, I believe I can sell off the cattle for enough money to renegotiate the loan."

"Good plan," Matt said.

When Matt and Kitty returned to the house, they saw a carriage parked in the driveway.

"Looks like you have company," Matt said.

"That carriage belongs to Marcus Kincaid," Kitty replied. "I wonder what he wants."

"Only one way to find out," Matt said.

Kitty urged her horse into a trot and Matt kept up with her. As they rode into the drive, the door to the carriage opened and a well-dressed man stepped out.

"Hello, Kitty," the man said.

"What are you doing here, Marcus?"

"Now, is that anyway to greet your own stepson? Who is this?" he asked, looking at Matt.

"This is Matt Jensen. He is a friend of mine. In fact, he has been a friend since we were children together."

Marcus extended his hand. "It's good to meet an old friend of Kitty's." he said. "I hope you find your visit to Idaho pleasant."

"I'm enjoying it so far," Matt replied. He was still mounted, so he was able to refuse the offered hand without it being too obvious. He nodded instead.

"You didn't answer my question, Marcus. What are you doing here?" Kitty repeated.

"I've been concerned about you," Marcus said. "I just came out here to see how you are getting along."

"You go to court to try and take everything away from me, and now you say you are concerned about me? Am I supposed to believe that?"

"I was wrong, taking you to court the way I did," Marcus said. "I guess I was hurt, and maybe a little angry, that Papa Tom left me out of his will. I mean, after all the years I was a part of his family, for him to just forget about me the way he did — well, it hurt my feelings. But I had no right to take it out on you. And now that I look back at it, I can see that what I did might be taken as an act against you, personally, and I don't want you thinking that."

"What are you saying to me, Marcus? That you will make no more attempts to take over Coventry?"

"That's exactly what I'm saying," Marcus said. "The issue was settled in court, and as far as I'm concerned, it's over."

"Well, I appreciate that. Does that also mean that I don't have to worry about Poke Terrell killing any more of my hands?"

"Now, Kitty, that isn't fair. You know I don't have anything to do with Poke Terrell. I have no idea why he suddenly showed up here."

"What about Madison and Jernigan? They worked for you at one time, didn't they?"

"Yes, they worked for me once, a long time ago. But they quit last year. As far as I know, they are out in California by now."

"They're dead," Kitty said.

"Dead? How do you know?"

"Because I killed them," Matt said. "Just like I killed Sam Logan."

"Logan, yes, he was a real bad sort. He tried to come to work for me once, but when I found out he had served some time in prison, I said thanks, but no thanks. And you say you killed Sam Logan?"

"And Madison and Jernigan."

"I suppose you had good reason to kill them?"

"They were trying to kill me," Matt replied.

Marcus nodded. "That's reason enough, I would say."

"But you knew nothing about it?" Kitty asked.

"No, how could I know anything about it? I told you, none of those men work for me. I have no way of keeping up with them."

"Yes, so you said," Kitty replied, the tone of her voice clearly challenging.

"Kitty, I wonder if your friend would excuse us, so we could talk alone for a few minutes?" Marcus asked.

"Anything you have to say to me, you can say in front of Mr. Jensen," Kitty said.

"Please, Kitty," Marcus said. "There are some things that are just too personal."

Kitty looked over at Matt.

"I'll put the horses away," Matt offered.

"Thank you, Matt," Kitty replied, offering him the reins to her horse. She watched as Matt led both animals toward the barn.

"May we step inside?" Kincaid asked.

"If you wish."

Kincaid made a motion with his hand, offering Kitty the lead. When they reached the top of the steps, Kincaid hurried ahead of her, then opened the door and held it.

"Ah, the suits of armor," he said, smiling, as they stepped into the hall. "Do you know that when my mother first married Papa Tom, and we came out here to live, I was frightened by these suits of armor? I was convinced they were all occupied by ghosts from Papa Tom's past."

"Kincaid, I know you didn't come out here to talk about ghosts and suits of armor."

"No, I didn't," Kincaid admitted. "Look, this is — well, it is rather awkward, but I don't know any way to say it, other than to come right out and say it."

"What are you talking about?"

"I'm talking about you and me. Us, actually," Kincaid said.

"Us?"

"Kitty, you can't possibly be blind to the fact that I have long been an admirer of yours."

Kitty laughed out loud. "You, an admirer? Well I must say, Kincaid, you certainly have a strange way of showing it."

"But it's true, Kitty. I've known it, from the moment Papa Tom brought you home. You have to know that you are a beautiful woman. Any man would admire you. I had to keep quiet about it of course. After all, you were my stepfather's wife. How would it look if I showed any romantic interest in you? It would have been, at best, shocking."

"It couldn't possibly be any more shocking than the conversation we are having now," Kitty said.

"I know this must come as a shock to you," Kincaid said. "After all, I have held my feelings in check for a long time now. First, there was the fact that I — well, as I said, I felt hurt and resentful over the fact that Papa Tom left everything to you. Then — foolishly I now know — I attempted to use the court to subvert Papa Tom's wishes. I had no right to do that. I can only hope that, by my foolishness, I haven't completely destroyed any possibility of paying court to you."

"Marcus, after all you have done, I can't believe that you would possibly say such a thing to me and expect any kind of a response," Kitty said.

"Don't say anything now," Marcus said. "All I ask is that you just think about it for a while. You are going to need a husband to help you run this place. You have a very good business head on your shoulders, I will give you that. But there are times when you will need a man around, and I'm willing to be that man."

"Marcus, I — I don't want to sound rude, but there is no way I could possibly have any feeling for you. What you asking is impossible."

"Why is it impossible? You can't tell me you actually loved Papa Tom. You know you married him just to — uh get out your situation. Well, you are in another situation now and I'm available. That's all I'm saying."

"You are wrong, Marcus. I did love Tommy. Oh, maybe not in some young, girlish romantic way. But I did love him. And there is no way I could say the same thing about you."

For a moment, Marcus looked angry, then, inexplicably, he smiled. "All right, Kitty, if you say so," he said. "But you can't blame a man for trying."

Matt came back in to the house before Kitty could respond. Noticing a pregnant silence and sense of awkwardness, he stopped just inside the door. "Have I returned too soon?" he asked. "Should I leave and come back?"

"No, I was just leaving myself," Marcus said. He smiled at Matt as he started toward the door. "Do enjoy your visit here," he said. "And if you get up toward Medbury, stop by and pay me a visit."

"Thanks, maybe I will," Matt said.

Marcus took Kitty's hand, then raised it to his lips and kissed it. "Until we meet again," he said.

Marcus's act of courtesy surprised Matt, but he said nothing until he heard the sound of the carriage driving away. Turning back toward Kitty, he saw a very strange look on her face.

"Katherine, are you all right?" he asked, reverting back to the name by which he had known her.

"Yes, I'm fine," Kitty said.

"What did he want?"

"Nothing in particular."

Matt knew that Kitty's response was disingenuous, but he didn't press the matter.

"You said I could speak with Prewitt?"

"Oh, yes. See Tyrone Canfield. He is the ranch foreman and his office is at the end of the bunkhouse. Tell him I said to take you to see Prew. I never go into the bunkhouse myself. I consider that to be the private quarters of the men who work for me."

"And I'm sure they appreciate that," Matt said.

Matt walked across the lawn and down to

the bunkhouse. He had seen a lot of bunk-houses in his life, had even spent about eight months in one when he worked as a cowboy, but he had never seen one like this. It was much larger than any he had ever seen before, painted white, with a red roof. A porch stretched down the length of it, onto which opened at least ten doors and twice as many windows. The porch had a roof, supported by a series of pillars that were set every ten feet. There were also benches and rocking chairs on the porch, many of them with cushions. It was obvious that Kitty, and probably her husband before her, treated the ranch hands with kindness and respect.

Matt tapped on the door to the office and it was opened by a white-haired man with steel blue eyes. He was weathered and bowlegged and he held the stump of a pipe clenched between his teeth. "I take it you are Mr. Jensen," the man said.

"Mr. Canfield," Matt said, extending his hand.

"Call me Tyrone," the man replied.

"Only if you reply in kind."

"What can I do for you, Matt?"

"Katherine said you would take me to Prewitt."

"Sure, right this way," Tyrone said, stepping out onto the porch and walking down to the next door. He pushed it open, then stepped inside.

"Prew, you awake?" he called.

"Yeah, I'm down here," a voice answered.

The inside of the bunkhouse was as nice as it was outside. There were at least ten potbellied stoves down the center aisle of the dormitory, all of them sitting in sand-boxes. Because it was summer, none of the stoves were lit, but the smell of last winter's fires still lingered, not strong enough to be unpleasant, but just enough to suggest the warmth the stoves provided.

Now, gourds of water hung from the rafters, the evaporation of the water helping to cool the interior. Every bed had a foot locker and wall locker, and there were decorations on the walls.

"How is your shoulder," Tyrone asked as he and Matt approached.

"Still a little sore," Prew answered. "I can't complain though, seein' as what happened to Timmy and Hank."

"Prew, this is Matt Jensen. He's a friend of —"

"Matt Jensen!" Prew said. "I know'd Miz Wellington was goin' to ask you to come out here. I'm sure glad you did, and I'm real pleased to meet you."

Prew stuck his arm out to shake hands with Matt, but he jerked it back with a quick spasm of pain.

"Ouch," he said, reaching up to grab his shoulder.

"Let me do the reaching," Matt offered, sticking his own hand out. Prew smiled broadly as they shook hands.

"I've read about you," Prew said. "You're the first famous person I've ever met."

"Fame is relative, Prew. There are a lot more people who have never heard of me than there are people who have."

"Yeah, I reckon that's probably right," Prew said.

"Prew, I want you to tell me all you can remember about the night you were shot."

Prew told how he, Hank, and Timmy were riding nighthawk, when Hank rode off to check on a colt. He told of hearing a gunshot in the night, then getting no response when they called after Hank.

"Me and Timmy rode right into it, Mr. Jensen," Prew said. "One minute we was lookin' for Hank, and the next minute there was bullets flyin' all around. I don't remember actually gettin' hit. I just remember lyin' on the ground with my shoulder hurtin'."

"But you saw the rustlers?" Matt asked.

"Yes, sir, I seen 'em all right. Only thing is

it was dark, so I couldn't say for sure. But I've seen Poke Terrell a lot of times in the Sand Spur, and, in the dark, this feller looked a lot like him."

"Did you recognize any of the others?"

"I thought one of them might have been Sam Logan," Prew said. "But then since Logan works for Poke, it might be I was just thinkin' it might be him."

"He don't work for Poke any more," Tyrone said.

"He don't?"

"Nope," Tyrone said. "Matt killed him."

"The hell you say," Prew replied with a wide grin. "When? Where?"

"Yesterday afternoon," Matt said. "Up on the top of Bruneau Canyon."

"Damn. What was he doin' up there?"

"He was trying to kill Mr. Gilmore and me," Matt said.

Prew laughed. "Good for you. You know what? I think gettin' you to come help her is 'bout the smartest thing Miz Wellington has ever done."

# CHAPTER THIRTEEN

"How long have you been here, Tyrone?" Matt asked when the two men returned to his office.

"Well, I worked for Sir Thomas for fifteen years before he and Mrs. Wellington were married. They were married for a year before he died, and I've been with Mrs. Wellington for the last three, so, all told I've been here nineteen years."

"So you were here when Marcus Kincaid was living on the place?"

"Oh, yes, I was here, all right. I was here when he and his mama come to live here. He was just a sprout then. No more than twelve or thirteen, I would say."

"What do you think of him?"

"Well, his mama, Miz Mary, now she was about as fine a woman as you'd ever want to meet."

"I'm asking about Marcus Kincaid."

"What do you mean?"

"I mean, do you like him?"

"Matt, you have to understand my position here. I'm the foreman, he was family. It was never my place to like or dislike him."

"Perhaps. But I'm not family. So you can tell me what your honest opinion of him is."

"He was a handful as a boy. Always gettin' into some kind of trouble. I think he broke her heart so many times that it's a wonder she didn't die before she did. But Sir Thomas, he never gave up on him. No matter what kind of scrape Kincaid would get hisself in, Sir Thomas was always there to take care of it for him."

"What kind of scrapes did he get in?"

"Once when they were all supposed to be in church, Kincaid snuck out and took Mr. Ebersole's surrey that was parked out front, drove it like a bat out of hell, and wound up wreckin' it and breaking the leg of one of horses. The horse had to be put down. But Sir Thomas bought Ebersole a new surrey and a new team. Then another time, Kincaid burned down the girls' toilet at school. It was all kid stuff, you understand, but it was mean kid stuff."

"I'm more interested in him as a man than as a kid. What do you think of him now?"

"I think he is a low-down, conniving, sorry example of a man," Tyrone said. "I know for a fact, that before he died, Sir Thomas split all his holdings in half. He gave half of it to Kincaid, even though Kincaid wasn't his. And he told Kincaid that the other half he was goin' to leave to Mrs. Wellington. 'Course, he was still alive at the time, I don't think he had any idea he would be leavin' it to her so soon."

"But Kincaid wasn't satisfied with that?"

Tyrone shook his head. "No, sir, he wasn't satisfied at all. That's why he took Mrs. Wellington to court to try and protest it. He called Mrs. Wellington, uh, he called her a, uh —"

"A whore?"

"Yeah, he called her a whore. I didn't want to come right out an' say the word, 'cause to tell the truth, I don't care what she was before she an' Sir Thomas got married. I know she was a good wife to him, and she's been a good woman ever since he died. She's treated ever' man that works here decent."

"Kincaid lost the lawsuit," Matt said.

"Yes, sir, he did."

"How has he been since that time?"

Tyrone stroked his jaw for a moment, then he cocked his head before he responded. "Well, sir, to tell you the truth, it's surprisin' the hell out of me, but he's been right decent about it. As far as I know, he hasn't tried nothin' else."

"How well do you know Poke Terrell?"

"I don't know 'im at all. He just come here a couple of months ago. I've seen him in the Sand Spur a couple of times, but he's not very friendly. He never talks to anyone, he just sits at his table and plays solitaire."

"Well, if Prew can't be any more definite with his identification than he was with me, the marshal is right, Prew's testimony wouldn't hold up in court."

"I got no reason not to believe Prew," Tyrone said. "He's seen Terrell more times that I have, so I figure he probably did recognize him. But it ain't just the stealin' horses that makes Poke Terrell a low-down in my book. In my book, anyone who would belong to the Idaho Auxiliary Peace Officers' Posse is about as low down as a fella can get. Why, there ain't no tellin' how many he kilt when he was ridin' with the Idaho Auxiliary Peace Officers' Posse."

"Yes, I heard about them. They are a wandering group of deputies?"

"Deputies my ass," Tyrone said. "They're a bunch of plundering murderers, if you ask me."

Some of the other riders started coming back in then and Tyrone excused himself.

"I have to set out the night riders," he said.

"Go ahead, don't let me stop you," Matt said. "Thank you for the visit and the information."

"How is Prew doing?" Kitty asked when Matt returned to the house.

"He's doing fine," Matt said.

"Was he any help?"

"Yes, I found his information useful. After talking to Prew, I'm convinced that Poke Terrell is the one behind the rustling, but you have to ask yourself, why is he taking only a few head at a time?"

"Maybe that's all he can handle."

"I don't think so. This ranch is perfect for stealing a two or three hundred head or more. Even driving livestock, you are less than a day from Utah, Nevada, or Oregon. You could go to any one of those states, or you could divide the herd into three easily managed groups and go off in three different directions."

"I guess you are right. I hadn't even thought about that," Kitty said.

"I'm sure Poke Terrell has thought about it. No, there has to be another reason why he just picking at you, rather than making one grand haul."

"But I don't understand. Why would he

do that?"

"It could be that he is just trying to cause enough trouble to keep you from being able to meet your loan payment."

"Why would he do that? He has no interest in the ranch."

"No, but Marcus Kincaid does."

"Matt, are you suggesting that Marcus is behind this?"

"Let me ask you this. If you go into default, is there any way Kincaid could take over Coventry?"

"I don't know, I'm not sure," Kitty said. "I suppose if the ranch fails and the bank forecloses, he could move in. But if the bank puts the ranch up for auction, there are people who have more money than Marcus, and who would love to have Coventry. I think they would simply outbid him. Besides, Marcus has another plan now."

"Oh? What plan would that be?"

"When he was out here this morning he began to pay court to me."

"I hope you set him straight."

"Why, Matt, could it be that you are jealous?" Kitty said.

Matt coughed, nervously, and Kitty laughed.

"I'm teasing, Matt."

"Oh. You mean he didn't come courting

this morning."

"No, I'm not teasing about that. I'm teasing about you being jealous."

"I don't know that I would call it jealous," Matt said. "But I would be concerned."

Kitty put her hand on Matt's cheek. "Matt, my old friend, you have nothing to be concerned about."

*Medbury, the next morning*

From the patio behind his rather large house, Marcus Kincaid could enjoy a panoramic view of the Soldier Mountains, which rose prominently some twenty miles to the north. However, because of the trick of light and dry air, the mountains, on which individual trees were visible, appeared to be within easy walking distance.

Kincaid was sitting at a small table, on the patio, having his breakfast. He had the same breakfast every morning: a soft boiled egg served in a silver egg cup, half a grapefruit, one slice of toast, two slices of crisp bacon, and coffee.

He was just beginning to eat his grapefruit when he heard his maid, Rosa, say, "Señor Kincaid is outside on the Patio, Señor."

Looking up, Kincaid saw Poke Terrell coming toward him.

"I thought I told you never to come to my

house," Kinkaid said as he spread butter on his toast. "No one is supposed to know that you are working for me, remember?"

"This man Jensen is going to be trouble," Poke said.

"How much trouble can one man be?"

"He's already killed Madison, Jernigan, and Logan. They were three of my best men."

"If they were your best, you either need to raise your standards, or I'm going to have to lower your expectations."

"What do you mean, lower my expectations?"

"Right now, you are keeping all the money you get from selling the horses you steal, right?"

"That was the deal. You said you didn't want anything out of it," Poke said.

Kincaid held up his finger. "Wrong, I do want something out of it. I want Kitty to default on her loan. I expect you to live up to our agreement. You see to it that Kitty Wellington is unable to make enough money to pay off her mortgage. That's all you have to do."

"Suppose she does go broke and can't pay off the bank. The bank will just put the ranch up for sale and it will go to the highest bidder. What if somebody outbids you?"

"You let me worry about that," Kincaid said. "You just keep up the pressure."

"Yeah, well, that's another thing. With them watchin' the horses as close as they are now, I'm not sure I can steal any more horses."

"You don't have to steal any more horses, all you have to do is keep her from getting any of them to market."

"That's not good for me. I've been taking my cut from the money I get from selling the horses."

"I've given you seven hundred and fifty dollars. How much have you made from the horses?" Kincaid asked.

"So far I've took a hunnert and fifty horses, I lost twenty-two of 'em during the drive down into Utah, and I only got twenty dollars a head for what was left. That mean's I've got just a little over twenty-four hunnert dollars."

"I'll give you twenty five hundred dollars in addition to what we've already agreed upon," Kincaid said. "All I need you to do is keep the pressure on."

"I'm going to have to hire some more men," Poke said. "So I'll need a little extra for that."

"Twenty-five hundred dollars, plus what you have already made, should be more

211

than enough to take care of that. At least for now."

"All right. For now," Poke said.

"Don't come to my house anymore."

"How am I going to get the twenty-five hundred dollars you just promised?"

"I'll have the money delivered to you by special courier," Kincaid said.

Poke nodded, then turned and walked away.

After breakfast, Kincaid went back into his office and took a paper from his desk. The paper was the mortgage agreement that now made him the holder of Kitty Wellington's loan. If she defaulted on the loan to the bank, the bank would put the ranch up for sale, take its money, plus interest, from the proceeds, and give the rest to Kitty.

But there was no legal requirement for him to do that. The terms of the loan were very specific. If Kitty couldn't make the payment, the ranch would become the property of Marcus Kincaid. There would be no extension of the loan, and there would be no auction.

# CHAPTER FOURTEEN

When Matt went into town that evening, he had dinner at a restaurant called the Railroad Café. It was dark by the time he finished dinner and walked down the street to the Sand Spur. This was his first visit to the most popular of the local watering places. Inside the saloon, the bartender was standing at the end of the bar, wiping the used glasses with his stained apron, then setting them among the unused glasses. When he saw Matt step up to the bar, he moved down toward him.

"I'll have a beer," Matt said.

The bartender set the beer in front of him with shaking hands, and even though this was Matt's first time in the Sand Spur, he knew he had been recognized.

Clutching the beer in his left hand — he always left his right hand free when he went in to a new place — Matt turned his back to the bar and looked out over the room. A bar girl sidled up to him. She was heavily painted and showed the dissipation of her profession. There was no humor or life left in her eyes.

"Mister, are you looking for good time?" she asked.

Matt wasn't interested, but he felt a sense of compassion for the girl, perhaps heightened by hearing the story Kitty told of her own experiences.

"How much?" he asked.

The girl smiled at the prospect. "Two dollars," she said.

Matt pulled two dollars from his pocket and gave it to her. "Suppose I give you two dollars and you let me buy you a drinki?" he asked. "Would you be interested in that?"

"Gee, Mister, thanks," the girl said, sticking the money down into the top of her dress. "Charley, I'll have a sarsaparilla."

"Coming right up," Charley said.

"Is that all you want?" Matt asked.

"I can't drink whiskey all day long, I'd be a helpless drunk," the girl said.

Matt chuckled. "I see your point," he said.

The bartender put the glass in front of the girl and for the next few minutes, Matt and the girl had a pleasant conversation. As she relaxed, her features softened, and Matt realized that, at one time, she was probably a very pretty girl. During the conversation, Matt saw the bartender go to a table over on the side and, as he was picking up an empty glass, speak to the man at the table. The man glanced up at Matt, though the glance was so fleeting that few would have caught it.

At the rear of the saloon the piano player, who wore a small, round, derby hat and kept his sleeves up with garter belts, was pounding out a rendition of "Buffalo Gals," though the music was practically lost amidst the noise of a dozen or more conversations.

The man the bartender spoke to got up and walked over to the bar, carrying his beer with him. It wasn't until then that Matt saw the star on his shirt.

"Mr. Jensen, I'm Marshal Bill Sparks. Welcome to Medbury."

"Thank you," Matt said.

"I can't help but wonder what you are doing in our little town, though."

"I'm visiting a friend."

"Word I got is that you've come to hire out your gun to Mrs. Wellington."

"I don't hire out my gun, Marshal," Matt said. "And, like I told you, I'm here to visit a friend."

"Very well, Mr. Jensen, I've got no call to dispute you. But I do know that Mrs.

Wellington has accused Poke Terrell of horse stealing, and she seems a little put out that I've done nothing about it."

"Why haven't you done anything about it?" Matt asked.

"What am I supposed to do? There is only Prewitt's word that Poke Terrell was one of the rustlers. And he saw Poke, if that is who he saw, in the dark. On the other hand, Poke had three witnesses who swore that they were with him that night, and he wasn't anywhere close to Coventry on the Snake."

"And I'm sure that his witnesses are all first-class citizens," Matt said. "Like Poke Terrell."

Marshal Sparks chuckled. "Well, you've sized that up pretty well," he said. "But I hope you can see that, legally, my hands are tied."

"Mine aren't," Matt said.

"What does that mean?"

"That means I don't have to prove Poke's guilt in a court of law. I only have to be convinced of it myself."

"I see. By the way, I assume you know that Poke Terrell used to ride with Clay Sherman and the Idaho Auxiliary Peace Officers' Posse."

"So I've heard," Matt said.

"Of course 'used to' may not be the correct term," Marshal Sparks said.

"You mean he is still with the Posse?"

"According to Tate, he's the telegrapher down at the depot, Poke has exchanged a few telegrams with Sherman since he arrived."

"What did the telegrams say?"

Marshal Sparks shook his head. "I couldn't tell you," he said. "Tate ain't allowed to divulge what's in the telegrams. Truth to tell, he probably wasn't even supposed to tell me that Poke and Sherman been sending them back and forth to each other. But I figure Tate thinks it's something I should know, otherwise he would never have mentioned it."

"I think your assumption is probably right," Matt said.

"But my point is, Mr. Jensen, that if Poke Terrell is still with the Auxiliary Peace Officers' Posse, he's not somebody you want to take too lightly. I would be a bit cautious around him, if I were you."

"That sounds like good advice," Matt said. He lifted his beer. "May I buy you a beer, Marshal?"

"Thanks, maybe later," Marshal Sparks said. "Right now I need to make my rounds."

Matt looked around the saloon. "Oh,

before you leave, Marshal, could you point out Poke Terrell to me?"

"Do you think I'd be talking about him like this if was in here now?" Marshal Sparks asked. He pointed toward a table near the stove. Though every other table in the saloon was full, this particular table was conspicuously empty. "When he is in here, which is most of the time, by the way, he sits at that table over there and plays solitaire."

"Solitaire?"

"Yeah, he's too damn mean to get anyone to play with him. And, get this, Jensen, this will tell you what kind of man he is. When he plays solitaire, he cheats. Can you imagine that? A man who cheats at cards, even when he's playing himself." Sparks laughed, then started toward the door. "Like I said, I need to make my rounds. I'll collect on that beer later."

"Anytime, Marshal," Matt said.

Matt turned back to the bar. The bar girl who was talking to him before had left when the sheriff approached. Now she came back to him, and though he was not looking for company, he smiled a welcome anyway.

The bar girl picked up her drink then held it in front of her mouth so that when she spoke, nobody could see her lips moving.

She spoke very quietly.

"Be very careful when you leave the saloon, Mr. Jensen. Someone may be waiting for you."

"Thanks," Matt said, covering his reply with the glass, just as the girl had.

When Matt stepped out into the street a few minutes later, he checked the false front of the building across the street, and looked toward the watering trough for any place that might provide concealment for a gunman. He expected the trouble, if it came, to be in the form of someone shooting at him. He wasn't prepared for and was surprised by two men with knives who suddenly jumped from the dark shadows between the buildings. It was only that innate sense that allowed him to perceive danger when there was no other sign that saved his live. Because of that sense, and his lightning quick reflexes, he was already moving out of the way of the attack even as the two men were starting it. The two assailants were dressed in black which, because of the darkness of the street, made it difficult for Matt to see them.

The attackers made low swinging, vicious arcs with their knives, and had he not moved when he did, Matt would have been disemboweled. Despite the quickness of his reaction, however, one of attackers did connect, and the flashing blade opened a wound in his side.

The other attacker moved in quickly to finish Matt off but Matt managed to slip to one side before sending a wicked right toward his attacker, hitting him in the side of the head and knocking him away. Almost immediately the other one moved in. Matt managed to avoid his thrust, then, before the attacker could draw his hand back, Matt grabbed him by arm and twisted it, causing the attacker to turn around. Matt pulled the attacker toward him, using him as a shield against another thrust by the first attacker.

The first attacker's knife plunged into the heart of the man Matt was holding. The first attacker realized with shock that he had not only just killed his friend, he was also now at a distinct disadvantage in this fight. Not willing to press his luck any further, he turned and ran off into the night.

The knife wound caused Matt to lose a lot of blood, and feeling faint and nauseous, he dropped the man he was holding, then managed to find his way back into the Sand Spur. His sudden and unexpected entrance startled everyone into silence. He stood just inside the door, holding his hand over his side while blood spilled between his fingers.

Despite his nausea and dizziness, Matt could see the expressions of shock on their faces. Even the piano player stopped playing and was now turned all the way around on his bench. Not one person was speaking, and it was so quiet that the only sound to be heard was the ticking of the clock and the quiet hiss of the burning lanterns.

Matt walked over to the bar, leaving a trail of blood behind him. He pulled a silver dollar from his pocket and put it down in front of the bartender.

"Better make it a whiskey this time," he said.

Without so much as one word, the bartender responded quickly, putting the glass in front of Matt. He started to pull the bottle back, but Matt reached out and put his hand on the bartender's arm.

"Leave the bottle," Matt demanded.

The bartender left the bottle. "Mr. Jensen, you need to see a doctor with that wound."

"I'll be fine," Matt replied, his voice strained. He poured some whiskey into the glass and drank it. Then he opened his shirt, and poured a considerable amount of the whiskey from the bottle over his wound. The whiskey washed away some of the blood, exposing the wound which, originally was but a thin slice, had been opened up by the exertion of the fight.

The bar girl who had warned Matt now came up to him, holding her petticoat in her hand. She tore it into two pieces, one of which she used to clean the wound, and the other to press over the wound.

"Thanks," Matt said.

"Damn, Mister, who did this?" the bartender asked.

"They didn't leave their names," Matt said as he closed the shirt over the wound.

"They? You mean there was more than one?"

"There's only one now," Matt said. "The other one is lying out in the street."

"Dead?"

"I don't know," Matt said. "I certainly intended for him to be."

Matt had saved enough whiskey for one more drink. He poured another glass, tossed it down, set the empty glass on the bar, then turned to address those in the saloon who, after halting all card games, conversation, and drinking at his entrance, continued to stare at the bleeding apparition who stood before them.

"I'll be going now," he said with a strained voice. "I don't want anyone to follow me. If I see anyone following me, I'll kill them."

"Like I said, Mr. Jensen, you had better

see a doctor," the bartender repeated.

"I thank you for your concern," Matt said. "But I'll be fine."

Matt looked at the bar girl who had warned him to be alert. He raised his hand to the brim of his hat.

"Miss," he said. "I'm obliged for your company and your conversation."

After that, Matt turned and walked away from the bar, growing more dizzy with each step. When he reached the batwing doors he had to reach out and grab the door frame to steady himself. Then, calling on every ounce of reserve strength, he took his hand down, leaving a bloody hand print behind as he stepped outside into the darkness.

Matt mounted Spirit and started away from the saloon.

# CHAPTER FIFTEEN

When Matt woke up he was lying in a strange bed. He felt some soreness in his side and putting his hand down, felt, not the petticoat he had pressed against the wound, but a well-constructed bandage that was wrapped all the way around his waist.

Matt looked around at the room. Embossed metal tiles covered the ceiling, while twelve-inch crown molding separated the ceiling from the wall. The wall itself was covered with white wallpaper embossed with a pattern of flowers. The furniture, like the bed, was massive and elegant. This was not his room and he had no idea how he got here. The last thing Matt could remember was mounting Spirit and riding away from the saloon, intending to return to Coventry on the Snake.

He tried to sit up, but winced with pain from the effort and had to stay still for a moment until the pain went away. After a moment, he tried again, and this time he was successful. He swung his legs over the side of the bed, then realized for the first time that he was naked.

At that very moment the door opened and Matt looked around, quickly, but unsuccessfully for his pistol.

"What are you doing sitting up?" Kitty asked, coming into the room then. "You shouldn't be getting up yet."

Frederica, who was carrying a tray, came into the room behind Kitty.

"Lay back down," Kitty ordered. "We've brought your lunch."

"This isn't my room, but I must be at your house."

"Yes, this is my room. And of course you are at my house," Kitty answered. "Where did you think you were?"

Matt looked around the room and chuckled. "To tell the truth, I wasn't sure I wasn't in Heaven," he said. "And when I heard someone coming through the door, I thought maybe it was St. Peter coming to tell me that there had been a mistake, and I was going to have to be on the next train out of here."

Kitty laughed. "I admit, this is much nicer than Captain Mumford's Home for Wayward Boys and Girls," she said, "but I wouldn't exactly call it Heaven. Now, you lie back down like I said."

"How am I going to eat my lunch if I lie back down?"

"I'm going to feed you," Kitty said. "Frederica, if you would, please, put his lunch there, on the small table."

"Si, Señora," Frederica answered, setting the tray on the table. Matt saw a bowl of soup, a large chunk of freshly baked bread, and a coffeepot.

"Thank you," Matt said.

"Señor," Frederica acknowledged with a nod of her head.

"Thank you, Frederica. I can handle it from here," Kitty said.

Frederica let herself out of the room and shut the door behind her.

"How did I get here?" Matt asked.

"You don't remember?"

"The last thing I remember is starting to ride away from the saloon."

Kitty dipped the spoon into the soup, then held it out for Matt. He hesitated.

"It isn't too hot," Kitty said. "I let it cool a bit before we brought it up to you."

Matt took the spoonful, swallowed it, then nodded.

"Oh," he said. "That is good. That is very good."

"Thank you. It's a duck soup that I made myself," she said. "I even made the noodles."

Matt took another swallow and smacked his lips appreciatively. "It is very good," he said again.

He picked up the piece of bread and tore off a piece, then stuck it in his mouth. "Good bread too," he said.

"So the last thing you remember is riding away from the saloon?"

"Yes. I don't remember riding out here at all."

"Not surprising that you don't remember riding out here, since you didn't do that."

"What do you mean?"

"I mean you didn't get very far," Kitty said. "You got only as far as the school before you fell off your horse."

"I fell off my horse?" Matt said incredulously. He shook his head. "No, I don't think so. That's not possible."

"Don't get your feelings all bruised. Maybe I worded that poorly. What I should have said is that you passed out from loss of blood, then you fell off your horse."

"All right, that explains that part of it. But if I didn't ride out here, how did I get here?"

"Millie brought you here.

"Millie?"

"She works in the saloon. It seems you made quite a good impression on her. Should I be jealous?"

"Jealous?"

"I'm teasing. Evidently, you were pretty badly hurt when you left the saloon, and Millie was worried about you, so she stepped outside to see how you were doing. You weren't doing very well, you were weaving back and forth in the saddle as you rode away. Then, when she saw you fall from your horse, she ran down to you. She said that, at first, she was afraid you were dead. But when she saw you move, she went to get Mr. Gilmore. Mr. Gilmore rented a buckboard for her, and helped her get you onto it. She drove it out here by herself."

"Gilmore didn't come with her?"

Kitty laughed. "Are you serious? A whore comes to his house in the middle of the night, and you think his wife is going to let him go with her?"

Matt laughed as well.

"Well, I owe her my thanks. Not just for bringing me here, but for warning me I was in danger. Because of that, when I stepped out of the saloon last night, I was on my guard. Of course, I have to admit, I didn't expect a knife attack."

"It wasn't last night," Kitty said.

"What?"

"It wasn't last night, it was two nights ago. You were out all day yesterday, and all night last night."

"You're kidding."

"No, I'm serious. You have slept, if you can call what you were doing sleeping rather than being unconscious, for two days and two nights."

"No wonder I'm so hungry," Matt said.

"Now, I don't know if you actually like my soup, or if you just like it because you are hungry," Kitty said.

"Couldn't it be both?"

"I suppose it could."

"Katherine. Who undressed me?"

"Millie and I both did. And we put on your bandage," Kitty replied. She chuckled. "Are you embarrassed?"

"No, I reckon not. It's not like I've never been seen by a woman before."

Kitty laughed out loud. "Then we are even, Matt. It's not like Millie nor I have never seen a naked man before."

"Where is Millie?"

"She had to go back into town yesterday. She said next time you come into town, be sure to drop in to the Sand Spur and say hello."

"I'll do that," Matt said. Again, he looked

around the room. "I'm sorry I put you out of your room."

"You didn't put me out."

"What do you mean?"

"I spent both nights right here, with you," Kitty said.

"Oh?"

"Don't worry, Matt, I haven't been compromised." She laughed, heartily. "As if someone like me could be compromised. But you have been drifting in and out of it so much that I thought you needed someone to keep watch over you. Although you are welcome to share my room, and my bed, for as long as you want, you could probably go back to your own room now if you feel up to it."

"I appreciate the doctoring, and I appreciate you watching over me," Matt said. "But it would probably be better if I went back to my own room."

"Don't get me wrong, Matt. It was delightful to feel you in bed beside me, the truth is, right now you are all I have to protect my investment, so keeping you healthy is more important than anything else," Kitty said. "I don't have a choice. I have to watch over you."

Matt felt up to getting out of bed later that

afternoon and Kitty said he could move to his room, but she insisted that he stay in bed at least one more day. To keep peace, Matt agreed to do so, and he did not get up, dress, and come downstairs until noon on the following day. He had eaten nothing but soup for the last two days so when he came downstairs, even though he was in the parlor, he smelled something cooking. The aroma, which was very enticing, promised a meal that was a little more substantial than soup, so his mood improved considerably.

"Smells good down here," Matt said.

"I had Frederica tell Maria to put a roast beef on this morning," Kitty said, explaining the aroma. "I thought you might be ready for some solid food."

"I'm more than ready," Matt said. "Truth is, I believe I could eat it whether it was cooked or not."

Kitty laughed, but her laughter was interrupted by someone banging the front door knocker.

"Wait here, I'll go see who it is," Kitty offered and, nodding, Matt walked over to have a seat in the rocking chair.

A moment later, Kitty came back into the parlor with Marcus Kincaid trailing behind her.

Matt stood up.

"No, no, don't get up on my account," Kincaid said, holding his hand out. "I heard about your — uh — trouble the other night. I wouldn't want to be the cause of you tearing something open."

"I'm fine," Matt said without further elaboration.

"I must say, you are the talk of the town," Kincaid said. "I mean, here, two knife-wielding ruffians tried to rob you, and you not only survived, you managed to kill Garcia."

"Garcia?"

"Carlos Garcia. He works down at the — that is, he *did* work down at the depot in the feeder lot. The other one who attacked you had to be Lopez. They were a couple of Mexicans who worked together and roomed together down at Mama Sanchez's boardinghouse. Anyway, the next day, Marshal Sparks went down to the feeder lot to talk to Lopez, but Lopez was gone, and his boss said he hasn't been seen since it happened."

"They weren't trying to rob me," Matt said.

"Of course they were trying to rob you. What other reason would they have for attacking you like that?"

"They were trying to kill me," Matt said. "They came out of the dark with their knives and they attacked me without a word. If they had been trying to rob me, they would have asked me for money."

"Why would they be trying to kill you? Do you know them?"

"They tried to kill me because someone paid them."

"What makes you think that?"

"Why was I attacked in American Falls? Why were Gilmore and I attacked on the way out here that first day? When you add that all together, it can only mean that someone wants me dead."

"As I understood it from the report Gilmore gave, you weren't actually attacked while you were on the way out here. Gilmore said that you saw someone on the lip of the canyon wall, then you stopped, then you went up to confront them. That's when you killed Sam Logan."

"Who shot at me first," Matt said.

"There's only your word for that, isn't there?"

"Kincaid, if you've got something stuck in your craw, spit it out," Matt said.

"Oh, don't get me wrong, I'm not disputing your claim. I'm just repeating what Mr. Gilmore said in the report he filed. And it does point out how difficult the marshal's job is in enforcing the law when there are no eyewitnesses."

"There were two eyewitnesses."

"Yes, Mole and Cooter. Perhaps I should have said, eyewitnesses who were would be willing to give testimony."

"Have they told the marshal a different story?"

"They told the marshal that it all happened so fast they didn't know what happened."

"Don't you think if they could convince the marshal that I was at fault, they would do so?"

"I suppose. I do wonder, though, why someone might be trying to kill you. Do you have any idea who that someone might be?"

"Yeah I got a very good idea who wants me dead. It's Poke Terrell."

"Ah, you've been listening to Prewitt, haven't you? Prewitt thinks he saw Poke Terrell the night the rustlers stole Kitty's horses. But there are eyewitnesses in the Mud Hole who will claim that they were playing cards with Poke the night the robbery happened."

"That's funny," Matt said. "According to what I hear about Terrell, he never plays cards with anyone but himself. Who were the three who were playing cards with him on the night Prew was shot, and his two friends were killed?"

"Sam Logan, Al Madison, and Ken Jernigan."

Matt laughed out loud.

"What's so funny?"

"All three of those men tried to kill me."

"And all three of them are dead, which means their testimony can no longer be challenged," Marcus said. "So, as you can see, your assertion that Poke Terrell is trying to kill you would never be sustained in a court."

"Are you actually saying that I can't prove in court that Terrell is trying to kill me?"

"Yes, that is exactly what I'm saying," Kincaid replied. "You can bring charges if you want to, but it will go nowhere. You have no collaborative testimony."

Matt laughed out loud.

"What is it?" Marcus asked. "What do you find so funny?"

"Kincaid, you don't understand, do you?" Matt asked.

"What is it I don't understand?"

"I don't need any collaborative testimony. I don't have to prove it in court."

"Then you are right, I don't understand. Why don't you have to prove it in court?"

"Because I only have to prove to me. In

this case I am the court, I am the judge, I am the jury, and when the time comes, I will be the executioner."

"Oh, my," Marcus replied, obviously unnerved by Matt's declaration. "If you don't mind, I would like to give you a word of advice, Mr. Jensen."

"By all means, feel free to do so," Matt invited.

"I, uh, would be careful about making threats toward Poke if I were you. He doesn't strike me as the kind of man who would take such threats easily."

"I'm not making threats, Kincaid," Matt said. "I'm simply stating fact."

"Oh, what is that I smell?" Marcus asked, breaking off the conversation. "It smells divine."

"I told Frederica to have Maria prepare a pot roast for lunch," Kitty said. "You are welcome to stay."

"Why, thank you, Kitty. I just believe I will accept your kind invitation," Marcus said.

Because the roast beef was too large for two people, or even three, considering the unexpected arrival of Marcus Kincaid, Kitty invited Tyrone Canfield to dine with them.

"Oh, Matt, I've got those numbers for you," Tyrone said as they were eating, "I meant to give them to you as soon as I came in, but this meal is so good that it plumb slipped my mind."

"What numbers are you talking about, Tyrone?" Marcus asked.

Tyrone looked over at Marcus, but didn't answer. Instead, he glanced back toward Kitty.

"Oh, I'm sorry," Marcus said. "I seem to have stepped into something that isn't any of my business."

"I don't mean to be rude, but I reckon that's about it," Tyrone said. "I figure if Mrs. Wellington wants you to know, she'll tell you."

"I don't mind telling you," Kitty said. "He's talking about horses, Marcus. The horses we'll be shipping to Chicago next week."

"That's the contract you were telling me about earlier?" Marcus asked. "The army contract?"

"Yes. Matt will going into town tomorrow to arrange for railroad cars."

"Twenty horses per car," Matt said.

"You can get a lot more than that in a car," Kincaid said. "Heck, when I ship cattle, I can get fifty to a car."

"I'm not shipping cattle," Kitty said, resolutely. "I'm shipping purebred horses, and if you put any more than twenty in a single car the chances are likely that some might be hurt. In fact, they might be hurt so badly that you would have to put them down."

"Even so, you should be able to at least double the number per car," Kincaid said. "I'm just looking out for you, Kitty. The cars are going to cost you at least one hundred dollars per car."

"I figure it's going to take a minimum of twenty-five cars," Kitty said. "That would be with twenty head per car. Now, suppose I doubled the number of horses in each car, and suppose a minimum of two horses per car are hurt. In fact, I would say that the number is too low. I could wind up with a many as three or four, or even five horses hurt, per car. I could be looking at four thousand dollars in losses. On the other hand, if I go along with the idea of limiting it to just twenty horses per car, it will cost me no more than twenty-five hundred dollars in railroad fees, which in the long run could be much cheaper. Also, we will more than likely transfer every horse without injury, and despite the money consideration, there is something to be said for the welfare of the horses."

"I'll drink to that," Marcus said. He lifted his wineglass in toast. "To my beautiful stepmother and all her horses."

"I'm not your stepmother," Kitty said, speaking the words in the flat monotone that suggested she had discussed this very subject with him dozens of times before now.

"Very well, then," Kincaid said, lifting his glass a second time. "To your horses."

The others lifted their glasses to the toast.

"What time are you going in tomorrow?" Kincaid asked, conversationally.

"I'm going to help Tyrone and Prew select the horses that will be shipped, then put them in a separate field before I start into town. I'd say about mid-morning. Why do you ask?"

"I have some business in town tomorrow as well," Kincaid said. "Perhaps you would like to have lunch with me."

"Maybe I will," Matt agreed.

"Good, I shall look forward to it," Kincaid said. Pushing the plate away, he stood up. "Kitty, I must be going back into town," he said. "I know it is poor manners to leave immediately after having eaten, but I really must get back, and you can't blame me for staying through lunch. It was delicious."

"You are welcome anytime, Marcus," Kitty said.

"I don't like that man," Matt said after Marcus Kincaid left.

"I feel sorry for him," Kitty said. "He was so certain that he would inherit everything, and then I came along. I'm sure it was quite a blow to him when Tommy left Coventry to me."

"Mrs. Wellington, I don't mean to be talkin' out of turn," Tyrone said. "I mean, bein' as this is sort of family and all. But I've known Marcus Kincaid a lot longer than you. I've known him since he was a sprout. Sir Thomas had a heart that was just too big, so he either couldn't see it, or wouldn't see it, but the fac' is, even as a boy Marcus Kincaid wasn't no good. He wasn't no good then, and he ain't no good now."

# CHAPTER SIXTEEN

*The next morning*
Cooter climbed up onto a rock from which he could see for nearly two miles back across the desert. A small rise hid everything beyond that point.

"See anything?" Mole asked.

"Nothin' but sand and rock," Cooter answered.

Mole, a short, hairy man with gray eyes and a pug nose, took the last swallow from a whiskey bottle, then tossed it against a nearby rock. The bottle broke into two pieces.

"Damn, I shouldn't of broke that," Mole said. "I wasn't thinkin', I guess. I could of got myself a penny for it back in town."

"A penny," Cooter snorted. "A penny ain't no money. Not compared to what we're goin' to be gettin' for this job."

"Yeah, well, if you remember, we tried to kill this feller once before and it didn't work

241

out all that well," Mole said. "What happened is Logan got hisself kilt. That's what happened."

"That's 'cause we didn't know who we was messin' with then. Logan didn't tell us nothin' about him, so we wasn't ready for him when he snuck up on us like he done."

"I don't intend to let 'im sneak up on us this time," Mole said. "You might not of seen nothin' yet, but he's close. I know it."

"How do you know it?" Cooter asked.

" 'Cause I can feel it in my gut, that's how I know it. He is out there, and he's close."

Cooter climbed down from the rock and walked over to his horse. He slipped his rifle out of the saddle holster.

"What are you fixin' to do?" Mole asked.

"If he really is comin' and he's all that close, like you say he is, I don't aim to let him get any closer than a rifle shot."

"Yeah," Mole agreed. "Yeah, now that's the best idea you've had yet. We'll just shoot the son of a bitch down, soon as he comes into range."

The two men, with rifles in hand, climbed back up onto the largest rock that afforded them, not only a good view of the approaching trail, but also some cover and concealment. They checked the loads in their rifles, eased the hammers back to half-cock, then hunkered down on the rock and waited.

"Let 'im come up to no more'n about a hundred yards," Cooter said. "That way, he'd more'n likely be out of pistol range."

"What if we miss?" Mole asked. "A hunnert yards is a pretty long shot."

"It ain't all that long a shot, and with both of us shootin', one of us is bound to hit him."

"What if we don't?" Mole asked. "What if all we do is just let the son of a bitch know that we're here. Next thing you know, he'll be on us like a fly on a horse turd, just like he was back at the canyon. And there won't be nothin' we can do about it."

"The thing to do is not to miss," Cooter said.

"I don't know. I'm beginnin' to think we shouldn't of took this job," Mole said.

"You ever had five hundred dollars before?" Cooter asked.

"Hell, you know damn well I ain't never had that much before. I ain't ever even seen that much money before," Mole answered.

"Then shut up your yappin' and just do what has to be done. Anyhow, we got all the advantage. He's out in the open, and we got good cover here, what with the rocks and all. Besides which, he don't have any idea we're even here at all."

"I guess you're right," Mole agreed.

"Damn right, I'm right."

At that moment, a rider came into view over a distant rise.

"Son of a bitch! It's him!" Mole said. "I told you he was close!" He raised his rifle to his shoulder.

"Hold it!" Cooter said, reaching out to pull Mole's rifle back down. "Be patient. You shoot now and you won't do no more'n spook him. Let him get close, like I said. Besides, you was the one sayin' you didn't think you could hit him at a hundred yards."

"All right," Mole said, nervously.

They waited as the distant rider came closer, sometimes seeming not to be riding, but rather floating as he materialized and dematerialized in the heat waves that were rising from the desert floor.

On he came: a mile — half a mile — a quarter of a mile — two hundred yards. Cooter raised his rifle and rested it carefully against the rock, taking a very careful aim. "Just a little closer," he said, quietly. "A little closer before we fire."

Mole shifted position to get a better aim. As he did so he dislodged a loose stone, and the stone rolled down the rock, right into the largest, unbroken piece of the whiskey bottle. The stone pushed the glass out into the sun.

As Matt approached the ridgeline ahead of him, a sudden flash of light caught his attention, and he stopped, looking toward the flash.

"What the hell did he stop for?" Mole asked.

Looking down, Cooter saw the sun flashing off the broken whiskey bottle. "You dumb bastard, when you pushed that whiskey bottle down like you done, it commenced to flashin' in the sunlight. You just gave away our position!" he said angrily. He raised up and fired his first shot.

"I didn't do it of a pure purpose," Mole said. "You got no call comin' down on me like that."

"Where is he, anyhow?" Cooter stuck his head cautiously over the rock and looked down where the target had been. "Where is he? I can't see him."

"I don't know," Mole admitted. "I seen him get behind that rock, but I ain't seen him since."

"There's a dry creek bed down there. I seen it when we come through," Cooter said.

Mole looked toward him. "A dry creek bed? Damn, he could be right on us before we even knew it."

Cooter shook his head. "I don't think so," he said. "It curves away a long time before it ever gets up here."

No sooner were the words out of Cooter's mouth than there was a puff of smoke and the bark of a rifle from a clump of bushes not too far distant. The bullet hit the rock right in front of them, then hummed off, but not before shaving off a sliver of lead to kick up into Mole's face.

"Ow! I been hit, I been hit!" Mole called, slapping his hand to his face. "I been shot right in the jaw!"

Cooter looked at him, then laughed.

"I'd like to know what the hell you think is so funny?" Mole complained.

"You are. You are funny," Cooter said. "You ain't been hit. That ain't nothin' but a little ole scratch."

Two more bullets hit the rocks then and chips of stone flew past them.

"I don't like this," Mole said. "He's gettin' too damn close." Mole fired a couple of shots toward the bush just below the puff of gun smoke.

"Hey, Mole, look down there," Cooter said. "Ain't that his horse comin' back up the road?"

"Yeah," Mole said. He giggled. "This is

great! Shoot the horse! We'll just leave the son of a bitch afoot."

Both men started shooting at the horse, but the animal was still a couple of hundred yards away and slightly downhill. As a result, it wasn't hit, though the bullets striking the ground nearby caused the horse to turn and run toward the shelter of a bluff, a quarter of a mile away.

"Damn it! We missed!" Mole said.

Another bullet hit the rock, very close beside them.

"Come on, Cooter, let's get the hell out of here!" Mole shouted. He started running for his own horse.

"Mole! Mole, come back here!" Cooter called, chasing after him.

Seeing the two men start to run, Matt tracked them with his rifle, firing at the second man. That man went down, but the one in the lead made it to his horse. He kicked his horse into motion and in just a few seconds was behind a rocky ledge, out of the line of fire.

"Don't leave me, you bastard!" the one on the ground shouted. "Don't you leave me!"

Matt approached the man on the ground, holding his weapon pointed toward him. Seeing him, the man sat up and threw up

247

his hands. "Don't shoot, don't shoot," he cried out. "I'm shot. You can see that I'm bad shot."

Matt picked up the rifle Cooter had been using, jacked all the bullets out of it — there were only three left — then threw the rifle over the edge of the hill so that it landed more than a hundred feet below.

"Mister, that rifle cost me sixty dollars!" Cooter complained.

"Give me your pistol," Matt said, holding out his hand. "Butt first," he added.

"You ain't goin' to throw it away too, are you?" Cooter asked as he complied with Matt's request.

Matt stuck Cooter's pistol down into his waistband.

"Your name is Cooter?" Matt asked.

Cooter looked surprised. "Yeah, it is. How do you know my name?"

"This is the second time you've tried to ambush me, Cooter," Matt said. "I remember you from before, when you were with Logan. Then, you said Logan paid you. But Logan is dead, so who is paying you now?"

"You got to get me to the doctor," Cooter said, without answering Matt's question. "If this wound ain't treated, I could wind up losin' my leg."

"Yes, I suppose you could," Matt said

laconically. Kneeling beside Cooter, he tore the trouser leg away and saw the entry wound. The bullet was still in the leg and the wound was still bleeding.

"Take off your belt," Matt ordered.

"What do you mean, take off my belt?"

"You want to bleed to death?"

"No."

"Take off your belt. I'm going to use it to make a tourniquet."

Cooter took off his belt, and Matt looped it around the leg above the entry wound, then cinched it down tight.

"Ouch, that hurts."

"Does it?"

"Do you know what you're a' doin'? I ain't never heard of nothin' called a tourniquet."

"It'll keep you alive, and more than likely let you keep your leg," Matt said.

"I need a doctor."

"This will do for now," Matt said.

"What do you mean, this will do for now? You ain't no doctor."

"Who paid you to ambush me?"

"Nobody. We just done it 'cause you kilt our friend a few days ago."

"Mister, if Sam Logan was your friend, all I can say is, you have a piss poor choice of friends. Now I'm going to ask you again. Who paid you to ambush me?"

"Why the hell should I tell you that?"

Matt pulled his gun and put the barrel of his pistol to Cooter' forehead.

"Because I will shoot you if you don't."

"You're bluffing."

Matt cocked his pistol. "When you get to hell, say hello to your friend, Logan, for me," he said, matter-of-factly. His finger twitched on the trigger.

"No, wait!" Cooter screamed.

Matt eased the hammer down on his pistol.

"Who paid you?"

"You got to understand that if I tell you who paid me, he'll kill me."

Matt shook his head. "Cooter, have you ever heard the term, first things first?"

"No."

"Well, let me tell you what it means. It means that you need to take care of the problem you've got now, before you start worrying about any problem you might have in the future. You are worried about someone killing you if you answer my question. But that is in the future. I am right here, right now," Matt said. "And if you don't tell me who paid you to ambush me, I am going to kill you, right here, and right now. Do you understand that?" Once again, Matt cocked the pistol.

"No, no!" Cooter shouted, crossing his arms over his face. "Don't shoot, don't shoot! I'll tell you."

Cooter was quiet for a moment."

"I'm listening."

"It was Poke Terrell."

"Now, that wasn't all that hard, was it?" Matt asked. Once again he eased the hammer down on his pistol, and this time he put his pistol back in is holster. Then he walked over to Cooter's horse and started to mount.

"Hey, wait a minute! What are you doin'? You're takin' my horse again, aren't you?" Cooter asked. "This ain't like the last time, when I had two good legs. I can't do no walkin' on this leg."

"I'm going to use your horse to ride down and get mine," Matt said. "You may recall that you and Mole tried to kill my horse. I'll be back."

When Matt rode down to retrieve his horse, he saw Spirit standing quietly behind the ridge he had run to when Cooter and Mole began shooting at him.

"Hey, Spirit," Matt said, speaking soothingly to his horse. Matt looked around at the ridge, then nodded. "Yeah, you're a smart horse," he said quietly. "This was a good place to get out of the line of fire."

Spirit whickered, and nodded his head.

"Yeah, I know, we do seem to be getting into a lot of trouble here, lately," Matt said. "But I told you that when you signed on with me."

Matt got off Cooter's horse then mounted his own. He started back with Spirit, leading the animal he had borrowed.

Shortly after Matt had ridden away on Cooter's horse, Cooter saw a pistol lying under a mesquite bush. At first he didn't know how it got there, but when he picked it up, he recognized it. It was the one Logan had given Mole on the day they tried to ambush Matt Jensen the first time. Mole must have dropped it when he ran and, in his panic, didn't even notice that it was gone. Of course, even if he had known it, he wouldn't have come back for it.

"Well, Mole, you yellow livered coward," Cooter said under his breath. "I thank you for leavin' me a gun like this, even if you didn't know you was doin' it. Now, I'm going to take care Matt Jensen and go see Poke to collect my money, then I'm going to take care of you for runnin' out on me like you done."

Cooter picked up the pistol, checked the loads, then stuck it down his waistband behind his back.

"All I have to do now is wait on Mr. Jensen," he said.

He waited.

"Damn! What if he don't come back? There ain't no way I can walk all the way back to town on this leg."

He waited a few more minutes, then, when he was convinced that Matt Jensen wasn't coming back, and just when he was about to panic, he heard the strike of hooves on rocks. Raising himself up, he saw Matt Jensen coming back, riding his own horse and leading Cooter's horse.

"I was beginnin' to think you had forgot me," Cooter said.

"I thought about it," Matt said. "Get mounted, we're going into Medbury."

Cooter mounted with some effort, his face grimaced with pain.

"I know damn well it's not hurting you that much," Matt said. "So you can quit the show, I'm not believing any of it."

"That's 'cause you ain't got a bullet in your leg," Cooter said.

Matt could have told Cooter that he had a knife slice on his side that was rib deep, but he said nothing.

Matt was correct in his belief that Cooter was faking more pain that he was actually feeling. Cooter was playing for time, waiting for the right opportunity, and when he saw Matt turn away from him, he was positive that the opportunity had presented itself. Reaching around behind, he pulled Mole's pistol from his waistband, then he brought it around and aimed it at Matt's back.

"I've got you now, you son of a bitch!" Cooter yelled, pulling the trigger at the same time he yelled.

Cooter should not have yelled. He did not count on Matt's phenomenal reaction time because, even as Cooter was yelling and pulling the trigger, Matt was falling off his horse. The bullet whistled just over Spirit's empty saddle, passing through the exact spot Matt's spine had been but a split second before.

The contact with the ground was hard and painful, doubly so because it slightly re-opened the wound on Matt's side. Halfway down to the ground, Matt pulled his pistol. But by the time Matt actually hit the ground, he had brought his gun to bear, and pulled the trigger.

Matt's bullet caught Cooter in the chest, causing him to let out one, large, expulsion of air.

"How the hell did I miss?" Cooter asked, his voice racked with pain. He raised his pistol and tried to shoot it again, but the gun began wobbling in his hand, then he dropped it and grabbed his chest, then fell.

# CHAPTER SEVENTEEN

When Matt came riding into Medbury, he was leading Cooter's horse behind him. Cooter was draped, belly down, across his saddle, and Matt's entry into town aroused immediate attention. Those who were riding or driving in the street, as well as those who were merely pedestrians, saw the body draped over a horse. Many of them interrupted their transit to their original destination in order to follow Matt. There were other townspeople engaged in commerce inside the stores and buildings, both as customers and merchants, who saw the macabre parade through the windows, and they came pouring out of the stores and buildings, including one man who ran out from the barber shop still draped in the barber's cape, with the barber, brandishing his razor, chasing after him. They joined the growing throngs of people who were now walking alongside Matt, keeping pace with the two horses as they moved down the street, the hoofbeats making loud, clopping sounds.

"Ain't that Cooter's horse?"

"Yeah, it's Cooter's horse. That's Cooter lyin' across the saddle."

"He looks dead."

"Hell yes, he's dead. You think he'd be lyin' belly down on his horse that way iffen he war'nt dead?"

"That's Matt Jensen leadin' him. I reckon you've heard of Matt Jensen."

"Yeah, but I didn't figure he'd ever come back into town after he kilt the Mexican the other night."

The curiosity of the crowd grew even greater when Matt stopped in front of the Sand Spur. The crowd followed, but kept a reasonable distance, because no one wanted to incur Matt Jensen's anger.

"What you reckon he stopped here for? How come he didn't go on down to the undertaker? I mean, what else for would he be bringin' in Cooter's body, iffen he wasn't bringin' him in to the undertaker?"

"Why don't you ask him?"

"No sir, not me. I ain't goin' to ask him nothin'."

Tying, first his own horse off, then Cooter's horse, Matt slid Cooter's body off the saddle, draped it across his shoulders, stepped up onto the porch, then pushed his way through the bat wing doors.

"Here! What are you doin' there?" one of the saloon patrons shouted. "You can't be bringin' no dead body into a saloon like that! They's folks drinkin' in here."

Matt looked at the man who had complained, fixing him with such a steely glare that the man blanched, then took a couple of steps backward.

"Of course, I reckon if you wanted to bring him in here, that would be your business," the man said, clearing his throat.

Upon seeing Matt come into the saloon with a body draped over his shoulder, most of the patrons jumped up from the tables and moved back out of the way. One man, however, was conspicuous in that, unlike the other patrons of the saloon, he remained seated. He was playing a game of solitaire, and he gave the impression that he was so engrossed in his game that he didn't even notice Matt.

Matt had never seen Poke Terrell, but the man sitting at the table was short and stocky, baldheaded, and with no neck, which was exactly the way Poke had been describe to him. Matt also saw Mole, and it was obvious that Mole had been talking to

Poke because, though he had moved away from the table, he was still in close proximity to it.

Matt walked back to the table. Not until then, did Poke look up.

"I've got a play for you, Poke," Matt said.

"What would that be?"

Without ceremony, Matt dumped Cooter's body onto the cards that were spread out for the game.

"Dead man on the black queen," he said.

Poke sighed, but made no abrupt movement.

"I was winning this game," he said. "Do you have any idea how hard it is to win at Ole' Sol?"

"This is number five for you," Matt said.

"Number five? I don't know what you are talking about."

"Al Madison, Ken Jernigan, Sam Logan, Carlos Garcia, and now Cooter. I don't know Cooter's real name," Matt said.

"Why are you telling me all this?"

"Because you are the son of a bitch who keeps sending them after me."

"Here, you got no call to be talkin' to Mr. Terrell that way," Mole said.

Matt jerked his pistol from his holster, pointed it at Mole, and cocked it. "You were there with Cooter, both times," Matt said.

259

"You were on the canyon wall, and you were with Cooter this morning."

"I don't know what you are talking about," Mole said.

"You don't?"

"I swear, I don't have the slightest idea."

"Then you are going to die dumb," Matt said. "I don't plan to give you any more chances to ambush me, so I'm going to kill you right now."

Several in the saloon gasped.

"No, no!" Mole said, throwing his arms up. "I ain't even carryin' a gun. You can see my holster is empty! I think Cooter stole it."

"Did he, now? Well, you can take that up with him when you see him in hell."

"No, no!" Mole said. "Please, Mister, don't kill me. Don't kill me!" Mole dropped down onto his knees, weeping.

"Get out," Matt said, making a motion toward the batwing doors. "Get all the way out of town. If I ever see you again, I'll kill you."

"I'm goin', I'm goin'," Mole shouted. Getting back on his feet, he ran toward the door, pushing through those who had gathered just outside. A moment later, everyone could hear the clatter of hooves as Mole galloped out of town.

"Mister, I don't know who you are," Poke said. "But you don't come in here and threaten me or my friends. I won't put up with — *unh!*"

The grunt came from a blow, struck by Matt. Matt was still holding the pistol in his hand, and he brought it around in a vicious backhand, hitting Poke in the side of the head and knocking his chair over. Poke wound up on his back, on the floor.

"You son of a bitch!" Poke shouted in rage, pulling his pistol from his holster.

Matt closed in on him in one step, and as Poke got the pistol out, Matt sent a swift kick against it, knocking the pistol out of Poke's hand.

Poke rolled over onto his hands and knees and stayed that way for a moment.

*"Arrghhh!!"* Poke yelled at the top of his voice. Coming up off his hands and knees, Poke launched himself in a bull-like charge toward Matt. The sudden charge caught Matt off guard and he dropped his pistol as Poke drove him across the room before slamming him into the bar.

The ferocity of the attack momentarily stunned Matt and he was unable to respond. Poke took advantage of Matt's immobility, then pulled back away from him just far enough to send a hammerlike blow into

Matt's side.

Poke was an incredibly strong man, and Matt felt as if he had been kicked in the side by a mule. The pain was excruciating, and he knew that the wound had been opened up. In fact, he could feel a dampness under his shirt, and he knew it was blood.

Thinking he had the advantage now, Poke threw a powerful right cross, hoping to connect and take Matt out. But Matt managed to jerk his head back just far enough to avoid the blow. Matt countered with a hard, straight left, landing it on Poke's nose. He felt the nose go under the blow, and had the satisfaction of hearing Poke grunt in pain.

By now the citizens of the town who had gathered just outside the saloon began to come inside, joining the saloon patrons who were already inside, in order to witness this fight. For a few of the townspeople, this was the first time they had ever been inside the saloon, and though under normal circumstances, they would avoid such a place with all that was in them, this was different.

This was a fight between two powerful men. And since neither of the men were from Medbury, it didn't really matter to the crowd who won, as long as the fight was entertaining.

Poke made another wild swing, and Matt managed to dance back away from it, shooting a right jab to Poke's chin as he did so. Poke shook off the blow, then saw that Matt was bleeding through his shirt on his left side. Poke smiled at him.

"Oh, now, did I do that?" Poke asked. "That must really hurt."

Poke picked up a chair, then swung it like a baseball bat at Matt. Matt ducked under it, and the swing caused Poke to be off balance. Taking advantage of that, Matt gave Poke a shove, causing him to stumble into the potbellied stove, knocking it over. When he did so, all the sections of the stove pipe came loose, and black soot poured out onto Poke, blackening his face.

Just as Poke regained his feet, Matt charged, putting his shoulder into Poke's stomach and driving him back against the stair railing. Poke went through the railing.

Matt stepped away again. Poke lay halfway through the railing onto the stairs. He shook his head, then got up but, as he did so, he grabbed one of the rungs from the railing. Lifting it over his head, he charged Matt, once again, bellowing in anger.

Matt picked up a section of the stove pipe and held it crosswise in front of him to take the blow from the club. The stove pipe was bent double by the force of the blow, but it prevented the club from actually hitting Matt. Poke threw away the club and made another roundhouse swing at Matt. This time, because Matt had been put slightly off balance by the club attack against him, Poke connected.

The blow knocked Matt back, and he fell onto one of the tables, smashing it into two pieces. Poke ran over to him and raised his foot with the intention of bringing it down hard on Matt's head. Matt grabbed Poke's leg and twisted it, causing Poke to go down. Matt rolled over to him then knocked him out with a blow to the chin.

Now, breathing hard, and bleeding from the reopened wound in his side, Matt got up from the floor and stumbled over to the bar.

"Whiskey," he said.

"Yes, sir," the bartender replied. "And this one will be on the house, Mr. Jensen. I reckon you've earned it."

"You dropped this," Millie said, handing Matt his pistol.

"Thanks," Matt said. "And thanks for the other night, not only the warning, but for taking care of me. Katherine told me what you did."

"It wasn't anything that anybody else wouldn't have done," Millie said.

"But that's the point, Millie. Nobody else did it."

By now everyone had crowded back onto the floor of the saloon. Many were repositioning tables and chairs, and a couple of men set the stove back up. They were unable to reconnect it to the flue though, because one of the stove pipes had been too badly damaged.

Poke was sitting up on the floor now, with his head hanging down. Nobody would dare approach him.

"Oh, honey, you are bleeding just real bad," Millie said, putting her fingers on Matt's shirt. "Come on up to my room, let me take care of that for you."

"Mister, look out!" someone shouted and Matt turned to look toward Poke, just as Poke shot at him.

"Uhn!" Millie grunted, going down beside Matt. Matt drew and fired back at Poke, hitting Poke in the middle of his chest.

"Millie!" Matt said, dropping down beside her.

Millie smiled at him. "Kitty told me what a good man you are. I said she didn't have to tell me that . . . I already knew."

Millie took two more gasping breaths,

then she stopped breathing.

Matt stood up, then looked over at Poke. He walked over and stood over him, then pointed his gun at Poke's head and cocked it.

"Mister, you'll just be wasting a good bullet on that worthless son of a bitch," someone said. "He's already dead."

By coincidence, the circuit judge was in town, so they were able to hold an inquiry as to the cause and circumstances of the deaths of Poke Terrell, Cooter, and Millie that very afternoon. After all the testimony was taken, Judge Marshall Craig issued his ruling.

"As to the death of Harold Cotter, there being no eyewitnesses to dispute Matt Jensen's claim that it was in self-defense, this court rules that there be no indictment.

"As to the death of Poke Terrell, all testimony being heard, this court rules that it was death by gunshot, said gunshot discharged in the defense of his own life. This court rules that the homicide be justifiable, and there will be no indictment.

"As to the death of the young woman known as Millie, all testimony being heard, this court rules that her death was the result of an act of murder committed by Poke Terrell, and only his own death prevents an indictment from being issued.

"This hearing is concluded."

Several came to congratulate Matt, and he accepted their congratulations and best wishes graciously.

When he rode back out to Conventry on the Snake that evening, he realized that not only had he not had lunch with Marcus Kincaid, he didn't even see him while he was in town.

He had also made no arrangements for the livestock cars, and that had actually been the sole purpose of his visit.

His day had become unexpectedly busy. He was sure that Kitty would understand that.

What he didn't realize was that it was about to get busier.

He felt the bullet, before he heard the sound. Actually, he didn't feel the bullet as much as he felt the effects of the bullet, because his hat flew off his head and he felt his hair fluff. Had the bullet been but one inch lower, it would have slammed into the back of his head.

Matt jerked the reins of his horse hard to the right, toward a large rock that would give him protection from whoever was shooting at him. Spirit needed no urging, the horse answered so quickly that Matt wasn't sure whether the horse was responding to his direction or reacting on his own.

Once he was behind the rock he jumped from the saddle, then climbed up onto the rock to see who had taken the shot at him. When he saw Mole, he wasn't surprised.

Mole took a second shot at him, and Matt shot back. One shot was all it took.

Matt walked back to look down at Mole's body, then he sighed.

"You just got yourself killed for nothing, Mole," he said. "With Poke dead, just who did you think was going to pay you?"

The next day, two grave diggers drove the undertaker's wagon out to the edge of town to Boot Hill, then back into the part of the cemetery known as Potter's Corner. There, the two men dug three graves, alongside the recent grave of Carlos Garcia, Mole having been brought in last evening. There was another recent grave in the cemetery, that of Sam Logan, but as Logan had not been without standing or funds when he died, he was spared Potter's Corner and was buried in the main part of the cemetery.

But, just as the town of Medbury had paid to bury Carlos Garcia, they were also footing the bill for Andrew "Poke" Terrell, John

"Mole" Mueller, and Harold "Cooter" Cotter. The three men had been put into plain pine boxes and, once the graves were opened, they were lowered by a rope into the ground. Not one person, other than the grave diggers themselves, was there for the interment.

Gene Welch, the undertaker and proprietor of the Eternal Rest Mortuary, had thought Millie would be buried in the same way. After all, she was a whore with no known relatives and the only thing that was known about her was that she had told one of the other soiled doves who worked at the Sand Spur that she was originally from Springfield, Illinois. All that changed, though, when Kitty came to town.

"You will not put her in a pine box," Kitty said, when she learned of Welch's plans.

"I beg your pardon, Mrs. Wellington, but the city is paying for her funeral, same as they done for Mr. Poke and Mr. Cooter. And with what the city pays, a pine box is all she gets," Welch said.

"I am paying for her funeral," Kitty said. "I want to see the finest coffin you have."

A big smile spread across Welch's face. "Yes, ma'am," he said. "I got one here for you to look at that is as fine a coffin as you'll find anywhere in the country. Why, you could bury the president of the United States in this coffin. It's called the Heaven's Cloud, and it's all lined with silk, don't you know. Why, I promise you, the young lady will be as comfortable lyin' in that coffin as she would be sleepin' in her own bed."

"Good. I want her in that coffin, and I want you to use all the artifice and skill at your command to see to it that she looks beautiful," Kitty said. "Also when she is taken to the cemetery, you take her in the glass-sided hearse. I will provide a team of horses to pull the hearse."

"Yes, ma'am," Welch said. "Mrs. Wellington, if you don't mind my askin', why are you willin' to go all out for this woman? She wasn't anything but a whore."

"I do mind your asking," Kitty replied. "You just do what you are paid to do, without asking questions. Otherwise I can hire Mr. Stallings from King Hill to conduct the funeral."

"No, no, you don't have to go be doing that, now," Welch said quickly. "There's no need for you to go over to King Hill. I assure you, Mrs. Wellington, I can give the young lady as nice, if not a nicer, funeral than anything Paul Stallings can do."

"Have her ready tomorrow afternoon. I'll be back with the team of horses then."

"Oh, you don't have to do that. I have a fine team of draft horses."

"I will bring carriage horses," Kitty said. "That is what you will use to draw the hearse."

"Yes, ma'am, if you say so. I'll have her all ready, looking as pretty as a picture. What about a marker? Will you be wantin' a marker?"

"Yes, of course I want a marker."

"The problem is, as far I know there don't nobody in town know her whole name. The only name anyone knows is Millie. And we don't even know if that's her real name or not, seein' as whores often takes other names that aren't their own. They do that to keep their family from findin' out what they are doin', don't you know."

"I know her real name."

"You do? You know her real name, do you? Well that's good. What is it?"

"Her real name is Millicent McMurtry," Kitty said. "I'll write it down for you."

"Yes, ma'am. Millicent McMurtry. I'll have that carved on her marker, along with a flower, or somethin' real pretty."

"You do that," Kitty said as she left the morturary.

"Mrs. Wellington?" Welch called.

At the call, Kitty stopped and turned around.

"About callin' Miss McMurtry a whore and all. I hope you didn't take that personal."

"Oh? And tell me, Mr. Welch, why should I take it personal?"

"You know, you bein', uh, I mean what some folks say 'bout you one time, uh . . ."

"Yes, Mr. Welch?" Kitty said, pointedly.

"Uh, nothin', I just, uh, like I say, I'll have the — young lady — all ready in time for the funeral tomorrow."

"You do that," Kitty said, as she walked out the front door of Welch's funeral establishment.

# CHAPTER EIGHTEEN

Shortly after Matt woke up on the day of the funeral, there was a light knock on the door to his bedroom.

"Yes?" he called.

"Señor Yensen, it is Frederica," a voice called from the other side of the door.

"Just a minute."

Quickly, Matt pulled on his pants, and put on a shirt. Then, with his shirt tucked into his trousers, he opened the door. Frederica was standing there, holding a cloth garment bag.

"Señora Wellington asks if you would please wear this for the funeral," Frederica said, handing him the garment bag.

"Thank you," Matt said, taking the bag from her. Closing the door, he took the bag over to his bed, unbuttoned it, and looked inside.

"All right, Katherine," he said under his breath. "If you want me to wear this, I will."

■ ■ ■ ■

"Oh, my," Kitty said when Matt came down into the parlor a short while later. "You look good in Tommy's suit. In fact, you look more than good, you look positively handsome."

"Frederica had to let the jacket out some for me to wear," Matt said, holding out his arms and looking down at himself. He was wearing a black suit, gray silk vest, and black string tie, the clothes having belonged to Sir Thomas Wellington.

"Yes, in the shoulders," Kitty said. "She told me." Kitty smiled. "In fact, I think her exact words were that you were a very strong man."

"Yeah, well, I have to tell you, Katherine, I don't feel all that strong right now. That fight with Poke took quite a bit out of me," Matt said, touching his side, gingerly.

"Are you sure you feel up to going?" Kitty asked. "I mean with your side, and all."

"My side is bothering me, some, I will admit," Matt said. "But I would go to Millie's funeral if I had to hold my guts in with my own hands."

Kitty chuckled. "Oh, my, how — descriptive — of you. But, hopefully that's not going to happen."

"Did you know Millie from somewhere before here?" Matt asked.

"Yes and no," Kitty said.

When Matt looked confused, Kitty continued.

"I never met Millie before the night she brought you out here. But I knew her, because I've known dozens of girls just like her. And, of course, as you know, I was just like her myself, once. I know it might be hard for you to understand why I have this feeling of connection to her but —"

"No," Matt said, interrupting her and shaking his head. "It isn't at all hard for me to understand."

There was a light tapping on the door of the parlor then, and looking toward it Matt and Kitty saw Tyrone Canfield standing just outside the parlor in the hall. Like Matt, Tyrone was wearing a suit, though even as he stood there, he tugged at the collar, giving evidence of his discomfort in such apparel.

"I have the team ready for the hearse," Tyrone said. "I chose a couple of black Percheron mares."

"Good choice," Kitty said. "Go ahead and take them on into town to Mr. Welch. Matt and I will follow in the surrey."

"Yes, ma'am," Tyrone said. "Prew has

hitched up the surrey and brought it around, but if you don't mind, he'd like to ride into town with me."

"Of course I don't mind."

"Thank you, ma'am," Tyrone said. "We'll see you in town," he added as he started toward the front door.

Kitty watched Tyrone leave, then she turned back to Matt. "Are you ready to go?" she asked.

"I'm ready," Matt replied, trying to hide the wince as he rose from the chair.

"Maybe I'd better drive," Kitty offered, noticing the wince as he stood.

"Yeah, that might not be a bad idea," Matt agreed.

The surrey was parked in the curved driveway, sitting right in front of the great, stone steps. It was a very attractive vehicle, polished black lacquer with yellow wheels, red leather seats, and a black leather top. And, adding to the overall attractiveness was the fact that it was being pulled by a team of very handsome, matching white Arabians.

Matt reached the top step of the porch, then he stopped.

"What's wrong?" Kitty asked. "Do you not feel up to going?"

"No, it isn't that," Matt said. He laughed, a low, almost self-deprecating laugh. "It's just that, well, I don't have my pistol with me, and this will the first time I've gone anywhere without my gun for almost longer than I can remember."

"Poke Terrell is dead," Kitty said. "His sorry carcass is lying under six feet of dirt in an unmarked grave in the back corner of the Medbury cemetery. Why do you need your gun now?"

Matt shrugged. "No reason, I guess," he said. "It's just that I feel naked without it."

"Honey, I've seen you naked," Kitty said. "And believe me, you aren't naked."

Matt laughed hard at the ribald comment.

There were some in town who thought it unnecessary to have a funeral for a whore — in fact, a few thought it was almost sacrilegious to do so. But the Episcopal priest, Father Walt Pyron, believed that everyone deserved a Christian burial, so when Kitty asked him if he would perform the service, he agreed without hesitation.

Surprisingly, the church was full, and whether the people had come out of a sense of piety and genuine compassion for the young fallen woman, or merely out of curiosity, Kitty didn't know, nor, did she care. She was just pleased that they were here. Kitty, Matt, Tyrone, Charley, the bartender, Amos, the piano player, and Jenny and the other girls who worked at the Sand Spur had seats on the very front row. The other seats were on a first come, first seated basis and, within moments after the church's red doors were open, the pews were filled. The spillovers lined the walls on each side, or stood at the rear, crowding even out into the narthex. In addition there were more people outside, waiting for the service to end so they could accompany the funeral cortege to the graveyard.

Father Pyron had come out of the study during the organist's prelude, and now sat quietly in his chair on the sacristy until the music ended.

Someone coughed.

Through an open window came the incongruous sound of a sudden burst of laughter, and, at a nod from Father Pyron, one of the ushers closed the window.

Pryon stepped up to the ambo.

"I know that there are some, perhaps even present in this congregation, who would take issue with me conducting funeral rites for someone like Millicent McMurtry," he began, "and yes, the young woman whose life we are met here to celebrate, was a prostitute. But I am told by those who knew her best that prostitution was not a profession she chose because of any prurient nature, or unholy desire for lucre. Instead, like many a young woman who has found herself thrust into the world with not one person to provide for her, Millie turned to the only means she believed was available to provide sustenance.

"That this was the only avenue open to her is the shortcoming of us all, for we, as a society, failed Millie, as we have failed all young women in similar circumstances.

"But know this. The fact that Millie was a soiled dove does not mean she is a lost soul. We are told in the Book of Matthew that a harlot, who is good at heart, will be welcome into the Kingdom of God. And those who knew Millie, know that she was, truly, a woman with a heart of gold, a child of God. It is my belief that Millie is in heaven today."

Matt, Tyrone, Prew, Charley the bartender, Amos, the piano player, and a cowboy from the Lazy J, identified by the other girls who worked at the Sand Spur as Millie's "favorite," acted as pall bearers. At the conclusion of the service, they carried Millie's coffin out of the church and loaded it into the back of the hearse. Then, Gene Welch, who was wearing a top hat, tails, and striped pants, snapped the reins against the team of

Percherons, and the horses moved forward in a stately manner.

St. Paul's Episcopal Church was at the north end of town, near the Union Pacific railroad track, and the cemetery was a quarter of a mile south of the town. That meant the funeral cortege had to traverse the entire distance right through the middle of town. The hearse led the way. Next came a green, three-seated touring wagon in which rode all the pall bearers except for Matt, who was in the surrey with Kitty, following. Behind Kitty's surrey was a spring wagon carrying the three remaining girls who worked at the Sand Spur. The three soiled doves were weeping; their tears and Kitty's were the only tears being shed in the entire funeral party.

There was no particular order after that, and surreys, traps, buckboards, and spring wagons fell in line. There were also riders on horseback, as well as many pedestrians.

The funeral procession moved solemnly through the town, with more people in the parade than there were standing on either side of the road watching. Many of those watching paid a moment of respect as the cortege passed them by, some by doffing their hats, some by bowing their heads, and some by crossing themselves.

When the cortege reached the cemetery, the coffin was taken from the hearse and everyone crowded around it. At the open grave, Father Pyron read from the *Book of Common Prayer.*

"Most merciful Father, who has been pleased to take unto thyself the soul of thy servant Millicent McMurtry; Grant to us who are still in our pilgrimage, and who walk as yet by faith, that having served thee with constancy on earth, we may be joined hereafter with thy blessed saints in glory everlasting; through Jesus Christ our Lord. Amen."

At a nod from Father Pyron, the six pall bearers, with ropes looped around Millie's coffin, lowered it gently into the open grave. Then, withdrawing the rope, Pyron invited Kitty and the other girls who worked at the Sand Spur to drop a handful of dirt onto the coffin.

As the dirt fell upon the coffin, Pyron gave the final prayer.

"For as much as it hath pleased Almighty God, in his wise providence to take out of this world the soul of our deceased sister, we therefore commit her body to the ground; earth to earth, ashes to ashes, dust to dust; looking for the general Resurrection in the last day, and the life of the world to come, through our Lord Jesus Christ; at whose second coming in glorious majesty to judge the world, the earth and the sea shall give up their dead and the corruptible bodies of those who sleep in him shall be changed, and made like unto his own glorious body; according to the mighty working whereby he is able to subdue all things unto himself."

# CHAPTER NINETEEN

From the *Medbury Advocate:*

### *Funeral for a Fallen Woman.*
### ENTIRE TOWN TURNS OUT.

Not since the funeral of Sir Thomas Wellington, have so many townspeople witnessed the interment of one of its citizens. Millicent McMurty was a woman of the line, a soiled dove who plied her avocation in the Sand Spur Saloon. It was, in fact, while practicing the oldest profession, that the young woman was shot down.

On the day in question, Matt Jensen, a man known by few locals, but with a reputation that is respected by many, entered the Sand Spur lacking fifteen minutes of the stroke of noon. As Mr. Jensen entered the saloon, he was carrying over his shoulder the corpse of

Harold Cotter, known by many as a barfly and ne'r do well who went by the sobriquet of "Cooter."

Jensen deposited Cotter's body on the table in front of Poke Terrell, a man just recently arrived in Medbury, but one who had already established his presence by virtue of his frightening demeanor and disposition, as well as the knowledge that he once rode with the Idaho Auxiliary Peace Officers' Posse. Jensen accused Terrell of having sent Cotter to kill him. Terrell denied the accusation, and a fight ensued.

It is said by those who bore witness to the events described herein, that it was a fight to behold. Two powerful men engaged in a desperate struggle for supremacy. Jensen, according to all eyewitness accounts, got the better of Terrell, then he retired to the bar to have a drink. Miss McMurtry, as per her profession, stepped up to Mr. Jensen in order to provide a calming effect. It was then that Terrell raised up from the floor and shot at Jensen. Unfortunately, he missed and hit Miss McMurtry, killing her almost instantly.

At the same time Terrell was shooting at Jensen, Jensen, with a dexterity and quickness that is rarely seen, pulled his own revolver and discharged it, his ball striking Terrell with devastating effect. All who bore witness testified in the hearing that followed, that Matt Jensen was completely blameless in the incident. The fault lay with Poke Terrell who, had he not been dispatched at the scene, would no doubt have been tried, convicted, and hung for the murder of Miss McMurtry.

Miss McMurty had no relatives in Medbury, nor in Idaho, nor in any of the surrounding territories. She was an indigent, and like the three other indigents who were buried within the last two weeks, would have been buried in Potter's Corner as well, had events run their normal course. But she was not buried in Potter's Field, she was buried in the main garden of the cemetery. There are those who have questioned why the town of Medbury would go to such expense for a harlot.

The answer is, she was not buried at the expense of the town. Mrs. Kitty Wellington, widow of Sir Thomas Wellington, paid all the expenses incurred by the funeral, from the finest coffin, to the use of the special hearse, to the purchase of a burial plot in the main part of the cemetery.

One may ask why Mrs. Wellington went to such personal expense. This newspaper thought to make an inquiry as to her reasons, but decided not to. Harlot or no, Millicent McMurtry was, as the reverend Father Walt Pyron said during the funeral rites, a child of God. And that, this newspaper believes, is reason enough.

## Boise

There was no railroad service directly to Boise, so Marcus Kincaid left the train at Thurman City and took a stagecoach for the ten-mile ride up to the territorial capitol. For all that it was the capitol, it was not a very large town, and it was but a short walk from the stage depot to the headquarters building of the Idaho Auxiliary Peace Officers' Posse. It wasn't hard to find the building; there was a sign suspended from the overhanging porch in front of the building; and another sign painted on the window itself, identifying this as the headquarters of the Idaho Auxiliary Peace Officers' Posse.

There were two men standing in front of the building. One was tall and broad shouldered, with a neatly cropped moustache.

He was wearing denim trousers, a light gray shirt, and a star-shaped badge on his left pocket. The other man was wearing a three-piece suit. The man in the suit was obviously just leaving, so Kincaid stopped short of going up to them and waited. After a few more minutes of conversation, the two men laughed, shook hands, then the man in the suit left, heading toward the capitol building.

The tall man with the moustache and star looked over at Kincaid.

"Have you come to see me?" he asked.

"Are you Clay Sherman?"

"I am Colonel Sherman, yes."

"Then, yes, I have come to see you."

"Who are you?"

"My name is Marcus Kincaid, Colonel Sherman. I'm from —"

"Ah, yes, I know who you are, and I know where you are from," Sherman said. Sherman pointed toward the man who had just left. "Do you know who that is?"

"No, I'm afraid not."

"That is Nathaniel Patterson, the assistant deputy attorney general for the territory of Idaho," Sherman said. "I am in good standing with the territorial government. And why shouldn't I be? My posse provides services that the territory is simply unable to provide."

"But you provide those services for private individuals too, do you not?"

"I do."

"I require just such a service."

"Come in, Mr. Kincaid. We'll talk," Sherman said.

The office could have been any sheriff's office, though without a jail cell. There were wanted posters on the walls, a rifle rack, and a heroically posed photograph of Clay Sherman, with a brass plaque beneath the photo that read COLONEL CLAY SHERMAN, COMMANDING OFFICER.

Sherman opened a silver humidor on his desk, took out two cigars, and gave one to Kincaid. Kincaid accepted, and, after biting off the end, waited for Sherman to provide the match. Sherman lit Kincaid's cigar first, then his own, and took several puffs before speaking.

"Have a seat," Sherman offered, pointing to a chair that was drawn up in front of his desk. Sherman sat behind the desk as Kincaid sat down across from him.

"What happened to Poke Terrell?"

"He was killed by Matt Jensen."

"But Matt Jensen isn't in jail, is he?"

"No. There were too many witnesses to the event. They all say that Terrell drew and fired first. In fact, Terrell killed one of the whores while he was trying to kill Jensen."

Sherman moved some papers around on his desk, then picked up a newspaper and showed it to Kincaid. "Then what you are saying is that the article in this newspaper is correct?"

"Yes."

"Poke was not only my second in command, he was my friend," Sherman said.

"I thought you fired him."

"That's what we wanted you and everyone else to think," Sherman said. "We felt that was the best way he could help you."

"Then you were aware of his activity on my behalf?"

"Yes, of course I was. In fact, he was keeping me informed by frequent telegrams."

"I'm sorry your friend was killed."

"It says in the paper that Poke is buried in Potter's Corner? Is that true?"

"Yes."

"You are a wealthy and influential man in Owyhee County, are you not, Mr. Kincaid?"

"You might say that."

"You are a wealthy and influential man, and Poke Terrell was working for you, yet you couldn't give him a proper burial?"

"How could I?" Kincaid asked. "Nobody knew that Poke Terrell was working for me."

"I see," Sherman said. "Now tell me, Mr. Kincaid, why have you come to see me?"

"Because the problem I had, the one that Terrell was working on, still exists. And evidently it is a much bigger problem than I anticipated. It's a much bigger problem than Poke Terrell anticipated."

"You are talking about Matt Jensen," Sherman said. It was a statement, not a question.

"Yes."

"I can understand how he would be a problem. From what I know of Matt Jensen, he can be quite formidable."

"Do you know him?"

Sherman took several puffs of his cigar, wreathing his head in the smoke, then he pulled it out and examined the glowing tip, before he answered.

"I've never met the man, so I don't know him personally," Sherman said. "But a man in my position must make it a policy to know as much as one can about people like Matt Jensen."

"You say he is formidable. How formidable?"

"Quite formidable."

"But, not too much for you to handle," Kincaid said. "I mean, you have a reputation of dealing with people like Jensen, right?"

"I will concede that I have run across people like Jensen a few times, yes," Sherman said.

Kincaid smiled. "And it is my understanding that, when you do encounter such people, you generally leave them dead."

"I've left my share of them dead," Sherman said.

"Good. Because I want you to kill Jensen."

Sherman glared at Kincaid through the tobacco smoke.

"Mr. Kincaid, I am commanding officer of the Idaho Auxiliary Peace Officers' Posse, duly deputized and authorized by the territory of Idaho to enforce the peace and uphold the law. Now, I admit that the law is often as I interpret it to be, and I also admit that in the performance of this duty, people are sometimes killed," Sherman said, "but I want it well understood that I don't kill on command, and I am not a professional executioner."

"I'm sorry," Kincaid said. "I guess I just didn't realize you were so particular about killing."

"I'm not particular about killing. In my business, it is sometimes necessary to kill. But I will choose the time, the place, and most importantly, I will choose who I am to kill. If you want someone killed, hire an assassin."

"I thought I had hired one when I hired Poke Terrell."

"Really? It was my understanding that what you really wanted was for Poke to help you take possession of Coventry Ranch. Am I wrong?"

"No, you are right. That is what I wanted. It is what I still want."

"Do you have a plan in mind?"

"Not a plan, exactly. But I do have the means of bringing it about. I hold the mortgage on the ranch," Kincaid said. "Kitty Wellington doesn't know this. She thinks the bank still has the mortgage. She believes that, even if she defaults on the loan, she will still have the opportunity to save the ranch by negotiating an extension. But her loan is due on July fourth, and if she defaults on repayment, even by so much as one day, the ranch comes to me. There will be no auction. I will simply take possession of it."

"Then the objective is to make her default on the loan."

"Yes."

"What does Matt Jensen have to do with that?"

"Kitty has a contract to supply horses to the U.S. Army. This contract will give her enough money to pay off the loan, but in order to fulfill the contract, she must deliver the horses to the army depot in Chicago. She has hired Matt Jensen to see to it that she gets her horses through to Chicago in time to pay off the loan."

"So as I understand it, Mr. Kincaid, you want us to see to it that her horses don't get to Chicago in time to pay off the loan," Sherman said.

"Yes," Sherman replied. "That's it exactly."

"I see," Sherman said. "But tell me this. What is the legal basis for using the posse?"

"I beg your pardon?"

"There are those who consider the posse a 'court of last resort' if you will. But if we are a court of last resort, that means you must have a case that could be argued in court. Now, if you were to take your case to court, what would be your argument."

"I took my case to court and I lost," Kincaid said.

"What was your argument?"

"My argument was that I had a greater right to inherit the land than did a widow of but a year."

"No, that won't do. What other legal basis

do you have for using the court of last resort?"

"I don't know," Kincaid admitted. "I mean, I am willing to pay you, whatever you ask. But I don't know any legal basis for using you."

"You do know, don't you, that I don't do anything unless I have some legal coverage?"

"Uh, no, I didn't know that. Poke was working for me, I didn't think it mattered whether it was legal or not."

Sherman chuckled. "You are right. You didn't think," he said. "But it did matter for Poke, and it matters for me. I don't commit the posse to anything, unless there is a legal basis for the commitment."

"I see," Kincaid said, crestfallen. "I thought maybe if I paid enough that maybe —"

Inexplicably, Sherman laughed. "Don't worry about it, Kincaid," he said. "Fortunately for you, I have found what we need. I have found a law that will cover any participation by the Auxiliary Peace Officers' Posse."

"What? Do you mean to say there *is* a law that will help me get control of Coventry?"

"Well, the law is not specifically drawn to give you control of Conventry," Sherman said. "But it is drawn in such a way as to prevent Mrs. Wellington from selling her horses to the army, or to anyone else. And that would accomplish the same thing, would it not?"

"Yes, of course it would," Kincaid said excitedly. "But I must confess that I am curious. What law would that be?"

"Have you ever heard of herd management law?"

"No, I can't say that I have."

"Let me read this to you," Sherman said, pulling a book down from a shelf behind him and opening it. It was obvious that he had given this particular law a lot of thought, because he was able to open it to a pre-marked page.

"This is from the Idaho Territorial Livestock Law, paragraph twenty-five, subparagraph three, stroke two. It is called the Herd Management Law."

Sherman cleared his throat, then began to read.

"The Livestock Commission of the territory of Idaho shall have power to create, modify, or eliminate herd management districts within such counties as hereinafter provided; and when such district is so created, modified, or eliminated, the provisions of this chapter shall apply and be enforceable therein. In a district that is set aside for cattle, no one shall run horses, mules, asses, sheep, or goats in excess of what is needed for the immediate operation of the ranch without specific authorization from the Livestock Commission. Such regulation or control is provided by the creation of a herd management district pursuant to the provisions of this chapter. The provisions of this chapter shall apply with immediate effect, subject to any modification as may hereinafter be enacted."

Sherman closed the book and smiled at Kincaid. "There is your legal basis," he said.

Kincaid shook his head in confusion. "I don't have the slightest idea what you just said to me."

"Is Kitty Wellington raising horses?" Sherman asked.

"Yes."

"Would you say she is raising more horses than are required to run her ranch?"

"Yes, absolutely."

"I have checked all the filings in the herd district that apply to Coventry on the Snake, and there has been no authorization specifically granted for her to run horses." Sherman thumped on the book he had just read. "Therefore, according to this, she is in violation of the law."

"She is? Then I don't know why the territorial government hasn't stopped her. Everyone knows she is raising horses, there was even an article about it in *The Boise Statesman*."

"The territorial government hasn't done anything about it, because they probably don't even realize she is in violation. This law was written primarily to prevent trouble by keeping the sheep herders and cattle ranchers separated."

"Then we should tell the government about her," Kincaid suggested.

Sherman shook his head. "No, that is the last thing you want to do," he said.

"No?"

"Not if you really want to stop her," Sherman explained.

"I don't understand."

"Look. If the agriculture commission realized that this law, which as I said was primarily designed to keep cattle and sheep apart, was stopping a productive horse ranching operation, they would simply grant her an exception to the law, and the posse would have no legal basis for involvement. But" — he said, holding up his finger to emphasize a point — "as it stands now, minus that exception, she is in violation of the law, and that is all the cover we need."

With that explanation, Kincaid understood, and he nodded his head. "Yes," he
said. "Yes, I see what you mean."

"Now, Mr. Kincaid," Sherman said. "As a
cattle rancher, if you wish to file a complaint
because someone in your country is violating the herd management law, that will give
the Idaho Auxiliary Peace Officers' Posse a
legal basis for getting involved. Do you wish
to hire the posse to enforce that law?"

"Yes, I do," Kincaid said.

"Good, good," Sherman said. "May I suggest that we go next door to the Palace Café
and have our lunch? Afterward, we will
come back to my office, reach some agree-
able settlement as to terms, then sign a
contract that authorizes us to come to your
aid in seeking a just prosecution of the law."

# CHAPTER TWENTY

For the ranchers and farmers who lived within a ten-mile radius of Medbury, Saturday was a big day. It was the day they came into town to get their business and shopping done, and just to visit with friends and neighbors. By mid-morning the town was crowded with people, horses, and conveyances. There was a parking yard near the livery, and it was filled with buckboards and wagons of all sizes and descriptions. The men tended to congregate in the feed and seed store or the leather goods store, while the women did their shopping at the mercantile and general stores. Children, excited over the prospect of getting their weekly prize of a piece of stick candy, ran up and down the boardwalks, laughing and playing.

It was into this atmosphere of happy commerce that Colonel Clay Sherman led his posse of Idaho Auxiliary Peace Officers. They rode in, in military precision, a column of twos, eight rows deep, with Clay Sherman in the lead.

Their arrival captured the attention of nearly everyone, and people interrupted their weekly commerce in order to wonder at this strange parade through the center of their town.

"That's Clay Sherman," someone said, speaking quietly lest Sherman actually hear him.

"I know who it is," another answered. "The question I got is, what in Sam Hill is he doin' here?"

"I don't know, but I don't like it. From all I've heard of him and his men, it means trouble of some sort."

It was a magnificent looking body of men. All were wearing dark blue denim trousers and light gray shirts. All had shining brass stars pinned to their shirts. Sherman was dressed exactly as the other men, except that, on his collar, in metallic thread, was embroidered an eagle, the symbol of his rank as colonel.

One young boy was so excited by the sight that he dashed out into the street and ran alongside, shouting "Bang, bang, bang!" So disciplined were the riders that not one of the men looked at the boy, nor did they glance around when his mother ran out into the street after him.

"Joey! Joey! Come back here!"

Several of the men of the town, who standing alongside watching, laughed when the mother caught up with the boy and, grabbing him by the ear, pulled him back out of the street.

"That'll teach you, Joey!" one man yelled.

"You better listen to your mama, boy!" another added.

When Clay Sherman and his riders reached the sheriff's office, Sherman held up his hand and the men stopped.

"Dismount and stand by your horses," Sherman ordered and, as one, the sixteen men swung down from the saddle. They stepped up to the front of their horse and held it by the halter. As Sherman went inside the sheriff's office, several of the townspeople moved closer to the body of men.

"Hey!" someone called out to them. "What are you fellas doing here?"

Not one man answered.

"Are you chasin' somebody?"

Like the first question, this one went un-acknowledged.

"How come there won't none of you answer?"

"They are like the army, George," on of

the other townspeople explained. "They are standin' in formation, and that means they can't talk or look around."

"That don't make no sense," George said.

"That's because you have never been in the army. I have, and I know what it's like when you are standin' in formation."

"I just want to know what they are doin' here," George said. "I mean, ever' one knows what these fellas are like. Whenever they get on somebody's trail, there is most always shootin'."

Like the others in town, Marshal Sparks had seen the posse arrive and he was now standing just inside his office, drinking coffee and looking through his front window as the riders halted in front of the building. He knew about the Idaho Auxiliary Peace Officers' Posse, and he knew about its leader. He watched Clay Sherman dismount, order his men to stand by their horses, then come in. One of the other men came in with him.

Sherman pushed the door open and looked around. Because Marshal Sparks was standing over to one side by the window, and because the door opened toward him, temporarily blocking him from view, Sherman didn't see him when he first came in.

"Anyone in here?" Sherman called loudly.

"I'm over here," Marshal Sparks said from the front window. In contrast to Sherman's shout, Marshal Sparks response was so quiet as to be conversational.

"Marshal, I'm —"

"Clay Sherman," Sparks interrupted. "I know who you are, Mr. Sherman."

"If you know who I am, then you know that I am more properly addressed as Colonel Sherman."

"What can I do for you, *Colonel* Sherman?" Sparks asked, emphasizing the word colonel to show a little irritation at being told how to address his arrogant visitor.

"Yes, well, it isn't what you can do for me, Marshal. It is what I, and my men, are going to do for you."

"You are going to do something for me? I don't recall asking for any outside support in running my town."

"We don't always have to be asked. Often when there is a clear and unaddressed violation of the law, we will respond for the good of the whole," Sherman replied.

"So, what brings you here?"

"Marshal Sparks, it has come to the attention of Governor Neil that you have been — let us say, lax — in your enforcement of a very important territorial law. We have been sent here to Owyhee County to enforce that law."

"I don't know of any law I'm not enforcing. What law would that be?" Marshal Sparks asked, surprised by the announcement.

"What law it is, is no longer of your concern," Sherman said. "As you have not worried about it before, there is no need for you to worry about it now. Like I said, we will take care of it for you. But you need not worry too much about it. The fact that we will be enforcing this law will not reflect adversely on you. Also, we will not interfere with your normal performance of duty. You just go on about your normal business and pay no mind to us."

"I should at least know what law you are talking about."

"How many rooms does the hotel have?"

"I beg your pardon?" Sparks asked, unable to follow the abrupt change of subject.

"The hotel, Marshal. How many rooms does it have? I must find quarters for my men. I shall require nine rooms, eight for my men, they can double up, and one for myself."

"Oh, that won't be possible. The hotel only has ten rooms and at least four of them are permanently occupied."

"Thank you," Sherman replied.

"Marshal, I got a question I want to ask you," the man who had come in with Sherman said. He had been silent until this moment.

"What is the question?" Marshal Sparks replied.

"How come it is, that you didn't do anything about the man who murdered Poke Terrell?"

"Who are you?" Marshal Sparks asked.

"Marshal, this Lieutenant Luke Scraggs. He is my second in command," Sherman said.

"Why didn't anyone do anything about the man who murdered Poke Terrell?" Scraggs asked a second time.

"Mr. Scraggs," Marshal Sparks started.

"It's Lieutenant Scraggs," Scraggs replied.

"We did do something about it, Scraggs," Marshal Sparks said, purposely omitting the use of the word lieutenant. "The judge conducted a hearing and determined that the shooting that took Terrell's life was justifiable. Matt Jensen was cleared of any wrongdoing. Everyone who was in the saloon at the time testified that Poke Terrell drew first. In fact, Terrell killed a young woman, and if he had not been killed himself, I have no doubt but that he would have been indicted by the hearing, tried, found guilty, and hung. Does that answer your question?"

"I heard it was a whore he kilt," Scraggs said.

"Like I said, he killed a young woman."

"If you see this man, Matt Jensen, you might tell him that he is going to have to answer to me for killing my friend," Scraggs said.

"You aren't making a threat, are you, Scraggs?" Marshal Sparks asked.

"You must excuse Lieutenant Scraggs, Marshal," Sherman said. "He and Poke Terrell were particularly good friends."

"Yeah," Marshal Sparks said. "I can see how he must be just all broken up inside, what with Terrell being such a nice fellow and all."

"Marshal, I get the impression that you don't much approve of us," Sherman said.

"That's pretty observant of you, *Colonel* Sherman." Again, Marshal Sparks emphasized the word colonel.

"I must say, that's rather disappointing. Don't you have respect for your fellow lawmen?"

"For fellow lawmen? Yes, I respect other lawmen. But I don't consider you and your group to be lawmen," Marshal Sparks said. "You are in this for yourselves."

"You don't understand, Marshal. Unlike you, we do not have our salary paid by the federal, territorial, or local government. That means that every case we undertake must pay for itself," Sherman said. "You call that self-serving, I call it practical. At any rate we are both doing the same thing, and that is enforcing the law. So, if we can't respect each other while we are here, we can at least stay out of each other's way."

"As long as you don't break any law while enforcing the law, you'll have no problem with me," Marshal Sparks said. "But break any of my laws, and I'll be down on you like a duck on a June bug."

"Break any of *your* laws, Marshal? Interesting. I would have thought they would be town or county laws."

"Town and county laws *are* my laws," Marshal Sparks said.

"I see." Sherman stared at Marshal Sparks for a few seconds, then he turned to Scraggs. "Come, Lieutenant," he said. "We need to get quarters for our men."

Sherman and Scraggs left the sheriff's office, and once again the town was treated to the sight of a well-disciplined body of men riding as one as they moved down the street from the sheriff's office to the Del Rey Hotel.

"Dismount. Horse holders, post," he said. "The rest, with me."

Sherman and every one of his men except for four who remained outside to hold the horses tramped into the hotel lobby.

"Yes, sir what can I — oh my," the hotel clerk said, looking up and seeing so many armed men, all of whom were dressed just alike. "What is going on?"

"Innkeeper, I am Colonel Clay Sherman, and we are the Idaho Auxiliary Peace Officers' Posse. We are here on official business, and I shall need nine rooms."

"Nine rooms?" The clerk shook his head. "Oh, I'm sorry, but I'm afraid that is impossible. I don't have nine rooms available."

"How many rooms do you have?"

"I only have six rooms available, but the Union Pacific asks me to keep at least two open until the late train arrives. That's for any passenger who might need one."

"You are telling me how many rooms you have available. But the question I am asking you is this. How many rooms does this hotel have?"

"Well of course the hotel has ten rooms, but four are . . ."

"You have ten rooms? That's perfect. Like I told you, I only need nine."

"And I am trying to tell you that four are

permanently occupied," the clerk said, speaking slowly as if explaining something to someone who clearly didn't understand what he was trying to say.

"Move them out."

"I beg your pardon?" the clerk replied, blinking his eyes in surprise, not sure he had heard what he clearly heard.

"I said move them out."

"Move them out? Sir, I can't do that."

"My men and I are here to enforce a territorial law," Sherman said. "I am exercising eminent domain. Move them out."

"Eminent domain? I don't understand. I don't know what that means."

"That means you have to give me the nine rooms I asked for, even if you have to move someone else out. Otherwise, you are in violation of the law, and I would be within my rights to enforce that law." He pulled his pistol. "By any means necessary," he added, ominously.

"Take the rooms, take the rooms! You can have them!" the clerk said, his voice on the edge of panic.

"A very wise decision," Sherman said. He put his pistol back into his holster. "Lieutenant Scraggs, go upstairs. Take Grimes with you," Sherman ordered. "If you find anyone in any of the rooms, turn them out."

"Yes, sir, Colonel," Scraggs answered. "Come along, Grimes."

Scraggs and Grimes went upstairs to carry out Sherman's orders.

Up on the second floor, there was a long hallway that ran from front to back. Ten doors opened onto the hall way, five doors from either side. Scraggs started down one side, and Grimes the other. The first four doors they opened were empty. Then Scraggs tried a door that was locked. He banged on it loudly.

"Who is it?" a muffled voice answered. The voice was obviously that of a woman, thin with age, and hesitant with fear.

"Open the door." Scraggs called out in a gruff voice.

"Go away," the woman's thin voice replied.

Scraggs stepped back from the door, raised his foot, and kicked hard just beside the doorknob. The door popped open and the woman inside screamed.

Scraggs stepped into the door way, filling it with his presence. The occupant of the room, a woman who appeared to be in her seventies, cowered on the other side of the bed.

"Get out," Scraggs ordered.

"What?" the woman asked.

"I said get out," Scraggs said. "We need this room."

"I won't get out. This is my room," the woman insisted.

Scraggs stepped quickly into the room, crossed to the other side of the bed, grabbed her roughly by the arm, then pulled her out into the hallway. "Get out," he said shoving her so hard that she hit the wall on the opposite side of the hallway and fell to the floor. She cried out in pain.

"Get up," Scraggs ordered, again grabbing her by the arm and lifting her from the floor. "Downstairs with you, you old hag. Get out of here."

By now Grimes had also dragged a woman out of the room. The two women moved quickly away from the men and, clutching each other in fear, watched as a third woman and an elderly man were pulled from their rooms. Like the first two women, they stood in the hall, terrified and confused.

"Who the hell are you? What are you doing?" the man shouted angrily. When Grimes reached for him, he pushed his hand away. "Get your hands off me, you son of a bitch!"

Scraggs laughed. "He's a scrappy old shit, ain't he?"

"Down the stairs," Grimes ordered. "Go downstairs now before I kick you downstairs."

More than anxious to get away from the frightening men, the four occupants of the hotel hurried down the stairs to the hotel lobby. They halted when they reached the bottom step and saw that there were several other men in the lobby, all of whom were dressed exactly as the men who had rousted them were dressed.

"Elmer," the first old lady said to the hotel clerk. "Elmer, who are these terrible men? Why did they come into our rooms and tell us we had to leave!" she complained.

"I'm sorry, Mrs. Rittenhouse, I had nothing to do with it," the clerk replied.

"Who are these men?" Mrs. Rittenhouse asked, looking at all the men in the lobby.

"I apologize, ma'am," Sherman said, dipping his head slightly. "I am Colonel Sherman of the Auxiliary Peace Officers' Posse. We are here on a matter of the law and I require quarters for my men. By the law of the United States Government, as well as the law of the territory of Idaho, I have the right of eminent domain. I have exercised that right to take your room, and all the other rooms in the hotel. I'm sorry if this has inconvenienced you, but it is a matter of necessity."

"But, where will I go? What will I do?" the woman asked. "I have no place to go!"

"I'm sorry, ma'am, but that isn't my problem," Sherman said.

"All the rooms are clear, Colonel," Scraggs said.

"Thank you, Lieutenant," Sherman said. "Burnett?"

"Yes sir, Colonel?"

"See to my horse. The rest of you men, get your horses boarded, then come back and find your rooms. We'll meet here in the lobby in thirty minutes."

All those who had come into the hotel with Sherman now hurried outside in response to Sherman's orders.

"Elmer, I'm holding you responsible for this," the old man said.

"I'll find a place for you, Mr. Pemberton." Elmer promised. "Don't worry. I'll find a place for all of you."

# CHAPTER
# TWENTY-ONE

The arrival of Clay Sherman and his Idaho
Auxiliary Peace Officers' Posse was the
subject of conversation all over town for
the rest of the day. It was discussed in
stores and shops, talked about at the barber-
shop and in the meat market, at the train
station and the stage depot, and by house-
wives over the back fence.

"They say they put poor old Mr. Pemberton out of his room at the hotel. Where will
he go?"

"I heard he has a room upstairs at the
Sand Spur. But the women are still lookin'
for a place."

"Father Pyron is putting up one of 'em."

"I've got a room where one of 'em can
stay."

"Me too."

"That will take care of all of 'em."

"Yeah, but it still don't say why Sherman
and that bunch of his has come to

Medbury."

"You want to know what I think? I think they come here to get even for Poke gettin' hisself kilt."

"Why would they do that?"

"Terrell used to ride for 'em."

"Yeah, but he war'nt ridin' with 'em when he was here. I heard he had been fired."

"Maybe, but he prob'ly still has a lot of friends among 'em. Wouldn't surprise me none at all if they war'nt here to settle scores with Matt Jensen."

"Yeah? Well from what I've heard of Matt Jensen, he can pretty much take care of his ownself."

"But they's seventeen of 'em, countin' Sherman. There can't no one man go up ag'in seventeen men. Not even Matt Jensen."

"I don't know, I wouldn't sell Matt Jensen short if I was you."

"I ain't sellin' him short. But I've heard a lot about Posse folks, and there ain't nothin' I've heard about 'em that's good."

That night Sherman and his men took their dinner in the Sand Spur. There were so many of them that they took up four tables and, by their very presence, dominated the saloon. Also, because so many were frightened of them, they had a tendency to run others away so that business was way down from normal. The Sand Spur was losing money.

The girls had approached the Auxiliary Peace Officers when they came into the saloon, smiling and flirting with them as they did with all customers who frequented the Sand Spur. The posse men wanted the girls' company, but they didn't want to pay for it, so there were no tips, so the girls, like the saloon, were losing money.

At eleven o'clock that night, the posse left the saloon, but by then it was too late for any of the regular customers to come.

"I tell you the truth, Jenny, I wish those fellas would take their business to the Mud Hole, and leave us alone," Charley said as he wiped down the bar. "I hardly made enough to keep the bar open."

"You certainly got that right," Jenny said. "I'll have a drink, Charley. Only this time, make it a real one."

Charley poured a drink of whiskey and slid the glass across to her, then poured one for himself. They held their glasses toward each other in an unstated salute.

"I wonder what they are doin' here?" Charley asked.

"I've heard some say they came here to

settle the score with Matt Jensen for Poke Terrell," Jenny replied as she tossed the drink down.

When Matt and Kitty rode into Medbury the next morning, they rode by an empty lot just south of town. On that lot were gathered several young boys, playing the game of baseball.

"Throw it to him, Jimmy, throw it to him! He ain't no hitter!" someone was chanting.

"Come on Carl, you can do it. All we need is a hit!"

Matt looked over toward the game just in time to see the batter swing and miss.

"Ha! I told you he ain't no hitter. What's a' matter, Carl? You got a hole in your bat? What was you swingin' at?"

"You can do it Carl, you can do it."

Matt watched the next pitch, then he saw Carl swing and connect. He heard the cracking sound of the bat hitting the ball, and saw the ball flying high over the outfielder's head, who turned and chased after it. With his efforts cheered by the other members of his team, Carl started running toward first base.

The circumstances of Matt's childhood had caused him to miss out on many childhood activities, including baseball. Sometimes he felt as if he had been cheated. Then he realized that he had been given personal tutoring by Smoke Jensen — and he wouldn't have traded that for all the baseball games in the world.

As it turned out, Matt had not made arrangements for the railroad cars when he came into town last week, so he and Kitty were here to finalize the arrangements and set the date that the twenty five cattle cars would arrive. But before they went to the depot, they stopped in front of a shop which had a sign boasting:

ANNA COOKE
*Seamstress*
Latest Fashions Sewn Here.

"You go on, I'm going to stop in here and talk to Anna for a few minutes," she said.

"I can wait out here for you," Matt offered.

Kitty chuckled. "You are sweet, Matt, but you don't want to wait on me. These are women's things, and if you knew anything about women, you would know that no matter what we might say, we never do anything in just a few minutes. I wouldn't dream of dragging you along with me while I take care of them, so you go have a beer, play some cards or something. I'll meet you at Railroad Café for lunch, then we'll go to the depot."

"All right," Matt agreed.

Kitty smiled at Matt as he rode on up the street, then she stepped inside the dress shop.

A small bell attached to the top of the door jangled as Kitty pushed it open and stepped inside.

"I'll be right with you," a voice called from the back of the shop.

"It's all right, Anna, I'm in no particular hurry," Kitty replied.

A moment later a middle-aged, rather buxom woman stepped through a door that led to a back room. She was holding a piece of material in her hand, and there were a couple of pins sticking out of her mouth. She removed the pins and smiled with she saw Kitty.

"Kitty," she said, happily. "It's so good to see you."

"Hi, Anna."

"What can I do for you?"

"I need a new dress for Chicago."

"Oh, my, Chicago," Anna said. "How exciting. What kind of dress are you looking for?"

"I'm not sure. I was hoping you might

suggest something."

"Let's start with the color," Anna said. "That will give me an idea."

"All right."

"Black or brown?"

"No, definitely not black or brown," Kitty said, shaking her head.

"Not black or brown. Good, that narrows it a bit. Let me make a few suggestions and see what you like. How about white and serene?

"White and serene? That sounds too — virginal," Kitty said.

Anna laughed out loud. "You are awful, Kitty."

"Aren't I?"

"All right, how about blue and regal?"

"Blue and regal might be all right if I were going to England to meet Tommy's family. But I'm going to Chicago."

"Then might I suggest red and daring?"

"Yes!" Kitty said. "Red and daring. I knew I could count on you."

"Hmm, now, I know why you are going to Chicago," Anna said.

"I'm going to sell horses."

"But you are going to meet someone there, aren't you?"

"No," Kitty said. "Nobody except the army agent who will be buying the horses."

"Kitty, you aren't telling me everything," Anna said. "If you aren't meeting someone there, then why would you want a dress that is red and daring?"

Kitty smiled. "You didn't ask me who I was going with," she said.

"Why, Kitty Wellington. You have a beau, don't you?"

"Yes," Kitty said. "The only thing is, he doesn't know it yet."

# Chapter
## Twenty-Two

This was the first time Matt had been inside the Sand Spur since the fight with Poke Terrell and he wasn't sure how he would be received. Any concerns he might have had were alleviated though when Charley, the bartender, smiled at him as he stepped up to the bar.

"Matt, it's good to see you again," Charley said.

"Hello, Charley," Matt greeted.

Without being asked, Charley drew Matt a beer. "I say it's good to see you again, but then, right now, it is good to see anyone besides these polecats," he said, indicating a table where four similarly dressed men were sitting. Matt also saw that all of them were wearing star badges pinned to their shirts.

"They look like lawmen," Matt said.

"Ha. If you ask me, outlaws is what they are. Oh, they wear their stars, and they call themselves lawmen, but believe me, they are nothing but outlaws. And they scare away my regular customers."

"How many are there?"

"I don't know exactly, I've never counted 'em. But I think someone said there are seventeen of 'em. At least, that's how many came into town. They call themselves the Idaho Auxiliary Peace Officers' Posse, and their leader is a fella by the name of Clay Sherman, only, he calls hisself *Colonel* Sherman. Have you ever heard of them?"

Matt took a swallow of his beer as he studied the men.

"Yeah, Marshal Sparks told me about them," Matt said. "I think he said that Poke Terrell used to ride with them."

"Yes, I heard that too," Charley said. "Oh, damn, you don't think they've come here after you to, uh . . . ," he started to ask, then he interrupted his comment in mid-sentence.

"You can finish the question," Matt said. "It won't bother me."

"No, I mean, well, they got here yesterday and that's near 'bout all the folks in town has been talkin' about. And ever'one is wonderin' why they come here. Some of 'em has been wonderin' if, maybe, they come here because of Poke Terrell. I mean him bein' one of their own and all."

"You are saying they may have come here to square things for Terrell?" Matt asked.

"Yeah, sort of like that, I reckon," Charley said. "Of course, there don't nobody who is in the posse that actually knows you, I don't reckon. At least, not on sight. I mean they looked up when you come in, but didn't none of 'em give any sign of recognizin' you. So I don't figure you're in any particular danger for now. And for sure, there ain't nobody in town goin' to be pointin' you out to them. But if I was you, I'd sort of stay out of sight until they're gone. Just to be on the safe side."

"Well now, that's going to be a problem, Charley," Matt said.

"What's goin' to be a problem?"

"I've never been one to be on the safe side," Matt said. He took another swallow of his beer. "As a matter of fact, I think it might be a good idea if I went over there and introduced myself to them."

"What? Matt, what in the hell are you talkin' about? Why would you want to do a dumb fool stunt like that?" Charley asked.

"It doesn't hurt to be friendly now, does it?"

Matt set his beer down on the bar, then walked over to the table.

"Good morning, gents," he said.

The four men who had been engaged in a private conversation glanced toward him for just an instant, but no one returned his greeting. They went back to their private conversation.

"Not very friendly, are you?" Matt said.

He still did not get an answer.

"I was going to try and do this in a friendly way, but for some reason you boys don't seem to be very friendly, so I'll just come out and say it. Move."

Finally one of them turned toward him. "What did you say, Mister?"

"I said move," Matt repeated. "You boys have my table. I don't like it when someone else takes my table."

There weren't many other customers in the saloon at the moment, but hearing Matt challenge the four posse members got their attention. All conversation stopped as everyone looked on with shocked surprise at the drama that was beginning to play out before them.

"Your table?" one of the four men replied.

"Yes. So I would appreciate it if you would move."

The four men looked surprised, then they all began to laugh.

"Your table," one of them repeated, and the laughter continued.

"Yes," Matt said again.

"All right, Mister, you've given us a good laugh. Now, if you know what is good for you, you will go away and not bother us anymore. There are plenty of other empty tables here."

"Yeah, I see that," Matt said, pointedly looking around the room. "But I don't want any of those tables. You see, this is my personal table, and this is the one I want."

"Now just what the hell makes you think this is your — *personal* — table?" the talkative one asked. He dragged out the word "personal."

"What's your name, Mister?" Matt asked.

"My name is Luke Scraggs. Lieutenant Luke Scraggs of the Idaho Auxiliary Peace Officers' Posse."

"Lieutenant Luke Scraggs of the Idaho Auxiliary Peace Officers' Posse," Matt repeated. "Well now, that's just really impressive. But I'll tell you why I think this is my table, Scraggs. You see, this used to be Poke Terrell's table. I'm pretty sure you've heard of Poke Terrell, haven't you? I hear he used to ride with you."

"Yeah, he did," Scraggs said. "As a matter of fact, he was a good friend of mine."

"Was he now? Well then, you should be particularly interested in why I consider this to be my table. You see, it used to be Terrell's table, but I killed him. Now, that makes this my table."

"You are the one who killed him?"

"That's right."

"You're Matt Jensen?" Scraggs asked, angrily.

"Oh, good, you already know who I am. That means I don't have introduce myself. Also, it's good to get this out in the open, don't you think? Because I don't like surprises."

"What do you mean by surprises?" Scraggs asked.

"What I mean is, if any of you have a bone to pick with me, I don't want you sneaking around to shoot me in the back."

"Mister, if we had a bone to pick with you, we wouldn't have to shoot you in the back. You may have noticed, there are four of us here and only one of you," Scraggs said.

"Gentlemen, Mr. Scraggs seems to be doing all the talking," Matt said. "Is he talking for all of you?"

"Yeah," one of the other men said. "Whatever Lieutenant Scraggs says, we all say."

"That's good to know," Matt said. "Because if any of you do start anything now, the lieutenant, here, will be the first one to die."

"Mister, we was just sittin' over here, mindin' our own business when you come over and started on us," the second speaker said. "So if somethin' was to happen, and we was to kill you now, there wouldn't be no jury anywhere that would say it is our fault."

"What difference would it make to you what a jury might say?" Matt asked.

"What do you mean, what difference would it make? I wouldn't want some jury to find me guilty for killing you."

"That's not anything you are going to have to worry about. All four of you will be dead, long before a jury trial."

"Mister, have you gone plumb loco?" Scraggs asked.

"Oh, I don't think so," Matt replied in an easy, unstressed voice. "Look at the way you are sitting. Scraggs, you are the only one who can get to your gun right now, so, like I said, I'll kill you first. But, unfortunately for you, you are sitting down. A man who is standing, can draw and shoot a lot faster than someone who is sitting down. What's your name?" he asked the man sitting next to Scraggs.

"Burnett," the man replied.

"Burnett, I'll kill you second. You are also sitting on the side of the table, so you could probably get your gun out almost as fast as Scraggs, but then you would have to bring your arm across to shoot at me, wouldn't you? So that's going to slow you down enough to give me time to kill you second. And you two, sitting behind the table?" Matt chuckled. "From the way you are sitting, it would take you two a week to draw and shoot. I can take as much time as I need to kill you two."

"Mister, I don't know who the hell you think —"

"Shut up, Burnett," Scraggs said.

"Are you going to let him. . . ."

"I said shut up," Scraggs repeated. "Let's get out of here."

Matt took a step back, but bent his knees slightly to be ready for anything that might happen.

Scraggs held his hand up.

"Take it easy, Jensen," Scraggs said. "We ain't doin' nothin' but leavin'."

"Yes, I think that is wise," Matt said. "From what I hear, you aren't very welcome in the saloon anyway. You frighten the other customers, and drive them away."

"I've about had it with you, Mister," Burnett said, pointing his finger, angrily at Matt.

"Burnett, I told you to shut up!" Scraggs said.

Burnett glared at Matt for a moment longer, then he went outside with the others.

As the men left the saloon, Matt walked back up to the bar and, with his left hand, retrieved his beer.

"Damn, I ain't never seen nothin' like that!" Charley said, his voice cracking with awe.

"Wait," Matt said quietly.

"Wait on what?"

"You'll see."

At that moment the batwing doors swung open and Scraggs stepped back into the saloon. He already had his pistol in his hand, but before he could bring it to bear on Matt, he found himself staring into the big .44-caliber hole at the business end of Matt's pistol.

"Hello, Scraggs," Matt said easily.

Scraggs stood there for a second, his face registering the shock of seeing Matt with his pistol already drawn and pointed toward him.

Scraggs lowered his gun. "I, uh, just thought I'd," Scraggs started, but he was unable to finish his sentence.

"Empty your gun, Scraggs," Matt ordered.

"Look, why don't I just . . . ?"

"Empty your gun," Matt said again. "Push

out all the shells and let them fall to the floor."

Scraggs made no move, and Matt cocked his pistol, the double click sounding dangerous.

"Empty your pistol," Matt said again.

Glaring angrily at Matt, Scraggs punched all the shells out of the cylinder. They sounded exceptionally loud as the hit the floor, one at a time.

"Now, walk over to the stove and toss your gun in."

"What good would that do you? I have another pistol," Scraggs said.

"Just do it," Matt said, making a small waving motion with the end of his pistol.

Scraggs continued to glare at Matt, but seeing Matt's unwavering insistence, he walked to the middle of saloon floor, opened the door, and dropped the pistol inside.

"That's a nice man," Matt said. "Now, find somewhere else to be. We're all tired of looking at you."

"Mister, you don't have an idea in hell what you have just done," Scraggs said.

"Yeah, I do," Matt said, and he kept his gaze fixed on Scraggs until the posse man left the saloon.

For a long moment after Scraggs left, it was deadly quiet in the saloon, as if no one would dare even breathe. Then Jenny walked over to the window and looked outside.

"They're gone," she said. "They are all goin' toward the hotel."

"Good riddance," Charley said.

Charley's comment seemed to open up the dam because now everyone started talking, describing in animated detail what they saw to everyone else who had seen the same thing.

"Gents," Charley called out. "This round is on the house."

With acclamations of appreciation, the other patrons rushed to the bar.

"What about Mr. Pemberton?" Jenny asked.

"Pemberton isn't down here now."

"No, but I'm sure the old gentleman would like a beer," Jenny said. "Especially since Mr. Jensen just ran off the men who threw him out of his home."

"Threw him out of his home?" Matt asked.

"He was livin' at the Del Rey Hotel," Charley explained, "but Sherman and his men took over the hotel. They threw Mr. Pemberton out, as well as the three old ladies, just so they could have the entire hotel for themselves. Pemberton didn't have anywhere else to go, so he's stayin' in the room that Millie was usin'."

"I think Millie would like that," Jenny said.

"Yeah, I do too," Charley said. He drew a mug of beer and handed it to Jenny. "Take it up to him, and tell him why."

Matt visited with the other saloon patrons while he killed time until noon.

"Say, young fella, you've got the name Jensen," one of the other patrons said. "Would you happen to know a man by the name of Smoke Jensen?"

Matt took a swallow of his beer and studied the questioner for a moment before he answered. Smoke Jensen was better known than Matt, and over the years, Smoke had made a lot of friends by doing the right thing, even when doing the right thing was hard, or unpopular.

But, like Matt, Smoke had also made a lot of enemies, probably even more enemies than Matt had made, primarily because Smoke was older and had been around a lot longer.

Matt lowered the beer and wiped some foam away from his lip. There was nothing in the tone of the questioner's voice, or the expression on his face, to indicate that he might be an enemy.

"Yeah, I know Smoke Jensen," he said. He didn't offer any more information.

The man smiled and nodded. "Uh, huh. I thought so. Well, let me tell you this, son. Smoke Jensen is as fine a man as ever drew a breath, and if you are anything like him, then I'm damn pleased to make your acquaintance."

The man offered his hand, and Matt took it. "Thanks," he said. "I share your opinion of Smoke." Looking over at the clock Matt saw that it was nearly noon. He finished his beer. "I have to be going," he said. "I've enjoyed my visit."

"That has to be either the most courageous, or the most foolish man I have ever met," Charley said after Matt left. "And I swear I don't know which it is."

# CHAPTER
## TWENTY-THREE

"That's him," Scraggs said to Clay Sherman, pointing to Matt as he left the saloon. "That's the son of a bitch that kilt Poke."

Scraggs and Clay were standing at the front window in the lobby of the Del Rey Hotel.

Sherman stepped up closer to the window to look at the man Scraggs had pointed out.

"So, that's the famous Matt Jensen, is it?" Sherman asked.

"Yeah. I don't mind tellin' you, Colonel. He worries me," Scraggs said.

"He's only one man," Sherman said.

"Yeah, well, he was only one man in the saloon too," Scraggs said.

Sherman made a tsking sound as he shook his head, slowly. "You know, Scraggs, if I were you, I don't think I would be all that anxious to tell how one man faced down four of you."

"I told you how it happened. There

335

weren't none of us in position to get to our guns. He had the drop on us."

"Oh? He had his gun in his hand when he braced the four of you?"

"Well, no, not exactly," Scraggs said. "But it was near 'bout the same thing, I mean what with him standin' there where he could get to his gun, and us sittin' where we couldn't. And then, when I stuck my head back in, well, he did have the gun in his hand. Almost like he know'd I was goin' to stick my head back in like I done."

"And here I thought I had rounded up the finest men in the territory to be members of the posse," Sherman said. "Maybe I need to raise the standards for recruiting."

"Here, now, Colonel, you got no call to say somethin' like that," Scraggs complained. "I told you how it happened. When it comes down to it, you know you can depend on me and ever'one else in the posse."

"I hope so, Scraggs," Sherman said. "We're sort of in a poker game here. And it's a high stakes poker game."

"He went into the café," Scraggs said.

"It's about noon, isn't it?" Sherman asked.

Scraggs looked over toward the front desk of the hotel and saw a clock hanging on the wall behind the desk.

"It lacks five minutes of twelve," Scraggs said.

"I think I'll drop in over at the Railroad Café and have some lunch," Sherman said.

"Want me to come with you?" Scraggs asked.

"No," Sherman said resolutely as he headed for the door.

When Matt stepped into the restaurant he saw that Kitty had already taken a table near the back.

"I'll be right with you, sir," a waiter said as he started toward a table carrying an order.

"I'll be joining Mrs. Wellington," Matt said, pointing toward Kitty.

"Very good, sir."

Matt sat at the table across from Kitty, and she greeted him with a smile.

"Did you have a pleasant morning?" she asked.

"Made some new friends," Matt said. He chuckled. "And probably a few enemies."

"Oh? What happened?"

Matt shook his head. "Nothing to speak of. I trust you got all your womanly things done?"

"I did. Do you like the color red?"

"What?" Matt asked, surprised by the

question that came out of the blue.

"I'm having Anna make a dress for my trip to Chicago," Kitty said. "A red dress. Do you like red?"

"Red? Yes, I like red."

"Are you sure? Because it isn't too late, you know. She could also do it in either white or blue."

Matt chuckled. "Katherine, you are a beautiful woman," he said. "And you would be beautiful no matter what color dress you wear."

"You're just being nice."

"No, I'm being truthful."

"Then, I'll stick with red," Kitty said. "Have you ever been to Chicago? I've never been there but . . ."

Kitty waxed on about Chicago but it faded into the background when Matt saw someone come into the café. He was a tall, rather impressive looking man with a closely cropped, graying moustache and brindled hair. He was wearing the same uniform as the men had been wearing in the Sand Spur, but this man was alone, and he carried himself with a degree of self-confidence, almost arrogance, that made Matt think it might be the head of the Auxiliary Peace Officers.

". . . sailing on Lake Michigan. Don't you

think so?" Kitty said.

"I'm sorry, what?" Matt asked.

"Matthew Jensen, you didn't hear a word I said, did you?" Kitty asked, petulantly.

"You're looking forward to going to Chicago," Matt said, taking a stab.

"Yes. I think it will be a wonderful trip."

"I'm looking forward to it as well," Matt said. He looked again toward the recent arrival, who was now being seated at his table.

"Matt, what has your attention?"

"That man over there," Matt said, pointing toward Sherman. "He may be trouble for us."

Kitty looked over as well.

"How can he be trouble? He's wearing a badge. He's a lawman."

Matt shook his head. "No," he said. "He's not any kind of lawman you've ever known before. He's with the Idaho Auxiliary Peace Officers' Posse. In fact, unless I miss my guess, he is Colonel Clay Sherman, the head of the posse."

"The Auxiliary Peace Officers' Posse? Yes, I have heard of them. Isn't that the group that they say Poke Terrell once belonged to?"

"Yes," Matt said.

"Well, they can't be all bad. I mean, from what I've heard, they kicked him out of the organization. And we both know what a despicable person Terrell was."

"Yes, I suppose that is true," Matt said.

"I wonder what he is doing here, in Medbury?" Kitty asked.

"I'm wondering the same thing."

Matt considered going over to Sherman's table and asking that very question, but he feared that doing so might bring about some sort of confrontation. He didn't want to start anything here in the restaurant, and he for sure didn't want to do it in front of Kitty. So he did nothing.

When he and Kitty finished their lunch several minutes later he glanced over toward Sherman, who, he saw, was looking directly at him. Sherman nodded, and Matt returned the nod.

The Railroad Café was appropriately named because it stood directly across from the depot, so it was a short walk across the street for them to take care of ordering the cars.

"Hello, Mr. Montgomery," Kitty said, greeting the dispatcher. "I'm going to need to order some cars for a shipment to Chicago."

"All the way to Chicago, huh? That's a long trip."

"I know. And a profitable one too, I hope."

"How many cars will you need?" Montgomery asked.

"I'm going to need twenty-five," Kitty said.

"Twenty-five cars?" the dispatcher responded in surprise. He gave a low whistle. "That's a lot of cars."

"I suppose it is."

"In fact, that's an entire train."

"Is that a problem?"

"No, it's not going to be a problem," Montgomery said. "But it's going to be pretty expensive. It's going to cost you a hundred dollars per car and five hundred dollars for the engine."

"Oh, I have to pay for the engine too?" Kitty asked. "I didn't know I had to pay for the engine. Isn't that a regular part of the train?"

"Yes ma'am, it is if you just put three or four cars on where there's other payin' freight as well. But when you got that many cars, you'll have to have a dedicated engine," the dispatcher said. "And when that happens, you have an entire train to yourself, which means you'll have to pay extra for the engine."

"Oh," Kitty said.

"Will that be a problem? I mean, if it is, maybe we can work something else out by, say, splitting up your shipment and putting no more than three cars on per train."

Kitty paused for a moment, then sighed before she answered. "No," she said. "That won't do. I'm afraid I am going to have to have the entire shipment go as one. So schedule the train for me. How soon can we have the engine and cars here?"

"How soon do you want them?"

"I'd like them as soon as possible," Kitty said.

The dispatcher moved some more papers around, checking inventory figures, then he nodded.

"We can have the cars and the engine here within three days," the dispatcher said. "Will that be soon enough for you?"

"Yes, that will be fine," Kitty said.

"All right. The train will probably get in sometime in the middle of the afternoon, on Wednesday. I can have it set on a side track, all ready for you on Thursday."

"How soon can we leave after it is loaded?"

"Very soon afterward, I would think, but I'll have to work out the track schedule," Montgomery said. He chuckled. "We wouldn't want your train runnin' into another one now, would we?"

Kitty smiled. "No, that wouldn't be good."

"I'll have the track schedule all worked out for you by Thursday. I expect you'll be able to leave pretty soon after you are loaded. The engineer will have his orders by then, and he'll know when to put aside to let the varnish have the high iron."

"The varnish?" Kitty asked.

"The passenger trains," the dispatcher replied. "They own the high iron. That means, they have the right of way on the through tracks. Freight trains are required to pull over and wait until they pass."

"I see."

"Well, you can understand, I'm sure," Montgomery said. "Say if you were on a passenger train going to Chicago, you wouldn't want to have to shift off the track to let every freight train pass now, would you?"

"No, I wouldn't think so. Oh, and I am going to Chicago," she added excitedly.

"When?"

"Why, Thursday, of course. I'm going on this train."

"Mrs. Wellington, there are no provisions for passengers on this train," Montgomery said.

"Well, can't you make provisions?"

"What you are asking for is a private car attached to the train."

"Can you order one of those?"

"Yes, but it's going to cost you as much as the engine."

"Another five hundred dollars?"

"I'm afraid so."

"So, now we are talking about thirty-five hundred dollars."

"Yes, ma'am, I'm afraid so," Montgomery said.

"I'm in the wrong business," Kitty said. "I should own a railroad instead of horses."

Montgomery laughed. "Railroads are the transportation of the future," he said.

"All right, order the private car," Kitty said.

"Yes, ma'am."

"Can we get it as quickly as we can the stock cars?"

"Yes, ma'am, no problem."

"Thank you very much, Mr. Montgomery. You've been very helpful," Kitty said.

"I am glad to be of service, Mrs. Wellington. I'll draw up the contract and routing orders," the dispatcher said.

While the dispatcher pulled out the necessary forms and began filling them out, Kitty walked over to look out over the depot platform. Matt, who had taken no part in the business negotiations, was already standing by the window. A passenger train was due shortly, and the platform was filled with people. Some were departing passengers, and a few were waiting to meet arriving passengers. But most of the people milling about on the platform were just citizens of the town to whom the arrival and departure of the trains was an exciting event. Matt had noticed also that, scattered through the crowd, were several men wearing the dark blue denim trousers, light gray shirt, and star of the Auxiliary Peace Officers' Posse.

He sensed Kitty coming up to stand beside him.

"Did you get all business taken care of?" Matt asked.

"Yes, I guess so," Kitty replied. There was a note of concern to the tone of her voice.

"What is it, Kitty?" Matt asked. "What's wrong?"

"Matt, this deal has got to go through," she said. "I've already borrowed as much money as I can borrow, and I am putting every penny I have left into it. If something goes wrong, I'll be ruined."

Matt chuckled. "Why, Katherine, considering your background, there are already people who would call you a ruined woman," he said. "So how bad could that be?"

For just a second Kitty was startled by Matt's response, then she saw the humor of it, and she laughed out loud.

"You're right," she said. "In for a penny, in for a pound."

"All you have to do is get your horses to Chicago, and you'll have enough money to pay off all your debts, with enough left over to carry forward. Am I right?"

"Yes," she said. "All I have to do is get my horses to Chicago."

"Then you don't have a problem," Matt said. "I promise you, Kitty, we will get your horses to Chicago."

Kitty took Matt's arm in her hands, then leaned into him. "Thank you, Matt. You don't know how important that reassurance is to me."

"I have an idea of something we might do when we get to Chicago," Matt said.

"What is that?"

"When we get to Chicago, how would you like it if we were to go sailing on Lake Michigan?"

"What?" Kitty laughed, then she hit Matt on the arm. "You *were* listening, weren't you?"

# CHAPTER
## TWENTY-FOUR

Back at Coventry on the Snake, even as Kitty and Matt were making arrangements for the stock cars, Tyrone Canfield had Prew and the other riders rounding up the saddle horses that were to be shipped out. Kitty had asked that they gather them into one holding field so it would be easy to move them when the time came.

"We'll put them in the north field. Castle Creek runs through that, so they will have plenty of water," Tyrone said.

"How long we goin' to keep 'em there?" Prew asked.

"As long as it takes. Which is until we move them down to the rail head," Tyrone answered.

"The reason I ask is, there's good grass in that field, but when you consider there's goin' to be five hunnert horses there."

"I think there will be enough grass to last them three or four days, anyway," Tyrone said. "And if we have to, we'll bring in some hay just to stretch it out."

"Yeah, I hadn't thought of that," Prew said. He chuckled. "I reckon that's why you're the foreman."

"You got that right, sonny, and don't you forget it," Tyrone said. "All right boys, let's go round up some horses."

Tyrone, Prew, Jake, Crack, and four other spent the morning rounding up the horses. The cavalry had purchased Arabian horses, selecting that particular breed because they were known for their courage, intelligence, disposition, and endurance. It fit the army requirements perfectly, that they could run at a gallop, or trot for miles without stopping. Also, because the army had promised a bonus if all the horses would be the same color, Kitty had given specific instructions to round up only chestnuts.

It took from early morning until mid-afternoon before all the selected horses were cut from the herd, then moved into the smaller field where they would be held until they were shipped.

"You fellas don't know it yet, but you're all joinin' the army," Prew said to the horses, laughing as they were moved into the field. "Yes, sir, no more wanderin' around free as the breeze. From now on you'll have to get up early in the mornin', work all day and listen to bugles and the such."

"Hey, the cavalry ain't a bad life for horses," Jake said. "Hell, I was in the cavalry. The horses has it better than the privates. I mucked out their stalls, fed them, rubbed them down. Didn't no horse ever do that for me."

The others laughed as the last of the horses were put into the field.

"Did you get a count, Crack?" Tyrone asked.

"Yeah," Crack answered. "I counted five hundred and twenty-three."

"That's good," Tyrone said. "All right, boys, let's get this fence up and stretched across the opening, here."

For the next hour, the men worked at constructing a fence that stretched some fifty yards across the south end of the field, thus closing off the field to keep the horses put.

When Kitty and Matt returned from their trip into town they rode out to the field where the horses had been gathered, arriving just as the last part of the fence was finished, completing the enclosure. Seeing his boss, Tyrone rode over to her.

"How do they look?" Tyrone asked.

"They are beautiful," Kitty said. "And it looks like they all match."

"I tell you the truth, Mrs. Wellington, they are near 'bout all as alike as peas in a pod," Tyrone said. "But you are right. They are a good looking bunch of horses. I bet you hate to sell them off."

Kitty laughed and held up her hand. "Well, let's not go that far with it," she said. "I don't have any choice. I have to sell them off."

"Yes, ma'am, I know," Tyrone said. "But don't it make you feel good to know that you got 'em right here, ready to go?"

"It makes me feel very good," Kitty replied. "You and the others did a really good job. And when you get back up to the house, I've got something that will show my appreciation."

"Now, Mrs. Wellington, you don't have to do nothin' to show your appreciation," Tyrone said. "You are real easy to work for, and the boys and me are glad to be here. And roundin' up these horses? Well, that was our job, that's all."

"Then let's just say we'll be celebrating the fact that the horses will be sold soon, and there will be enough money to keep you and all the others working here."

"Yes'm, well, keepin' a job, now, that is

somethin' worth celebratin'."

Even before the riders returned to the compound they could smell the rich, enticing aroma of cooking meat. Then, when they rode up the bunkhouse they saw, on the lawn between the bunkhouse and the big house, a huge haunch of beef on a spit, glistening a deep brown as the cook turned it slowly over an open fire.

"Yahoo!" Crack yelled, taking his hat off and beating it against his trouser leg. That action raised so much dust that some of the riders nearest him had to cough.

"Tell you what, boys," Tyrone said. "I think maybe before we set down to this meal, we ought to get cleaned up."

"Hell, I always wash up before I eat," Crack said. "That's somethin' my mama taught me a long time ago."

"I don't mean just wash your face and hands," Tyrone said. "I mean take a bath and put on clean clothes. This here is an occasion, and we need to act like gentlemen."

"Tyrone is right," Prew said. "We need to take us a real bath."

"Hell, I took me a bath no more than two weeks ago," one of the riders said.

"You're goin' to take another one today," Tyrone said. "That is, if you want to eat with the rest of us."

"All right, all right, I'll take me another'n. Hell, it wouldn't surprise me none if you didn't start sayin' we had to take a bath ever' other week, or so."

Tubs were hauled out, filled with water, and the men, in turn, began washing away the dirt. As Matt and Kitty sat together on the back porch of the big house, they couldn't see the ranch hands because the tubs were blocked by the bunkhouse, but they could hear the loud laughter and teasing as the men took their baths.

"Damn, Jake, look at that! You were so dirty you done turned that water into mud!" somebody shouted, and the taunt was met with more laughter.

The cook brought out a big pot of beans and several loaves of freshly baked bread to augment the meal. The aroma of the cooking meat continued to fill the entire compound.

"I hope they enjoy it," Kitty said.

"Are you kidding? Listen to them. They are having the time of their lives," Matt replied.

"They are one of the reasons I so want this to work," Kitty said. "I've never had a family, Matt. The closest I ever came was at the orphanage, and Captain Mumford was so cruel that any sense of family was eliminated just by the effort of surviving. These men are truly my family. It's not just for selfish reasons I want to save the ranch. I want to save this family."

"You are not going to lose this ranch, Katherine. I promise you," Matt said.

"Matt, after we go to Chicago, sell the horses, and get the money, you will come back with me, won't you?"

"Yes, of course," Matt said. "The way I see it, delivering the horses is only half of the job. The job won't be finished until the bank has been paid off, and the ranch is in your hands, free and clear."

"Then what?" Kitty asked.

"What do you mean?"

"What will you do after the bank is paid off, and the ranch is mine, free and clear?"

"All right, here we are," Prew shouted, coming around from behind the bunkhouse, bathed, and wearing clean clothes. His appearance and shout precluded Matt from answering Kitty's question.

"Yeah, when do we eat?" Crack asked.

By now, every rider had appeared, freshly scrubbed, all wearing clean, and in some cases, new clothes. Jake was particularly proud of his new yellow shirt, for which he was soliciting compliments.

"Hah, if you ask me, it looks like somethin' a whore house piano player would be wearin'," Prew said.

"All right, fellas, come and get it!" the cook called, and there was a rush of all the ranch hands to get plates, and get them filled. Kitty had even bought a barrel of beer, and within minutes, the evening meal had turned into a party.

"The only thing we need now is some women and music," Crack said. "Iffen we had that, why we could dance and have us a fine time."

"I'm a woman, and I can dance," Kitty said. "And Jake, I've heard you play the harmonica."

"No, that won't do," Prew said. "Mrs. Wellington, you're a fine lady. You wouldn't want to dance with the likes of us."

"Sure I would," Kitty said. "Tyrone, you're the foreman, it's only right that you get the first dance."

Tyrone looked shocked at first, then he smiled and nodded. "I'd be right proud to dance with you, Mrs. Wellington," he said.

There was something in the expression in Tyrone's face that caught Matt's attention. Then, he remembered that Tyrone had been foreman here long before Kitty ever arrived. Matt was certain that Tyrone knew about

Kitty's background, and he was equally certain that Kitty knew that he knew.

Jake pulled out his harmonica and began playing, and as he played, the other men stood around clapping and stomping their feet in time to the music.

Because the eating and the partying and the dancing went on until long after nightfall, Matt never did have to answer Kitty's question.

Sleep did not come easily to Kitty that night. She lay in bed, tossing and turning as she thought about the question she had asked Matt — the question that had gone unanswered. It wasn't as if he had specifically avoided answering the question, they were interrupted before he could do so. And yet Kitty could not escape the feeling that it was a question he didn't particularly want to answer.

She couldn't blame him, especially when she considered what she had been before she had married Tommy. Of course, Tommy had known that she was a whore when he married her, because that was where and how he had met her.

In marrying one of her clients, Kitty had realized the dream of nearly every soiled dove she had ever met. They all dreamed of meeting a man who would marry them and take them away from "the life."

In Kitty's case she had been particularly lucky, because the man who took her away from life on the line had not only been a loving and caring husband, he had also been exceptionally wealthy. And, most important, he had never, even once, made her feel guilty about her past.

That was why she told Matt what she had been. She sincerely believed that whatever relationship they were going to have, even if it went no further than the current relationship, would have to be based upon the truth.

Maybe she shouldn't have told him.

No.

Whatever was causing Matt's hesitance in deepening the relationship had nothing to do with her past life. She was sure of that.

She heard the clock strike one before she finally fell asleep.

At half past one in the morning, the Auxiliary Peace Officers approached Coventry on the Snake. Sherman held up his hand to halt the band, then he pointed. The moon was bright, and several horses could be seen bunched together in one field.

"Scraggs, you and Grimes go down and take a look. If there is anyone watching over the herd, take care of them. If no one is watching, come back and let me know," Sherman ordered.

Sherman, and the other men with him, waited as Scraggs and Grimes checked out the herd. One of the men took out the makings and started to roll a cigarette but Sherman rode over and knocked the makings from his hand.

"You light up a cigarette and you may as well just ride down there and tell them we are here," Sherman said.

"Sorry, Colonel, I wasn't thinking," the man said.

"A man in this business who doesn't use his head, can easily lose his head," Sherman said.

"I know. I'll be more careful from now on."

"You damn well better be. It's not just yourself you are putting in danger. It's all of us," Sherman scolded.

About five minutes after Scraggs and Grimes had ridden down to check the herd, they returned.

"What did you see?" Sherman asked.

"Nothin', Colonel," Scraggs reported. "There ain't nobody down there at all."

"Are you sure? You mean to tell me there is not one rider watching over the herd?"

"That's what I'm sayin' all right. Me'n Grimes rode all the way around. I'm tellin' you, there ain't nobody out there watchin' 'em."

Sherman smiled and nodded. "Damn, they are making this too easy for us. All right, Scraggs, take Carson, Anderson, and Burnett with you. You four go down to the south end of the field and take the fence down. The rest of you, move on down as quietly as you can, and start driving the herd south, away from the house."

"How many are we going to take?" Scraggs asked.

"Why, we are going to take all of them, of course," Sherman replied.

"All of them?"

"At least all of the horses they have gathered here. According to Marcus Kincaid, they were goin' to gather all the horses they were planning on shipping in one small field. These are all saddle horses, the field isn't all that big, so this has to be them."

"Hah," Scraggs said. "And without nobody watchin' the herd, this here is goin' to be about the easiest thing we've ever done."

As Scraggs and the men with him rode out to take down the fence, Sherman led the rest of his men into the field with the horses, then spread them out around the herd. Because there were so many of them, the herd was easily moved and within less than five minutes the field was completely empty as the horses moved at a rapid trot away from the main house. Within another ten minutes, the entire herd had passed over a low lying ridge two miles to the south, and nothing remained of where they had been but the un-cropped grass, moving in a gentle, night breeze.

"Prew, Jake, Crack, you boys wake up," Tyrone said as he walked through the bunkhouse just after dawn.

All he got in response was a few disgruntled groans from the men whose names he had called.

"Come on get up, get up. This day is half over," he called.

"Damn, Tyrone, don't you ever sleep?" Crack asked, and a few of the others chuckled.

"Yeah, I sleep when it's dark, and I'm awake when it's light. If you hadn't stayed up till midnight last night, you'd be all rested, and ready to go, now."

"Midnight? We was all in bed by ten o'clock. You know that, you was right here with us."

"As far as I'm concerned, ten o'clock is

damn near midnight," Tyrone said. "Now, come on, everybody get up. We have to feed the horses."

"Can't they eat grass like every other horse in the world does?" Prew asked, groggily.

"It's your fault," Tyrone replied.

"What do you mean, it's my fault?"

"You're the one that pointed out to me that there are too many of them put into too small a field."

"Yeah, but you said there was enough grass for a few days."

"There probably is, but I think we should get some hay out for them anyway, just in case."

"Those damn horses live better than we do," Jake said. "They get their breakfast in bed."

"You want breakfast in bed?" Tyrone asked. "I'll be glad to bring you breakfast in bed."

"Really? Yeah, you do that, I might feel more like gettin' up this morning."

"All right, I'll get you a handful of hay, right now," Tyrone said, and the others in the bunkhouse laughed.

"Serve that hay with some bacon and eggs, and I might just take you up on it," Jake said, sitting up and rolling out of bed.

"I have some coffee in the office," Tyrone said, softening his tone a bit. "You boys can grab yourselves a cup before you come out to the barn. Then, soon as you get the hay out, you can come on back for breakfast."

"That sure was nice of Miz Wellington to throw us that party last night," Prew said.

"And to actually dance with us. Who would'a thought a lady like that would dance with regular hands like us?" Crack asked.

"I hear'd tell they was a time when she done more'n just dance with cowboys," one of the newer hands said.

The laughing banter in the bunkhouse stopped as all the hands looked over toward the speaker.

"You need to watch that mouth of you'rn, Asa," Prew said.

"What? What did I say? Are you boys sayin' you don't know that our boss lady used to be a whore?" Asa chuckled. "Folks say she was the best lookin' whore in Ketchum."

"Asa, there's no need for you to help the boys this morning," Tyrone said, his voice almost conversational.

"What do you mean, there's no need?"

"I mean, you don't work here any more," Tyrone replied. "So, there's no need for you to help out. In fact, why don't you just gather your tack and get on out of here now?"

"You can't fire me."

"Yeah," Jake said. "Believe me, Asa, Tyrone can fire you."

Asa looked incredulous over the reaction of all the hands. "I can't believe this. I tell the truth about something and you want to fire me?"

"Not just want to, Asa. I did fire you," Tyrone said.

"How'm I goin' to go? Shank's mare? You know I don't have no horse of my own. The horse I'm a ridin' belongs to the ranch."

"You can ride your horse into town. Just leave it at the livery," Tyrone said. "We'll pick it up, later. And, Asa, if I go down to the livery and find out that you didn't leave the horse, I'll see that you are hunted down and tried as a horse thief."

"All right, all right," Asa said angrily. "I don't want to work for no damn whore anyway."

Crack stepped up to Asa then and, without another word, knocked Asa down.

"What the hell was that for?" Asa asked, lying on his back and rubbing his chin.

"I just didn't want you to leave without somethin' to remember us by," Crack said, and the others laughed.

"And, Asa," Prew said. "If word gets back to us that you're talkin' about Mrs. Wellington, I guarantee you, you'll get a lot more than a punch on the chin."

"I've never seen such a bunch of . . ."

"A bunch of what?" Jake asked.

Asa rubbed his chin and looked into the glaring faces of the other hands.

"Nothing," Asa said. "I'm going."

"Yeah, you do that. And don't let the door hit you in the ass on the way out," Crack said.

# CHAPTER
## TWENTY-FIVE

Awakening fairly early this morning, Matt got out of bed and went downstairs, then stepped out onto porch even as a rooster began crowing. To the east, the rising sun was an orange-red ball just clearing the rounded domes of the Bruneau Dunes and touching the Snake River to turn it into a flowing stream of molten gold. He watched as the hands hitched a team to a wagon, then began loading it with hay. It took about ten minutes to load the wagon, then he watched as Jake and Crack started driving down to the field where the saddle horses were gathered for shipment to the army.

He could smell the aroma of bacon and biscuits coming from the cook house, and recalling the season he had worked as a cowboy in Wyoming, he almost wished that he was staying in the bunkhouse with the other men, rather than in the too elegant and too soft bedroom upstairs.

From behind him, he heard Maria, the house cook at work, preparing breakfast. The aroma of brewing coffee drifted out onto the porch, and that caused him to go back inside and step into the kitchen.

"The coffee smells good," Matt said.

"Señor, if you go into the dining room, I will bring you a cup of coffee," the cook offered.

Matt chuckled. "Maria, you have a very good way of getting unwanted people out of your kitchen," he said. "I will get out of your way and, thank you, yes, I would love a cup of coffee."

"Oh, Señor, now you make me feel bad," Maria said.

"Do you mean I make you feel bad because you actually do want me to stay in your kitchen?"

"No, Señor. I do want you out of my kitchen," Maria answered. "But you make me feel bad because you know that I want you out."

Matt laughed, then went into the dining room to wait for his cup of coffee.

Upstairs, the cock's crow had awakened Kitty, but she had not yet gotten out of bed. She stretched, then looked at the patterns formed by the shadows cast on the wall by the morning sun as it peeped through the aspen tree that grew just outside her bedroom window. The tree limbs were moving gently in compliance with a soft early morning breeze, and she could track their movement across the wall.

Through the open window, she could hear the men talking, and even though it had been very late when she was finally able to go to sleep last night, she felt a sense of guilt knowing that she was still in bed while the men who worked for her were already at work.

It had now been a little over a month since the last rustlers had hit Coventry, and ten days since Poke Terrell was killed. Clearly, with that evil man gone, and with all shipment horses safely confined in one field, the worst was over. It had been a peaceful ten days, and now, for the first time, Kitty was beginning to feel confident that she was going to get her horses to market in Chicago. Nevertheless she wanted to keep Matt around until the horses had been safely delivered.

The question she had asked Matt last night had been interrupted, and the opportunity to ask it had never repeated itself. This morning, upon reflection, she was glad that she had not been able to ask it again.

Deep down inside she knew what the answer would be, she knew that he would tell her that he was going to be moving on, and she didn't want to actually hear it expressed. She knew inherently that no deeper relationship between them was ever going to happen. Matt Jensen was not the kind of man who could settle down, and it would be like caging a wild bird and if she tried. Besides, if he did settle down, it might very well kill that which she loved most about him.

On the other hand, only two days remained until she could load the horses onto the train. Then she and Matt would share a private car all the way to Chicago. If that was all of Matt Jensen she could get, she would take it with gratitude for the opportunity.

Smiling at that pleasant thought, she got out of bed and dressed to go down to breakfast.

"Well, good morning," Matt said, lifting his cup of coffee in greeting.

"Good morning yourself," Kitty answered. "Did you get up with the chickens?"

"What do you mean get up with the chickens?" Matt replied. "Who do you think woke the rooster up this morning?"

Frederica came into the dining room with

a cup of coffee which she handed to Kitty.

"Uhmm, thanks, Frederica," she added. "Does Maria know I am up?"

"Si, Señora."

"Did you sleep well?" Matt asked, as Kitty took her first swallow of coffee.

"Yes, I slept like a log," Kitty lied.

"Señora, Maria has breakfast ready. I can serve you and Señor Yensen now if you want," Frederica said, returning to the dining room.

"Yes, thank you, Frederica," Kitty replied.

"Are you ready for Chicago?" Matt asked.

"Oh, yes," Kitty answered. "Not just because I will be able to sell the horses, but because I've never been to a city that big. Actually, I've never been to any big city. Oh, Matt, can we stay for a few days to just visit?"

"When do you have to pay off the loan?"

"I have to pay the bank by the fourth of July."

"That's not for two more weeks," Matt said. "Sure, we can spend some time in Chicago."

Jake and Crack drove the wagon up to the five-acre field, then stopped.

"Where are the damn horses?" Jake asked. "Hell, last night they filled the field. Now I don't see a damn one."

"They're prob'ly all gathered around the creek. We just can't see them because they're below the rise," Crack said.

Jake stood up in the wagon, put his fingers to his mouth, and let out a loud, piercing whistle.

He got no response.

"Even if they were below the rise, I should be able to see 'em by standin' up here on the wagon seat like this."

"Drive on up there, Crack," Jake said.

Crack slapped the reins against the back of the team and the wagon lurched forward. When they reached the crest of the rise, they not only saw that all the horses were, indeed, gone, they saw why they were gone.

"The damn fence fell down," Crack said.

"Fell down hell. Look at it. It was took down," Jake said.


Matt and Kitty were still at their breakfast and making plans for the trip to Chicago when Tyrone Canfield stepped into the dining room.

"Good morning, Tyrone," Kitty greeted, smiling at her foreman. "Have the men recovered from the party last night? I hope they had as good a time as I did."

Kitty's smile left when she saw the expression on Tyrone's face.

"Tyrone, what is it?" she asked. "What is wrong?"

"They're gone, Mrs. Wellington," Tyrone said.

"Who's gone?" she asked. "Good heavens, are you talking about the men? Where have they gone?"

"No not the men," Tyrone said. "The horses we put together to ship to Chicago. They are what is gone. Ever' last damn one of them."

"But that can't possibly be," Kitty said. "Five hundred horses? Not even the rustlers ever took that many."

"Five hundred and twenty-three to be exact. When Jake and Crack went out to take some hay to 'em this mornin', there weren't none of them there. At first, I thought maybe they might have found a break in the fence, and just wandered back out into the field. But I went down to have a closer look at the field. The fence at the south end of the field? The one we put up yesterday? It hadn't just been broke through by the horses. The fence had been taken down."

"Tyrone, I noticed Asa riding out this morning," Matt said. "Is he the one who discovered it?"

"No," Tyrone answered. "Well, the thing is, I don't know if Asa saw that the horses was gone or not. Even if he had, he prob'ly wouldn't of told us. I fired Asa this morning."

"You fired him?" Kitty said.

"Yes, ma'am. You remember, Mrs. Wellington, you give me the authority to hire and fire. Asa needed firin'." Tyrone gave no explanation as to why he fired him.

"You are right," Kitty said. "I did give you the authority, so I won't question it now. If you fired him, I'm sure you had a good reason."

"Yes, ma'am, I did."

"Tyrone, is it possible that Asa might have taken the fence down, then run the horses back out onto the range in anger over being fired?" Matt asked.

"I wish that was it, Matt, then all we would have to do is round 'em up again," Tyrone replied. "But the truth is, he rode off no more than a couple of minutes before Jake and Crack did. He wouldn't have had time to take the fence down and run off all the horses before Jake and Crack got there. No, sir, these horses was stole."

"Rustlers?" Kitty said in a distressed voice. "I thought with Poke Terrell gone, that we were through with rustlers." She sighed, then sunk back in her chair. "Oh, Matt, what am I going to do?" she asked. "That was more than half of my saddle horses. I don't have enough left to meet the terms of the army contract."

"I'm sorry Mrs. Wellington," Tyrone said, contritely. "I should have put some night riders out. But there hadn't been nothin' happen for more than a month now, and what with Poke Terrell dead, well, like you, I just sort of figured that we wouldn't be havin' no more trouble."

"No, no, Tyrone, you mustn't blame yourself. It isn't your fault. If I had thought we needed night riders, I would have asked you to put them out."

"But you shouldn't have had to ask me, Mrs. Wellington, that's the point," Tyrone said. "I'm the foreman, it's my job to look after things like that."

"Don't worry about it, either one of you," Matt said. "I'll find the horses and we'll get them back."

"How are you going to find them?" Kitty asked with a sense of defeat. "This isn't the first time we've had horses stolen and we've never been able to get them back before."

"They've never stolen this many before," Matt said. "This time they took over five hundred horses. That's going to be a lot harder for them handle."

"But there is no telling where the horses are now," Kitty said.

"It doesn't matter where they are now. I'll get them back," Matt insisted.

"Matt, I know you are just trying to make me feel better. But I don't see how you are going to find them."

"I know you have some wonderful horses, Kitty. But they can't fly, can they?"

"Fly? No, of course not."

"Since they can't fly, they are going to have to go over the ground and that means they will leave a trail," Matt said. "And there are five hundred of them, which means the trail is going to be as easy to read as if the rustlers left arrows painted on the ground."

"Yes," Kitty said, brightening a little. "Yes, I guess that is right, isn't it?"

"They can't have that big of a lead on me, and with five hundred horses to drive, it's going to slow them down. I don't think it'll take more than a couple of hours for me to find them."

"What are you going to do when you do find them?" Kitty asked.

"I'll bring them back."

"You can't drive five hundred horses all by yourself," Tyrone said. "We'll come with you."

"No," Matt said. "Get the men ready. Once I find the horses, I'll need them. But for now I don't want you to come with me. Too many men along with me will make it harder to track."

"What if there are people watching over the horses when you find them?"

"They won't be watching over them long," Matt said.

"Sure they will. If they've gone to all the trouble of stealin' 'em, they aren't goin' to just leave 'em somewhere without watchin' over 'em," Tyrone said. Then, he suddenly realized what Matt was implying.

"Oh," he said. "Oh, I see what you mean. But, in that case, I would think you would want some help."

Matt shook his head. "Tyrone, this is what I do," he said. "I don't want to get you or any of your men killed, and I don't want to be worrying about you and the men because that might take my mind off what I'm doing and get me killed. Do you understand?"

Tyrone nodded. "Yeah, I reckon I do," he said.

"Good. You just have the men ready to come bring the horses back, once I have recovered them."

"All right, Matt, whatever you say," Tyrone said resolutely.

# CHAPTER
# TWENTY-SIX

Back in Medbury, Clay Sherman stepped into Marshal Spark's office. Sparks had parts of a kerosene lantern spread out on his desk and was busy trimming the wick. He looked up as Sherman came in.

"What can I do for you, Colonel?" he asked.

"No doubt Mrs. Wellington is going to come see you sometime today, reporting that some of her horses have been rustled."

"Why do you think that?"

"Because I took five hundred horses from her during the night. It was the horses she had ready to sell to the army."

"What the hell, Sherman?" Marshal Sparks replied angrily. "You steal five hundred horses, then you have the audacity to come to my office and tell me about it? What is this, a challenge?"

"Take it easy," Sherman replied, holding out his hand. "I didn't steal the horses.

That's what I came here to tell you."

"What do you mean you didn't steal them? Didn't you just tell me that you took five hundred horses from Kitty Wellington in the middle of the night?"

"I did."

"What is that, other than stealing?"

"Legal confiscation," Sherman replied.

"What?"

Sherman pulled a piece of paper from his pocket and handed it to Marshal Sparks.

"Kitty Wellington was, and is, in violation of the herd management law. If you will read this, you will see that it is a violation to raise anything but cattle in this herd management district, unless you have specific authorization from the territory and county herd management council. Kitty Wellington has no such authorization. Therefore, I confiscated the horses on behalf of the territory of Idaho."

"I'm sure Mrs. Wellington never even heard of that law," Marshal Sparks said. "Nor have I heard of it."

"It is obvious you haven't heard of it, Marshal," Sherman said. "If you had, you would have done your duty and prevented her from raising horses in cattle country."

"I wouldn't have arrested her," Sparks said. "I would just have told her about the law so she could get a permit. I can't imagine the county or the territory, for that matter, withholding the permit."

"It's too late for the permit," Sherman said. "The law has been violated, the penalty must be paid."

"Where are the horses now?" Marshal Sparks asked.

"That's really none of your concern, Marshal," Sherman said. "Let's just say that the horses are somewhere safe."

"Sherman . . ."

"Colonel Sherman," Sherman said.

Marshal Sparks glared at Sherman for a moment. "Sherman," he repeated. "I may not have known about the herd law, but I do know that before you can confiscate anything, you have to have a court order, and you have to serve it. I'm just guessing, mind you, but I don't believe you served Kitty Wellington a court order. Not in the middle of the night, you didn't."

"Yes, well, here is the thing, Marshal," Sherman said. "My authority differs from yours. Your jurisdiction is limited to Medbury. Mine, on the other hand, extends throughout the entire territory of Idaho. I can issue my own court order and warrants."

"As city marshal of Medbury, I am also a

deputy sheriff for the county of Owyhee, which means I have jurisdiction throughout the county," Sparks said. "And I don't believe, for one moment, that you have the authority to serve a court order in this county, much less issue such an order."

"It doesn't make any difference whether you believe it or not, Marshal. I have already exercised my authority and I came here to tell you about it, only as a matter of courtesy. If Kitty Wellington, or her hired gun, Matt Jensen, comes to report that their horses are stolen, you might tell them that. Oh, and tell Matt Jensen that if he tries to recover the horses, or opposes me, or any of my men, we will be within our legal right to kill him."

Matt had learned his tracking skills from the legendry Smoke Jensen, and had learned so well that it was said of him that he could track a fish through water. However, it required no particular skill to track the herd of horses the rustlers had taken. Even a novice could have followed the wide band they left, not only tracks, but also their droppings.

But it was the latter, the horse droppings that provided additional, vital information. This information was something that only someone with Matt's remarkable skills and specialized education would be able to ascertain. The droppings of the range horses were filled with the Kentucky Blue Grass that Kitty had imported for her pasture land. But here and there could be found droppings that contained only Fescue hay. The hay droppings stood out from the others as if they had little signs attached to them, and those horses, Matt knew, belonged to the rustlers.

It was difficult to ascertain just how many rustlers there were, though Matt was sure there were fourteen or fifteen of them, and maybe more. Then, when they crossed Mill Creek, many of the rustlers turned away, leaving only four that he could still account for. He was glad to see that none of the range horses had turned away, because if the herd had been split, it would make the recovery a lot more difficult.

As he continued to trail the rustlers and the herd, he could tell by a close observation of the droppings that he had nearly caught up with them. The droppings he was seeing now were less than half an hour old.

When he approached a long, low lying ridge, he dismounted before he reached the top. Then, with a word for Spirit to remain in place, he crawled to the top to look over to the other side. There, in a natural bowl, he saw the horses. The herd was contained on one side by Blue Creek, and on the other three sides by the natural walls of a dead end canyon. Four mounted men were keeping watch over the horses.

Matt returned to Spirit, mounted, then pulled his pistol. Slapping his legs against the side of his horse, he rode up the ridge, then down the other side, his cocked pistol raised.

"Hold it right there!" he shouted at the four riders.

"What the hell?" one of the men shouted. "Who is it?"

"It's Matt Jensen! Shoot 'im down!" another called. Matt recognized the one who identified him as being one of the four he had confronted in the Sand Spur.

The four riders pulled their pistols then and opened fire. Matt returned fire and one of the men dropped from his saddle and skidded across hard ground. All hell broke loose as muzzle flashes and drifting gun smoke filled the air, while the crashes of gun fire rolled back from the canyon walls.

Matt was in command of the situation as he rode down the hill, well positioned to pick out his targets. The rustlers, having been surprised by his sudden and unexpected appearance were mounted on horses that were rearing and caracoling about nervously as flying lead whistled through the air and whined off stone.

Matt picked out another rider and shot him from the saddle.

"Shoot him! Shoot the son of a bitch!" one of the two remaining outlaws shouted in panic.

Matt fired two more times, and the last two riders fell. Then it was quiet, with the final round of shooting but faint echoes returning distant hills. A little cloud of acrid bitter gun smoke assailed his nostrils as Matt dismounted, then walked out among the fallen rustlers, moving cautiously, his pistol at the ready. He need not have been cautious in his approach. None of the rustlers were left alive.

The entire battle had taken less than a minute.

George Gilmore was bent over some papers on his desk when Marshal Sparks stepped into his office. He looked up in surprise.

"Marshal Sparks," he said. "Is something wrong?"

"I don't know," Marshal Sparks said. "Maybe nothing. But something is going on that I don't feel right about."

"What is it?"

"Are you aware that the Clay Sherman and his so-called Auxiliary Peace Officers' Posse are in town?"

"Who isn't aware?" Gilmore replied. "That's all anyone in town has been talking about ever since they arrived, wondering why they are here."

"I think I know why. Have you ever heard of something called the herd management law?" Marshal Sparks asked.

Gilmore shook his head. "No, I can't say that I have."

"This is why they are here," Sparks said, showing Gilmore the paper Sherman had given him. "According to Sherman, they are here to enforce the herd management law."

Gilmore perused the document for a moment, then handed it back to the sheriff. "Enforce it in what way?" he asked.

"Last night Sherman and his men visited Kitty Wellington's ranch and took five hundred head of her horses. Confiscated the horses is how Sherman put it. He confiscated the horses on behalf of the territory of Idaho, because, he claims, by running horses, she was in violation of the herd management law. Though why he confiscated exactly five hundred, rather than serving a notice that he was confiscating the entire herd, I don't know."

"I know," Gilmore said.

"Then I wish you would tell me."

"Five hundred head is the number of horses Mrs. Wellington is contracted to furnish the army. He took those horses to prevent her from fulfilling that contract."

"Damn! You're right," Sparks said. "That is exactly why they took five hundred head."

"Did Sherman have a court order to confiscate the horses?"

"I asked him that same question," Sheriff Sparks replied. "He says that he doesn't need a court order. He said he has the authority to issue his own court order."

Gilmore shook his head. "He's lying," he said. "Not even a federal marshal could confiscate an entire herd of horses on his own initiative."

"What about this herd management law? Would he be able to use it to get a court order that would allow him to confiscate Kitty Wellington's horses?"

"Let me check something," Gilmore said. He walked over to his book shelf and took down a book called *Codes for the Territory of Idaho.*

After looking through it for a moment, he shook his head. "There is no judge in the territory who would grant a court order to allow that. For all intent and purposes, this is absolutely meaningless."

"What do you mean, meaningless?"

"I mean it would have no effect on Mrs. Wellington. Listen to this. This is the next paragraph, paragraph twenty five, subparagraph three, stroke three.

"Any land owner, owning more than twenty percent of the land in said proposed herd district and who has a herd that is separated by more than two miles from a herd of dissimilar stock, who is a resident in, and qualified elector of, the territory of Idaho is not subject to the herd law, unless special petition is made and filed by land owners whose aggregate holdings total more than fifty percent of the land in said district. Such petition, if granted, shall be served upon the land owner by the county sheriff or his deputy."

"I haven't served any such notice," Marshal Sparks said.

"Then if notice has not been served, and Sherman really did take the horses, he stole them," Gilmore said. "That means you can arrest him and the entire posse."

"Yeah, I guess I could, couldn't I?" Marshal Sparks replied without enthusiasm. "Or, maybe I can just show him the error of his ways. Mr. Gilmore, would you copy that law out on a piece of paper for me so I can show it to Sherman."

"I'll be glad to do it for you, Marshal, but what will that accomplish?" Gilmore asked. "If Sherman knows about the part of the law that he showed you, the part he used as justification to steal Mrs. Wellington's horses, then you can bet that he knows about this part of the law."

"Yes," Sparks said. "But at least this way, he will realize that I know about this part of the law as well."

It was mid-afternoon by the time Matt and the other riders from Coventry on the Snake managed to retrieve the horses and put them back in the field where they were being held, pending the shipment to Chicago. As soon as all the horses were recovered, Tyrone detailed some of the men to repair the fence the Auxiliary Peace Officers had destroyed when they took the horses.

"I don't understand," Kitty said. "I thought Poke Terrell was behind all this. But he's dead and the rustling continues."

"Do you remember in the café yesterday, when I pointed out the head of the Auxiliary Peace Officers to you? I told you he was going to be trouble."

"Yes, I remember."

"The four men I killed were wearing the uniforms and badges of the Auxiliary Peace Officers."

Kitty gasped. "Oh, Matt. Have I gotten you in trouble with the law?" she asked. "If I have, I will never be able to forgive myself."

"If so, it won't be the first time I've come close to the line," Matt said. "But don't worry about it. Whether they are wearing badges or not, I don't believe, for a minute, that they are actually law officers. They may be some sort of posse with deputies' badges, but they are not legitimate law officers."

"Where are they now?" Kitty asked. "The men who stole the horses, I mean."

"Tyrone sent Prew back out with a wagon to pick up the bodies. I'll take them into town tonight."

"What are you going to do with them?"

"I'll figure something out," Matt said.

# CHAPTER
## TWENTY-SEVEN

It was mid-afternoon when Hodge Deckert stepped down from the 4:20 west-bound train at the Medbury Depot. He checked his sample case to make certain nothing had been broken during the trip.

A traveling salesman from Denver, Deckert had been on the road for just over a week, having served clients in Greely, Colorado, Cheyenne, Rawlins, and Green River, Wyoming, Squaw Creek, American Falls, and King Hill, Idaho, before arriving here in Medbury. So far his trip had been successful, and he had taken orders for almost a thousand dollars worth of goods, which meant he had earned one hundred dollars in commission. Medbury was the end of his sales territory. He would spend the night here at the Del Rey Hotel, then call on the mercantile and general stores tomorrow in time to take the noon train back.

Satisfied that his samples were undamaged, he closed the case then started across the street to the hotel. As he started through the door, though, two large men blocked his way.

"Where do you think you are going?" one of them asked. Both were dressed just alike, and both were wearing star badges on their shirt.

"I'm going to check into the hotel," Deckert said.

"No, you ain't."

"Why not?"

"There ain't no rooms left."

"Of course there are. Elmer always keeps a couple of rooms open for travelers. I stay here every time I come to Medbury."

"You ain't stayin' here tonight."

"I'd rather hear that from Elmer," Deckert said.

The two burly men looked at each other for a moment, then one of them laughed. "Let him talk to Elmer," he said.

"Yeah, why not?"

The two men stepped aside and Deckert, a bit apprehensive now, crossed the lobby to the front desk. Elmer was standing behind the desk.

"Hello, Elmer. Is my room ready? I'd like the same one I always have, on the front, overlooking the street."

"There is only one room left, Hodge, and I don't think you will want it," Elmer said.

"What do you mean I don't want it? Of course I do."

"No, you don't," one of the men with the star on his chest said.

"What's going on here, Elmer?"

"Pearl and I have a spare room. You can stay with us tonight," Elmer said. "In fact, you can join us for supper, and it won't cost you a cent."

"Well, then, if you are willing to do that for me, of course I will accept your offer. But I would like to know what's going on."

"I'll tell you all about it, later," Elmer said. "Come on, I'll walk down to the house with you and tell Pearl we're having company tonight."

"Does your wife like perfume?" Deckert asked.

"Oh, heavens, we can't afford to be buying something like perfume."

"You won't be buying it, I'm giving it to you. I have a spare bottle in my samples kit. I would be pleased if Mrs. Reinhardt would accept it."

Crack Kingsley was riding into town just as Elmer and Deckert were walking up the street toward the little cluster of houses that made up the residential area of Medbury. He touched his hat and nodded at them, and they returned the gesture.

Crack rode past the Sand Spur and wanted, very much, to stop and have a beer and maybe visit a little with one of the women. But he had told Matt that he would come straight to town, make his purchase, then return immediately.

Crack could understand the need to get back to the ranch, especially if the rustlers hit them again tonight. What he couldn't understand was why Matt had sent him in town to make such a frivolous purchase.

Dismounting in front of the Medbury Mercantile, Crack stepped up on the porch, then went inside. He passed by the candy shelf and saw a large jar of horehound candy. He thought of Hank, who always bought himself a stick anytime he came to town, and asked one of the others to buy it for him if they came to town and he didn't.

The thought caused Crack to experience a moment of melancholy, and, in memory of Hank, he reached down into the jar and pulled out a penny stick. He walked up to the counter holding the stick of candy.

"Hello, Crack," the store keeper asked. "How is Mrs. Wellington getting along?"

"She's doin' just fine, Mr. Dunnigan, I'll be sure and tell her you was askin' about her."

"You do that," Dunnigan said. He pointed to the stick of candy and chuckled. "You didn't ride all the way into town just to spend a penny, did you?"

"What?" Crack held up the stick of candy and looked at it. "Oh, no sir, I just picked this up on account of Hank."

"Hank? Isn't he . . . ?" Dunnigan let the question hang.

"Dead, yes sir, Hank's dead all right. But you mind how much he loved horehound?"

"I sure do. That boy bought him a piece ever' time he come in here," Dunnigan said.

"Well, sir, this here candy is for him, sort of a way I've got of rememberin' him."

"Yes, and a very good way that is too," Dunnigan said. "Now, what else can I do for you?"

"It's comin' up on the Fourth of July," Crack said. "I was just wonderin' if you had any of them fireworks in yet?"

"I sure do. Out here, you got to order them things early if you want to make sure you get 'em in time for the Fourth. What do you need?"

"I need me a sky rocket," Crack said.

"A sky rocket? Just one?"

"Yes, sir, just one will do me."

"All right," Dunnigan said, walking down behind the counter until he came to the fireworks' shelf. He picked up one rocket, then brought it back and showed it to Crack.

"Will this leave a trail when it goes up?" Crack asked.

"Indeed it will," Dunnigan replied. "If you send this thing up in the night it will leave a shower of sparks behind it, then, when it gets to the top, it will burst open into a whole bunch of little balls of different colored lights."

"I'll take it," Crack said.

"Is this all you want? I got me a lot of firecrackers too. You can't hardly celebrate the Fourth of July without you set off a bunch of firecrackers."

"Mayhaps I'll come back a'fore the Fourth and get some of them," Crack said. "But for right now, this here rocket is all I want."

"All right. The rocket and the piece of horehound candy come to eleven cents," Dunnigan said.

Crack paid for his purchase, put the rocket and half a piece of the candy in a sack, stuck the other half piece in his mouth, then went back outside. He saw a couple of cowboys he knew from a neighboring ranch. They were standing near the watering trough.

"Hey, fellas," he said. "What you doin' out here? Anytime you boys come into town, you near 'bout always go to the Sand Spur."

"Ain't no fun at the Sand Spur right now," one of the two cowboys said.

"Yeah, not as long as them deputies are here," the other one said. "They go into the Sand Spur and all the fun comes out of it."

"I don't know what they are after, but I'll sure as hell be happy when they leave."

"What are you doin' in town, Crack?"

"I just come into town to buy somethin'," Crack said.

"Horehound candy," one of the cowboys said with a chuckle. "You come into town to buy horehound candy."

"Yeah, well, I like it," Crack said. "What's wrong with that?"

"Ain't nothin' wrong with it. I like it too, but I don't think I'd ride five miles just to get me some."

"Maybe you just don't like it as much as I do," Crack said. He untied his horse, mounted, then looked back down at his two friends. "You boys take it easy now, you hear?" he said as he rode away.

"Good job," Matt said. He looked down at the rifle pit which was deep enough to stand in, and wide enough for three men to occupy.

"We dug one here, and another one over there," Tyrone said. "This way we've got the entrance covered, no matter which side the rustlers might come in on."

"Move some brush over in front of them," Matt said.

"Yeah, that's a good idea. That way they won't be as likely to see us, even if we are shooting at them."

"I'm going back to the house," Matt said. "When Prew gets back with the bodies, have him come up."

"Here comes Crack," Jake said.

Matt waited until Crack got there before he left for the house.

"Did you get the rocket?" he asked.

"Yeah, I got it."

"Good. Now, go back to the cookhouse, have the cook fix you a lunch to take with you."

"Take where?"

"Do you see that bluff there?" Matt said, pointing to a rather prominent feature about two miles away. "I want you to go up onto that bluff and stay. And stay awake. If you have to, get yourself a handful of coffee beans and chew on them tonight. From there, you will have a good view of anyone who approaches the ranch. If you see anyone coming, shoot the rocket off."

"Ahh, it's a signal," Crack said. "I was wonderin' what you were wantin' this rocket for."

"Don't shoot it until they pass you though," Matt said. "We don't want them to know they've been seen."

"How do you know they'll be coming tonight?" Jake asked.

"I plan to leave them a message tonight," Matt said. "Once they get the message, they'll come."

Matt was sitting at the dining room table with Kitty when Prew came in. "Excuse me, but Tyrone said you wanted to see me."

"Did you recover the bodies?" Matt asked.

"All four of them. With their hats, just like you said."

"Are they still in the buckboard?"

"Yeah. I tell you the truth, Matt, I don't know why we're goin' to all the trouble. If it was up to me, I'd let 'em just lie out there and rot."

"Have you had your supper?"

"Not yet."

"Have the cook make you a sandwich, then bring it with you. You can eat it on the way into town."

"We're actually going to do it, aren't we? We're takin' these bastards into to town to the undertaker."

"Something like that," Matt said.

Clay Sherman was staying in the room that had belonged to Mr. Pemberton, taking it because it was better furnished than any of the other hotel rooms. This room had, in addition to the bed and a comfortable chair, a small kitchen table and kitchen chair. At the moment, Sherman was sitting at the kitchen table in the soft, golden glow of the lantern, figuring his profit on the back of an envelope.

Marcus Kincaid had paid him ten thousand dollars to make certain Kitty Wellington did not get her horses to market in time to save her ranch. But Kincaid had made no reference of any kind as to the disposition of the horses. He hadn't mentioned them because he was certain that once the ranch came into his possession, then everything on the ranch would also be his, including all the horses.

Sherman hadn't mentioned the horses either, because he had his own plans for them. Poke had already made an arrangement to move the horses at fifty dollars a head, though he had told everyone but

Sherman that he was only getting twenty-five dollars a head.

Fifty dollars a head for five hundred horses was twenty-five thousand dollars. That twenty-five thousand dollars, plus the ten thousand he was getting from Kincaid, would make this, by far, the most profitable business arrangement he had ever entered in to.

Smiling, Sherman drew a circle around the figure, thirty-five thousand dollars, then he folded the envelope and stuck it down in his pocket. Glancing toward the window, he saw that it had grown very dark outside and, since he had not yet had his supper, he decided he would have it now. Sherman extinguished the lantern, then stepped out into the hallway and started down the stairs.

The wall sconces in the lobby had not yet been lit, so it seemed darker than usual. The only lantern providing any light was sitting on the front desk.

"Hey, hotel clerk," he called as he reached the bottom of the stairs. "Why ain't you lit the wall sconces yet?"

Sherman did not get a reply."

"Reinhardt, where the hell are you?" Sherman called again.

Of course, when one thought about it, there was really no reason for the clerk to be at his desk at all. The Auxiliary Peace Officers' Posse occupied every room but one, and nobody was likely to occupy that one, remaining room.

Sherman stepped up to the front desk, and banged his hand down on the call bell.

"Reinhardt?"

He didn't care whether the hotel had any new guests or not. As far as he was concerned, the clerk should still be at work, if for no other reason than to provide services for Sherman and his men. And one of the things he should do, was light the sconce lights in the lobby. A man in Sherman's position couldn't help but make enemies, and dark lobbies were places that a man with enemies should avoid, when possible.

"Never mind," Sherman grumbled. "I'll light the lanterns myself."

Reaching over the desk, Sherman found a box of matches, then he turned and started out into the lobby.

That was when he saw them.

Four of his men were sitting in chairs in the lobby. Their chairs were arranged in a square, as if the four were engaged in a friendly game of cards. But there were no cards, and there was no card table. There were just the four men, setting in a square, looking at each other.

"What are you men doing here, just sitting in the dark?" he asked with a little chuckle. "Did they run you out of the saloon?"

When not one of the four answered, he started over toward them. "You men aren't very — uhnn!" he shouted, and he jumped back as the hair suddenly stood up on the back of his neck. All four men were dead!

After he caught his breath, he moved close enough to identify them. The four men were Garrison, Edwards, Reid, and Kennison. These were the same four men he had left to guard the horses.

"Scraggs!" Sherman yelled at the top of his lungs. He ran up the stairs, taking them two at a time. "Scraggs!" he yelled again. "Grimes! Schneider! Anderson? Anybody?"

Nobody answered his calls, and he moved down the hallway, opening every door and looking inside. Then, deciding they must all be over at the saloon, he ran back downstairs and trotted up the street to the saloon.

Celebrating the fact that they had taken the five hundred horses without any problems, the posse members were quite animated tonight. As a result, the saloon was more lively, the piano was playing, and the men of the posse were laughing and engaging in loud conversation. However, their presence still seemed to intimidate the rest of the town though, because there were very few in the saloon, other than his men.

"Scraggs, damn it!" Sherman shouted as soon as he stepped into the saloon. "What the hell happened?"

Sherman's voice was so loud and angry that it brought everything to a halt, the laughter and conversation, and even the piano music. Everyone in the saloon stared at Sherman in curiosity.

"What are you talking about, Colonel?" Scraggs asked, clearly confused by the outburst.

"You know damn well what I'm talking about," Sherman replied, still shouting at the top of his voice. He pointed toward the hotel. "They are down there now, just sitting in the lobby of the hotel."

"Who is down there?" Scraggs asked. He still had no idea what was bothering Sherman.

"You know who is down there. I'm talking about Garrison, Edwards, Reid, and Kennison. They are in the lobby. All four of them, just sitting there as plain as you please."

"What? What the hell did they come back for?" Scraggs asked. "They got no business bein' back here. They was supposed to stay with the herd until tomorrow. Don't worry, Colonel, I'll take care of it." Scraggs started toward the door.

"How are you going to take care of them?" Sherman asked.

"What do you mean, how am I going to take care of them? I'm going to send their asses back into the field."

"You can't do that," Sherman said.

"Why not?"

"Because, you dumb son of a bitch! They are dead! All four of them are dead!" Sherman screamed.

# CHAPTER
# TWENTY-EIGHT

As soon as Matt and Prew returned from town, Matt mounted Spirit, then rode out to the rifle pits. Tyrone and all the ranch hands except for Crack were gathered around one of the pits, drinking coffee. The fire for the coffee was down in one of the pits so it didn't show.

"Good idea to keep the fire down there," Matt said. "Now, you boys know what to do, right? As soon as you see the rocket, get down into your pits. Do you all have rifles?"

"Ever' one of us," Tyrone answered.

"Where are you going to be, Matt?" Jake asked.

"I'm going up with Crack. After they pass us by, I'm going to come down behind them."

"That's goin' to be dangerous, isn't it? I mean if you are behind them, you are likely to be in our line of fire," Tyrone said.

Matt took out a cigar. "I'm going to be

smoking this cigar," he said. "I'll be the only one with a glow. Don't shoot at the glow."

"Don't shoot at the glow," Tyrone repeated, and the others laughed.

"Are you sure they're coming tonight?"

"Yeah, I'm sure," Matt said. "Prew and I left them a calling card."

"A calling card?"

Prew laughed out loud. "Wait till I tell you what we did," he said. "You think we were taking the bodies into the undertaker? Hah! We didn't do that. No, sir. Not by a long shot did we do that."

As Matt rode away to join Crack up on the bluff, he heard Prew telling the others the story of how they had taken the bodies into town, then carried them, one at a time, into the hotel lobby.

At the Sand Spur, there were only three customers beside the members of the Peace Officers' Posse and they had withdrawn into a back corner of the room as Sherman vented his anger with his men. Charley had signaled for the two girls, Jenny and Suzie, to come behind the bar with him, and they stood there watching in stunned silence.

Charley had reached under the bar and wrapped his hand around a double-barreled twelve-gauge shotgun. He hadn't shown the gun to anyone, and didn't intend to, except as a last resort.

"Charley, what's going on? I'm scared," Jenny said.

"Shh. Hush, girl," Charley said soothingly. "It's best we just stay out of this for now."

"I don't understand," Scraggs said. "Who the hell would bring four dead bodies into the hotel and just set them there?"

"Well, I'm just guessing, Scraggs, but I would guess it was the same one who killed them. It was Jensen, you idiot!" Sherman shouted angrily.

"No, they was four of them left guardin' the horses. There ain't no way Jensen could'a kilt all four of 'em," Scraggs said.

"Funny you would say that, Scraggs, seeing as how he braced four of you in the saloon," Sherman said.

"No now, that wasn't no way near the same thing and you know it," Scraggs said. "We was all four of us sittin' down so as not to be able to get to our guns. Garrison and the others was out in the open."

"Whether you were in the open, or sitting down, it doesn't make any difference," Sherman said. "The man is a devil."

"Wonder what happened to the horses?"

"I'm sure he took them back. But we're

going to go after them."

"No, you aren't," Marshal Sparks said. He had just come into the saloon and was now standing by the front door.

"What do you mean, no we aren't?"

"If you go after those horses again, you will be stealing them, not confiscating them," Marshal Sparks said. He held up a piece of paper. "This is the herd management law you were talking about," he said. "Without a specific order to the contrary, there is nothing to prevent Kitty Wellington from raising horses on her ranch. And if you actually took horses from her, you are guilty of rustling."

Inexplicably, Sherman smiled, then he clapped his hands. "Very good, Marshal," he said. "You found a law book. But my authority comes from the territorial capitol at Boise," Sherman said. "Which means my authority is greater than yours. So I'm ordering you now, to get out of our way and let us do our duty."

"And I'm ordering you out of my town," Marshal Sparks said. "I want you and all your men, out of the hotel now. And that includes the four dead men that are in the lobby. If you leave them here, they're going be buried in the Potter's Corner."

"I don't take orders from a town marshal,"

Sherman said, spewing the words in derision. "Get out of the way, Marshal," Sherman said.

Marshal Sparks started toward his gun, but that was a fatal mistake. At least three of the Posse already had their guns drawn, and all three of them fired. Jenny and Suzie screamed as Sparks went down.

"Let's go," Sherman ordered.

"What are we going to do with the marshal?" Scraggs asked.

Sherman looked down at him.

"Leave him," Sherman said. "Let the town bury him in their Potter's Corner." He laughed, a brusque laughter from hell. "Soon there will be more people lyin' in Potter's Corner than in the regular cemetery. And I intend to see that there are a few more that wind up in there tonight."

Crack and Matt were both on top of the bluff, waiting for Sherman and his posse to come try and reclaim the herd. It was dark, and looking back toward the north was a strain on the eyes, and made it difficult to stay alert. Matt and Crack were taking turns keeping watch. For the moment it was Crack's time to be looking.

He had been staring, unceasingly, to the north for at least the last half hour. And when he did spot them, and made the announcement, he did so in a voice that was as calm as if he was pointing out a cloud formation.

"Here they come," Crack said.

Matt had been sitting on a rock, sucking on the soft under part of a grass stem when Crack spoke.

"Are you sure?" Matt asked, standing up and moving to the edge of the bluff to look north. "I don't see anything."

"That's 'cause they just rode down into a little draw," Crack said. "They'll come out in a second, and you'll be able to see 'em."

"Yeah, I can hear them now," Matt said. He stared in the same direction for a moment longer, then saw them emerge.

"Get your rocket ready, but don't light it until I tell you," Matt said.

"Matt, it looks like there's at least a dozen of 'em. And we only have four men down there."

"It will be all right," Matt said. "Sherman doesn't know we only have four men and, believe me, when they start shooting from the rifle pits, Sherman will think he's facing an army."

Crack chuckled. "Yeah," he said. "Yeah, I forgot about the rifle pits."

"They are getting closer," Matt said. He

struck a match and, shielding the light from view, lit his cigar. Then, with his cigar lit, he swung into the saddle and rode out to the edge of the bluff and looked down. The posse had passed by now, but they were still a good mile away from Tyrone and the others.

"All right, send up the rocket," Matt said.

Crack lit the fuse to the rocket. It sputtered for a moment, and then raced up into the sky, leaving a long, glowing golden trail streaming out behind it. Even as he heard the hiss of the rocket's ascent, Matt slapped his legs against Spirit's side and started down the trail to the valley floor below.

"Tyrone, there goes the rocket!" Prew said.

"All right, you and Clem get over there in the other pit. Jake, you stay here with me."

"Come on, Clem," Prew said as he started across the field.

"Prew!" Tyrone called.

Prew stopped and looked back.

"Remember, Matt is going to be out there, smoking a cigar. Don't shoot at the glow."

"I ain't goin' to shoot at the glow," Prew said. "But I tell you the truth, you couldn't get me out there for a thousand dollars. I mean, even if we don't shoot at him, there's goin' to be bullets flyin' around."

"There's goin' to be bullets flyin' around ever'where," Tyrone said. "So hurry on over there, and remember to keep your head down."

"Halt!" Sherman said, holding his hand up. "Hold it up here for a moment!"

Sherman had twelve riders with him and they all stopped on his order. "Pull your pistols and be ready," he said. "Spread out. We'll go in abreast."

"What if we see someone?" Scraggs asked.

"If you see anyone, kill them," Sherman said.

"Even before they shoot at us? You're always wantin' them to shoot at us first."

"They killed Garrison, Edwards, Reid, and Kennison, didn't they? That means they have already shot at us."

"Yeah, I guess you are right."

"We'll go in at a gallop," Sherman said. He laughed. "It'll be a regular cavalry charge. I'd like to see how a bunch of cowboys are going to be able to handle a cavalry charge."

Sherman moved slightly out front, then looked back at his men, and waited until they were spread out twelve abreast. Then, he turned back toward the field and brought his hand down sharply.

The posse thundered across the field.

When Matt saw the posse begin its cavalry charge, he urged Spirit into a ground eating gallop, quickly catching up to them. He rode in between the two riders at the left end of the line, and as it happened, one of them had been sitting at the table with Scraggs when he confronted them.

"Hey!" Matt called. "Where are we going?"

"It's Jensen!" one of them called, and both of them turned their pistols toward Matt.

Matt hauled back on Spirit and the horse came to an almost immediate stop, just as the two men fired. Both men fell from their saddles, having shot each other.

Hearing the gunshots, but not realizing what happened, Sherman ordered the others to open fire. The fire of the attacking posse was immediately returned by the Coventry riders who were shooting from the rifle pits. Bright muzzle flashes from pistols and rifles lit up the night as the battle was joined. Although the posse had superior numbers to the Coventry riders, the advantage was to the latter. The rifle pits not only gave them cover, it also gave them concealment, whereas Sherman's men were riding in the open, without cover, and concealed only somewhat by the darkness.

The bullets were flying as thick as if someone had struck a hornet's nest, and four more posse men went down. Within less than a minute, the number of men riding with Sherman had been degraded by half.

"We'll all be killed!" Scraggs screamed in terror, and he turned his horse away from the charge.

"Scaggs! You cowardly son of a bitch, come back here!" Sherman shouted. In his anger, he shot Scraggs.

Now there were only six left, counting Sherman himself. But at that moment, Sherman made the same decision Scraggs had made a moment earlier. If they stayed here, they were all going to be killed.

"Let's get out of here!" he shouted, wheeling his horse around.

The others broke off the attack, then turned and chased after their leader.

Matt watched them gallop away and, for a moment, contemplated going after them. But they no longer represented a threat to the horses or to the ranch, so Matt let them go, deciding instead to check with Tyrone to see how the men had done during the brief but ferocious gun battle. He rode in

411

slowly, puffing on the cigar to keep the tip bright, hoping they would remember not to shoot at the glow.

Evidently it was working because all the shooting stopped, and the only sound that could be heard was the slow but steady clop of Spirit's hooves as Matt rode toward them.

"Tyrone, it's me," Matt called, when he got close enough for them to hear him.

"Yeah, we didn't figure the cigar was floating in by itself," Tyrone's voice called back from the dark. "Come on in, Matt."

Matt crossed the last few yards, then saw Tyrone standing alongside the pit. Tyrone was the only one standing, and for a moment, Matt was concerned.

"Where are the others?" he asked.

"They're fine," Tyrone said. "I told them to stay in the pits until we were sure."

Matt chuckled. "Yes, that was probably a pretty good idea. Anyone hurt?"

"Nobody was hit," Tyrone said. "How did we do against the posse?"

"Pretty good, I think," Matt said. "There were a lot fewer of them who left, than came."

The sun was just coming up when Sherman and what remained of his posse returned to Medbury. Most of the town was still asleep, though two men were loading a freight wagon, and Mr. Dunnigan was sweeping the front porch of his store.

Sherman stopped in front of the marshal's office.

"Why are we stopping here, Colonel?" Burnett asked.

"It's our duty," Sherman said. "The marshal is dead, someone has to be the law for these people."

Burnett chuckled. "Yeah," he said. "Yeah I see what you mean."

"Burnett, take Burke and Walker with you. Go down to the café and bring breakfast back for us," Sherman ordered.

"Uh, I don't have enough money to buy breakfast for all of us," Burnett said.

"You're the law. You don't need any money."

"What if they don't go along with that?" Burnett asked.

"You've got a gun, don't you?"

Burnett chuckled. "Yeah," he said. "I've got a gun."

The men were just finishing their breakfast when Marcus Kincaid came into the office.

"Kincaid," Sherman said. "What are you doing here? I thought we weren't supposed to be seen together."

"Sherman, what are you doing?" Kincaid asked. "I was just told that you killed Marshal Sparks yesterday."

Sherman cut open a biscuit, then lay a piece of bacon on it. He closed the biscuit and took a bite.

"Well, did you?" Kincaid asked, his voice high pitched and agitated because Sherman hadn't answered him.

"Did I what?"

"Are you deaf, man? I asked if you killed the marshal?"

"Yeah, I did. Now, I'm the marshal," he said with a wave of his hand, and the others with him laughed.

"This has gotten out of hand," Kincaid said. "Our deal is off. Do you hear me? Our deal is off. Nothing is worth this. I've changed my mind, let Kitty sell her horses. In fact, I own the loan contract to her ranch and I'm going to give it her."

"Huh uh, it isn't that easy, Kincaid," Sherman said. "I've already lost too many good men for you to back out now. You hired me for this little adventure. We're not pulling out."

"Oh, yes you are. You are fired. Do you understand that? I want you and all of your men to leave, now!"

"I expect Matt Jensen will be bringing in

Kitty Wellington's horses today. When she does, I intend to be here, waiting for him."

"Why? I told you, our deal is off. I'm not paying you one more cent."

"Do you have any idea how many of my men Jensen has killed?"

"I don't care how many of your men Jensen has killed," Kincaid said. "I told you that I want you to leave, and I mean now. If you don't, I will contact the sheriff in Silver City."

"Will you now?" Sherman asked.

"Oh, yes, I most definitely will do that," Kincaid said.

Sherman pulled his pistol from his holster and, without another word, shot Marcus Kincaid.

"What?" Marcus gasped, shocked and disbelieving. He staggered back a few steps, then collapsed.

Burke walked over to look down at him.

Sherman took a swallow of his coffee. "Is he dead?" he asked, giving the question no more emotion than if he had just asked if it was raining.

"Yeah, he's dead," Burke said. "What will we do with him?"

"Drag him out in the street and leave him there," Sherman said. "Someone will come along and take care of it."

"Damn, Colonel, ain't this the fella that's supposed to be payin' us? How we goin' to get paid now?" Burke asked.

"Five hundred horses at one hundred dollars each, is fifty thousand dollars," Sherman said. "You think that's pay enough?"

"Fifty thousand dollars? Wow. I didn't know there was that much money in the whole world."

"We've got to earn it though. We're going to have to take the herd."

Burnett shook his head. "How are we going to do that?" he asked. "We tried it last night, remember?"

"I made a mistake," Sherman admitted. "We attacked them on their ground, and they were dug in and waiting for us. And even if we had taken the herd, we would have had to bring it in. Now they are going to bring the herd to us, and when they do, we will be ready for them."

# CHAPTER
# TWENTY-NINE

"Mr. Gilmore?"

George Gilmore looked up from his desk and saw one of the soiled doves who worked at the Sand Spur. He remembered her from Millie's funeral, and knew that her name was Jenny.

"Yes, Jenny, can I help you?"

"I know that Millie came to you once when she needed help, so I thought, I mean, with the marshal being dead and all, well, you might be the best one for me to tell."

"Tell what?"

"All of the posse men are down at the saloon right now," Jenny said. "Mr. Gilmore, they plan to ambush all the riders from Coventry Ranch when they come in. They plan to kill them all, then take the herd."

"Oh, surely, they won't do anything like that," Gilmore said, trying to assuage young woman's fears.

"You don't know these men," Jenny said.

"Last night I saw them kill Marshal Sparks in cold blood. And this morning they killed Mr. Kincaid."

"Kincaid? They killed Marcus Kincaid?"

"Yes, sir, they were in there talking and laughing about it. Mr. Gilmore, Prew works for Conventry on the Snake. He — he has always been very nice to me. I wouldn't like to see anything happen to him. Or to Mrs. Wellington either, her being so nice to Millie and all."

Crack and Jake rounded up the dead posse men. There were six of them, including Scraggs, who had been shot in the back. Now, all the bodies were laid out alongside the barn.

"I hate taking them into town," Tyrone said. "What with the four that Matt killed the other night, that would be ten bodies we've given the good people of Medbury to have to bury and pay for."

"I sure can't see buryin' them out here though," Prew said. "No sense in spoilin' good range land by plantin' scoundrels like these polecats in the soil."

"Somebody's comin'," Crack said.

Looking through the arched gate and out onto the road, they saw an approaching team and light wagon.

"That's somebody in a surrey. More'n likely it's Kincaid," Jake said.

"No," Matt said. "It's George Gilmore."

"Who?" Crack asked.

"Gilmore," Prew said. "You know, that little lawyer fella."

"Wonder what he wants?" Tyrone asked.

Matt and the others watched as Gilmore drove through the gate, then around the curved driveway, the wheels making a crunching sound as they rolled through the pea gravel. From inside the house, Kitty had seen him as well, and now she came out to greet him. Matt walked over to join her.

"Mr. Gilmore," Kitty said. "What a pleasant surprise."

"Mrs. Wellington, Mr. Jensen," Gilmore said. He took out a handkerchief and wiped the sweat from his face. "I wish I had better news to report."

"What is it?" Kitty asked.

"Mr. Kincaid is dead," Gilmore said.

"Marcus, dead?" Kitty replied. "How?"

"Clay Sherman killed him. Sherman also killed the marshal."

"Oh, my!" Kitty said.

"Right now, Sherman and his men have taken over the town," Gilmore said. "Jenny heard some of them talking. I believe it is their plan to ambush you when you come

419

to town, then confiscate the herd."

"Confiscate? Is that a fancy name for stealing?" Matt asked.

"To be truthful, it is nothing but stealing. Sherman is using something called the herd management law as his authority, but it would never stand up to scrutiny."

Kitty shook her head. "I've never heard of the herd management law."

"It is a law that nominally prohibits someone from raising anything but cattle in a district that is set aside for cattle."

"If I was violating the law, why didn't someone tell me?"

"It was not to Marcus Kincaid's advantage for you to be in concurrence with the law. That's why he hired Sherman to enforce the law, and thus prevent you from fulfilling your contract with the army."

"But you said Sherman killed Marcus," Kitty replied.

"Yes, he did."

"Why?"

Gilmore shook his head. "I'm not sure. Evidently they had a falling out of some sort."

"Mr. Gilmore, do you have any idea what Sherman has in mind now?" Matt asked.

"Yes, I do. He plans to set up an ambush for you. I believe he intends to kill every one of you when you come to town, then take the herd to Chicago himself."

"That's it," Kitty said. "We aren't going to town."

"Kitty, do you think if we don't go to town, they will just go away?" Matt asked.

"Oh, I-I don't know what I think," Kitty said.

"You hired me to see to it that your horses get to Chicago. Why don't you just let me do my job."

"I told you, Matt, these men are my family," Kitty said. "I lost Hank and Timmy. I don't want any of the others to be killed."

"I'll handle it," Matt said. "There is no need for any of the men to go into town."

"What are you talking about? I don't want you killed either. And you can't go into town to face them, all alone."

Matt looked at the bodies of the posse men who had been killed the night before.

"I won't be alone," he said, mysteriously.

Word spread quickly around town that Sherman had now lost a total of eleven men to failed attempts to take the horses Kitty Wellington was planning on shipping to Chicago. Word also spread that Sherman and the five men he had remaining were planning on ambushing Matt Jensen and

Kitty Wellington's riders when they brought the herd into town today.

Because of that, all businesses were closed and all the residents of town were off the streets. If there was going to be a battle in Medbury, and it looked as if such a battle was going to take place, there would be bullets flying everywhere, and if that was the case, the street was no place to be.

Clay Sherman established his command post, as he called it, at the railroad depot. Burnett was over at the Dunnigan's store, behind the porch, Walker was on the roof of the apothecary, concealed by the false front. Burke and Carson were in the loft of the livery stable. Grimes was in Anna Cooke's dress shop which, because it was at the south end of the street, would make the first contact with Jensen and the others when they came into town.

Hearing a whistle, Sherman looked west on the track and saw a train approaching. He watched as the engine came into the station, then left the main track and switched over to a side track. The engine was pulling a long string of empty stock cars, with a parlor car attached at the end. The train came to a squeaking halt, then the engineer released the steam as the huge, powerful locomotive sat on the spur track.

Sherman watched the dispatcher walk out to the train and call something up to the engineer. The engineer and fireman came down from the cab, and the three of them hurried across the tracks before disappearing in the depot.

Sherman climbed up onto the water tower, then looked south. That was when he saw the approaching herd of horses, being driven expertly toward town.

"Ha!" Sherman said, speaking aloud. "This is working out well. You are bringing the herd right to us."

Sherman cupped his hands around his mouth. "Walker!" he called to the man on the apothecary just across the street. When Walker looked toward him, Sherman pointed toward the herd. "They are coming! Get ready! Tell the others!"

He heard Walker shout to Burke and Carson, then he heard the alarm passed on to the others.

Looking back toward the herd, he saw that it had been stopped. At first, he wondered what was going on, then he saw a wagon coming up the road from the herd. There were two men on the driver's seat of the wagon, both were carrying rifles. And as the wagon got closer, he saw four men in the back, also carrying rifles. Damn, he thought.

They were making this too easy.

"Walker!" he shouted. "They are coming in, in a wagon. Tell the others! Start shooting as soon as they get in range!"

Kneeling down on the ledge that ran around the water tower, Sherman cocked his rifle and waited. For a moment, the wagon was out of site on the other side of the blacksmith shop, but as soon as it appeared again, Sherman fired.

Sherman's opening shot alerted the others and they began shooting too. For several seconds the street reverberated with the sound of rifle fire.

Matt had come into town riding in a second bottom underneath the wagon. Looking through a narrow opening, he watched for the best opportunity to leave the wagon, slipping out just as it passed behind the blacksmith shop, during which time it was momentarily out of sight from anyone in town.

Running around behind the blacksmith shop, he began moving up the alley, keeping pace with the wagon as the team pulled it, and its grisly load of dead passengers, dressed, not in the uniform of the posse, but in old shirts belonging to the Coventry riders.

When the shooting started, Matt determined where each of the shooters was. Seeing that one of the shooters was in the dress shop, he decided to take care of that one first, believing the seamstress might be in the most danger.

Matt ran up to the back of the dress shop, and saw a woman outside, standing behind a tree as he did so.

"Anna!" he called.

Startled, the woman looked toward him. "Who are you?" she asked in a frightened voice.

"I'm Matt Jensen, I'm —"

"Kitty's friend," Anna said.

"Yes. Who is inside?" he asked, pointing toward the shop.

"There is a man in the front of the store," Anna said. "He has a gun."

"Go into your house," Matt said, pointing to the house that was behind the dress shop. "Stay away from the windows."

Anna nodded, then complied with his directions as Matt slipped in through the back door of the dress shop.

There were a couple of dress forms in the back room of the shop, and one of them was on wheels. Matt picked it up and moved quietly toward the front. He stopped at the door that separated the two rooms and saw the shooter standing at the open front door of the shop, shooting his rifle and cocking it, and shooting again.

Matt gave the dress form a push, and it rolled across the floor of the front room. Startled, the man jerked around, and fired at the rolling dress form. Matt shot back, and the man tumbled out onto the front porch.

Running up to the front of the building, Matt looked out across the street and saw someone rise up from behind the porch of the mercantile to shoot at the wagon. Matt took him down with one shot.

Sherman could actually see the bullets hitting the men who were in the wagon; he even saw dust coming up from the impact, and yet not one of the men reacted in any way to the bullets.

"What the hell?" Sherman said aloud.

"It's Scraggs!" Walker shouted from the top of the apothecary. "Stop shooting! It's our own men! They are all dead!"

Matt dashed out of the dress shop then, and seeing him, both Sherman and Walker started shooting. Bullets whizzed by his head and popped dirt up from the street as Matt ran in a zigzagging fashion until he reached the open door of the livery.

"Burke! Carson! He's in the livery!" Sherman shouted from the water tower.

Once inside, Matt heard a sound from the hayloft above. He also saw little bits and pieces of hay falling down between the cracks.

"Where is he? Where did he go?" a voice asked.

"I don't know. Sherman said he came in here," another voice answered.

There were two lofts in the barn, one, on the north end of the barn, was for hay. The other, at the south end of the barn was for equipment. The two lofts were separated by an open space of about forty feet. Matt climbed up onto the equipment loft, then he moved quietly to the edge and, taking concealment behind some wooden barrels, looked across. There were posse members standing on the other side, trying to look down into the barn to find the intruder.

Matt saw a rope tied off onto one of the supporting pillars. The rope looped through a pulley just under the peak of the roof, then the other end of the rope was tied off on one of the support pillars on the opposite loft. Matt untied the rope, and with a running start, leaped from the equipment loft and swung over to the hay loft.

"Carson! There!" Burke shouted and he

and Carson fired at Matt as he swung across the opening.

Matt hit the floor on the hayloft, rolled once, then fired back. Carson fell forward, Burked tumbled backward, through the loft window, and onto the ground in front of the livery.

Matt was climbing down from the hayloft when a bullet hit the ladder rung just above his head. Looping his arms and legs over the outside of the ladder, Matt slid down quickly, even as another bullet whizzed by him. Once he was on the ground, he turned toward his assailant and fired.

Making certain that he was dead, Matt took a moment to reload. He had just finished reloading when he heard Sherman calling to him from the street.

"Jensen! Jensen! Come on out and face me like a man! Jensen! Where are you?"

Matt left by the back door of the livery, ran down the alley for about half a block, then darted between two buildings and came out onto the street. He was behind Sherman, who was standing in front of the livery.

"Burke! Carson! Walker! Where are you?"

Matt put his pistol in his holster, and walked up to within sixty feet of Sherman.

"Jensen!"

Matt said nothing.

Sherman turned then, and was startled to see Matt standing so close to him on the street. For a second he was frightened, then he saw that Matt's gun was in his holster. Sherman actually had his pistol was in his hand, but his arm was down by his side.

"Well now," Sherman said, with an evil grin spreading across his face. "Here we are, just you and me. Only I have my gun in my hand, and you have yours in your holster."

"It doesn't matter," Matt said.

"What do you mean, it doesn't matter?"

"I'm going to kill you anyway."

With a loud, angry yell, Sherman brought his pistol up.

# EPILOGUE

The wind whispered as it came off the sails, and the sun created a million dancing diamonds on the surface of Lake Michigan. Matt and Kitty were seated on the afterdeck of the yacht, eating the meal the chef of the yacht had prepared for them. The yacht was about a mile offshore and from here, they had a great view of the city of Chicago. A passenger train was racing south along the lake shore.

"Where do you think that train is going?" Kitty asked.

"I don't know," Matt answered. "New Orleans, maybe?"

"Oh, wouldn't you like to go to New Orleans?"

"Some day, perhaps," Matt said. "But not today. I'm enjoying where I am right now."

"So am I," Kitty said. "I have had such a wonderful time in Chicago that I don't even want to go back. I hate to say this, but I could almost be convinced to sell the ranch."

"And do what?" Matt asked.

"The same thing you do," Kitty said. "Just wander around."

Matt shook his head. "No, Kitty, you don't want to do that."

"Why not?"

"Didn't you say Tyrone, Prew, Crack, Jake, and the others were your family?"

Kitty was silent for a long moment. "Yes," she finally replied. "Yes, I did say that, didn't I?"

"Besides, you don't want to quit now. The army not only bought all your horses, they told you they would buy as many as you could provide them."

"Did you hear them say that it was the finest bunch of horses they had bought all year?" Kitty asked, proudly.

"Yes, I did hear that," Matt said. "And now, without the pressure of paying off a loan, the money you got from selling your horses to the army, and the guarantee you got for future contracts, you could just enjoy your ranch and your horses."

"Do you think you could?" Kitty asked.

"Do I think I could what?"

"Enjoy my ranch, my horses, and me?" Kitty said.

"Kitty, I —"

"No," Kitty said, holding up her hand and interrupting Matt in midsentence. She smiled at him. "Don't answer that, Matt. Let me keep my dream."

"Let you keep your dream? Oh, I don't know. I'm not so sure about that," Matt said, smiling.

"What do you mean, you aren't so sure?"

"Kitty, you have just proven to me that your dreams seem to have a way of coming true."

# ABOUT THE AUTHORS

**William W. Johnstone** is the *USA Today* bestselling author of over 130 books, including the popular *Ashes, Mountain Man,* and *Last Gunfighter* series. Visit his website at www.williamjohnstone.net or by email at dogcia@aol.com.

**J.A. Johnstone** is a Tennessee-based novelist.

The employees of Thorndike Press hope you have enjoyed this Large Print book. All our Thorndike, Wheeler, and Kennebec Large Print titles are designed for easy reading, and all our books are made to last. Other Thorndike Press Large Print books are available at your library, through selected bookstores, or directly from us.

For information about titles, please call:
  (800) 223-1244

or visit our Web site at:
  http://gale.cengage.com/thorndike

To share your comments, please write:
  Publisher
  Thorndike Press
  295 Kennedy Memorial Drive
  Waterville, ME 04901

10-18-17

CPSIA information can be obtained
at www.ICGtesting.com
Printed in the USA
FFOW02n1322310315
12292FF